Mother Trucking Monsters

Book One of Magic and Motherhood

A. L. Tippett

Ebook ISBN: 978-0-6488121-8-0

Paperback ISBN: 978-0-6455730-4-6

Cover designed by Taurus Colosseum in collaboration with Ravenborn Covers

Published by FireFly Books

Australian spelling and grammar used throughout this book.

Contents

Author's Note

Dear reader,

Just a friendly PSA: this series is based in Australia, and guess what? There are Australians in Australia. Many of us are foul-mouthed and use Aussie slang on a daily basis and this is reflected in this book. So heed my warning, all who enter here. There are a few F-bombs scattered within these pages. Don't say I didn't warn you! If you require clarification on any Australian terms, please reach out. I'd love to hear from you!

The Magic and Motherhood series incorporates names of real locations in Australia that are used for authenticity but fictionalized. Please ensure you do your own research if you decide to visit these landmarks. For example, at the time of publication, the Big Mango in Bowen was not privately owned in real life, but it did sell fantastic mango sorbet!

If you want to keep up to date with the latest news from me, make sure you sign up to my monthly newsletter.

https://altippett.com/latest-updates/subscribe/

Thanks for taking a trip down under with me!
A. L. Tippett

Chapter One

"Frick-a-frack-frogs-legs!" I swore as a portal opened up in front of me.

The vertical oval of darkness on the other side of my office grew larger as I watched, a violet so dark, it was almost black. Adrenaline surged through my body as the thin tendrils encircling the portal's edge groped towards me, threatening to caress my office desk. I grimaced when the scent of brimstone permeated my office. Even knowing the creature that was about to step through the portal, I couldn't help my body's natural instinct to flee from the perceived danger. But I forced myself to remain professional. Smoothing my dark hair away from my face, I took a deep breath. Placing my shaking hands on my lap, I plastered a pleasant smile on my face as the emerald demon stepped through the pulsing purple light of the vortex.

"Gargolegmew. Always a pleasure to see you."

The horned creature grunted in response before folding his leathery wings tightly against his body. His black horns weren't far off scraping against my office's eight-foot ceiling.

"Trix," he rumbled in greeting and offered a slight bow, his black ponytail falling forward over his shoulder. He wasted no time in announcing his reason for visiting. "I need to lodge a claim."

"Of course, Garg. Please take a seat." I gestured to the dedicated client's seat that always sat on the other side of my desk, silently thanking whatever god was listening that, although the demon wasn't wearing a shirt, he was at least wearing pants today. I wouldn't need to throw the chair out. It creaked in protest as he folded his large frame into it, his hips barely squeezing between the chair's arms. Perhaps I would need a new one after all.

I didn't bother with my usual offering of refreshments since demons generally employed a strict diet of raw meat and the occasional freely offered soul. I pulled up his client file on my monitor and opened his business insurance policy.

"All righty." I quickly scanned his schedule, the document showing his sums insured and special endorsements. "Tell me, Garg. What's happened at the pet shop?"

He rubbed an anxious hand across his bare pecs, drawing my gaze to his green skin and dark chest hairs. There was plenty of eye candy on offer; if you were into that sort of thing. But I was his insurance broker and refused to let his muscly chest or insanely broad shoulders distract me. I cleared my throat and pulled my gaze up to his face. His black eyes met my brown eyes, and his features crumpled into an expression of distress.

"You know that big storm we just had?" he asked.

I nodded. The storm had hit the Queensland coast to the north of us, but even though the suburb of Maroochydore hadn't suffered a direct hit, the heavy rain had battered the entire Sunshine Coast region for days. Thanks to the friendly water kelpies who worked with the Natural Emergency Service (NES), only one human life had been lost in the ensuing floods. "Has the shop sustained water damage?"

"No," he replied. A fist as large as my head pounded my desk, and I winced internally, praying the timber would hold up to the weight. "We closed for a few days while the storm raged... Well, you know how much I hate getting wet. So each day, I portalled into the shop to feed my charges. I don't have the space in my apartment to keep the animals there; otherwise I would have brought them all home. On the third day, we lost electricity. But I couldn't abandon them. The fish need power running to their tanks at all times; if the water isn't kept filtered and aerated, they'll die. But I couldn't set my petrol generator going inside the shop because then the five kittens I have there would have perished from carbon monoxide poisoning. So I set the generator up outside and ran the cord through the gap at the bottom of the back door. But someone stole it overnight," he howled, his voice rattling my window panes.

I started at his outburst but managed to keep my automatic fearful reaction under wraps. My heart twisted in my chest at the greed of the human race. Because I had a strong suspicion it had been humans who had stolen from Garg. It wouldn't be the first time man had decided to steal from a magica. It rarely happened the other way around, no matter what the zealots at the local church claimed. Gingerly placing a comforting hand on his fist, I said, "I'm so sorry this happened. Did you lose any animals?"

He shook his horned head. "Thankfully, no. I went back to the shop first thing the next morning to check on all of my little ones and noticed the generator was gone. I had my cousin bring his in while I sorted out the shop. The electricity came back on that afternoon."

I typed everything the demon told me into a claim form. Turning my monitor towards Garg, I asked him to confirm that I had the details correct. He nodded an affirmation before I asked, "How many days were you closed for? I may be able to add loss of income to this claim since it was caused by the storm event."

He cocked his head, his black eyes squinting as he thought about it. "Four days."

"Okey-dokey. I'll talk to your insurer about it, and we'll let you know what information they ask for. The most likely items they will request is a police report number and a replacement quote for your generator. They'll also require details of your financials if we do lodge a business interruption claim, but I'll get back to you about that. Have you reported the incident to the police yet?"

The demon stood up, and I flinched at the sudden change in his height. Pulling a mobile phone from his trouser pocket, he quickly tapped the screen. It looked tiny in his massive hands. "Here it is," he murmured, his deep voice sounding like a distant thunderstorm. Sitting back down, he turned his phone towards me to show the thirteen-digit police report number.

Flicking my eyes between his screen and mine, I quickly noted the report number. "Perfect, thanks, Garg. Were the police...okay to deal with?"

Garg snorted at my thinly veiled question. "I initially spoke with Officer Harrow, who was ready to send me on my way without lodging a report when his superior took over. Think his name was Barracks. He was...polite enough."

My shoulders relaxed at the fact that at least one of the local cops was being civil. "Just giving you a heads up, even though it's not your fault, it's likely the insurer will charge you an excess, which is" —my eyes darted to his schedule again to confirm— "two-hundred and fifty dollars."

Garg bowed his head in acceptance. "I understand. Thank you, Trix. I will send you the quote for a new generator and then await your advice."

"Thanks for coming in. But next time, maybe you could use the stairs?"

He flashed me a terrifying grin, his sharp teeth protruding at odd angles from his gums, before standing up and weaving his hands in an intricate pattern, reopening his portal. He shrugged one shoulder and, with a mischievous wink, said, "It's quicker this way."

As the demon disappeared, I dropped my head into my hands and wondered how in the heckin' name of Hellscape's sake I was supposed to remove the distinct scent of brimstone from my office before my next client came in. It was pointless lighting my vanilla-scented candle; there was no way it could combat this stench. Glancing at the pretty pink glass container housing my candle, I couldn't help but smile. I rarely splurged on what I considered superfluous purchases. But there had been a musty smell in my office after the last wet season so I'd decided to treat myself for once. It would be nice to buy things for myself more often, but I simply couldn't afford it. I'd already spent the leftover money from this month's pay on my daughter's fifteenth birthday party. It had been a simple outing to the movies with two of her friends but she didn't mind. My sweet girl never minded. Pulling myself out of my reverie, I checked my clock and groaned. The next client was due in ten minutes. There was no way I'd get the smell out by then. But I was saved by the bell. Or rather, by my boss opening my door and sneezing.

"Ugh. Did Garg come by unannounced?" Fiona wrinkled her nose.

I offered a wry grin. "How could you tell?"

In response, Fiona made a melodramatic gagging sound before turning my ceiling fan on high and striding to my window to slide it open. The bright blue pantsuit she was wearing made a bold statement. Precisely what that statement was, I wasn't entirely sure. I didn't speak clothes.

"Mrs Hinschen had to cancel," she announced. "So according to your calendar, you're free of appointments for the afternoon. But I need you to pull up the monthly report, memorise the figures, and present it to Woodsy after work."

I whimpered. "Not Woodsy!" The man was insufferable. Arrogant and rude, he thought the sun shone out of his...bottom. We had to endure his company at the monthly meetings, and every now and then he'd swing into the office and surprise us. If Woodsy brought everyone a coffee, he seemed to expect something in return; not that any of us gave into his piggish ways. His lustful gaze followed anything that wore a bra, including myself. I didn't use the word "hate" very often, but I'd make an exception for him.

Fiona's mouth twisted in sympathy. "I know. He's not my favourite person either. But as much as I don't like it, he is the director of the business and the only reason we get paid. Meet him at Murphy's Bar if you like. Take the company card." She pulled the credit card seemingly out of thin air and presented it to me with a flourish. I didn't take it, instead studying her form-fitting ensemble, trying to figure out where she'd hidden the rectangular piece of plastic. "You'll be in a public space, so he won't say or do anything too foolish; plus you get to have some alcohol and maybe relax a little. Have some fun for a change." She gave the card in her hand a wobble, the name on the card, Maroochydore Mundane and Magica Insurance Brokers, shining in silver.

My brain worked furiously, desperately trying to figure out how I could get out of the meeting when I realised I had a legitimate excuse. "I'm sorry, Fi, but I can't. I have parent-teacher interviews tonight. I have to leave right on five o'clock if I'm going to pick up Millie from netball practise and make it back to the school in time. Training is over at the Maroochydore Netball Courts and it will take me at least twenty minutes to get her back to school."

Her brows pulled together before her shoulders dropped in defeat. She returned the credit card to her clothing, and I still managed to miss where it was hidden.

Did that thing have hidden pockets? I was flat out finding any clothes with real pockets, let alone a stylish pantsuit with hidden ones.

Fi raked her fingers through her black hair, being careful not to mess up her styled pixie cut before returning to her standard power pose. "That's okay. I'll do it. Send me the figures, please."

"Sorry, Fiona. I could maybe do it another night..." I detested the idea of spending time with Woodsy but hated the idea of disappointing Fiona more.

She reached over my desk and squeezed my hand. With a smile that lit up the room, she said, "It's fine, Trix. Your family is your priority, and I can respect that. Woodsy has asked for the figures today, so I'll make sure he gets them. Don't stress, lovely. You know I've always got your back."

Chapter Two

With no other clients booked and my renewals up to date, I didn't have too much to do before close of business. I sent through the sales figures for the month to Fiona with a brief overview. Then all I had left to do was lodge Gargolegmew's claim and check if there were any new emails that required urgent action. Before I summoned the energy to do one last push of focus, I stared at the white walls of my office. Aside from a small succulent in a purple glazed pot, my vanilla candle, and a framed photo of Millie on my desk, the only other decoration was a painting of the beach Fiona had hung on the wall before I'd started working here. It made me feel oddly calm when I looked at it for long enough. I could almost hear the gentle rush of the waves. Added to the view of an actual palm tree in the garden out of my office window, it lent my office a relaxed vibe. For a moment, I allowed myself to dream about spending a day at the beach. A whole day to myself. What a wonderous thing that would be.

Giving myself a shake, I reproached my wayward imagination. I didn't need time to myself. I had Millie. I might be a single parent, but Millie was the best thing that had ever happened to me. I didn't need alone time to be happy. I returned my attention to my computer and emailed the claim form to the insurer. With an ease that only comes from doing the same action many times on repeat over the years, I swiftly created a claim file on our system, wrote up the progress notes, and saved a copy of the claim form. I made a reminder on my calendar to follow them up in two business days for an update. As the afternoon drew to a close, my focus flagged. Flicking back to my Inbox, I stared blankly at the eleven new emails that had come through while I was in my appointment with Garg.

To distract myself, I rolled Gargolegmew's name around my tongue. His nickname almost sounded like a noise I'd make cleaning my teeth, but friendly as the demon was, I daren't ever tell him that. One never knew what joke would offend a resident of the Hellscape, an alternative dimension that housed the dark magicas. Much to the confusion of some bigoted humans, not all dark magicas were inherently evil, as proven by Garg. Thankfully, mankind didn't have access to the Hellscape; other-wise the demons would have nowhere safe to run when the going got tough on Earth. Although, was Garg really a resident there anymore? He lived here now, caring for his animals. Which made me wonder whether he had access to his full demonic power since he no longer lived in his home dimension. Did their magic die if they stayed up here for too long? I wasn't brave enough to ask him.

I gave myself a stern talking to. This was no time for procrastination. The more tasks I finished this afternoon, the less I had to work on tomorrow. Which would mean I could have a relaxing Friday to ease into the weekend. I took a long drink from my water bottle, managed to drop the lid, and in my scurry to grab it from under the desk, knocked over my water bottle and hit my head on the desk leg as I tried to save it.

"Cackle a kookaburra and cook a kangaroo!" I flung out my version of a swear word along with a yelp of pain, holding my throbbing head. Scrambling up, I raced into the office kitchenette and grabbed a hand towel. Scooting back under my desk, being careful to avoid taking out any more furniture with my head, I soaked up the spill. I was clumsy. Al-ways had been since before I could remember. Growing up, my mother often used to tell me I had a hard head. Whenever I ran into a stationary object, like now, she would never check if I was okay, instead asking if the offending item was still in one piece.

Cheers, Mum. Nothing like some maternal ribbing to keep your ego in check.

Luckily, my bottle had been less than half full, and it had avoided watering my desktop's tower. Muttering to myself, I stood and stretched, sucking in some deep breaths before settling back into my chair. I clicked the first unread email, giving it a quick scan. It was just an insurer sending a bulk email to their subscribers to let them know about an upcoming seminar on cyber insurance in Brisbane. Delete.

The next email was from Nicole, our receptionist and my best friend. She was a couple of years older than me, with no children of her own, but she welcomed the title of Aunty from my daughter. Blonde, tanned, fit, and blue-eyed, she was the epitome of what the rest of the world thought Australians looked like. Nicole was always ready for a laugh and a drink but had also stayed with me through some pretty tough times.

Her email said Woodsy had called, asking what I drank so he could have it ready for me. She also added a personal comment with some derogatory profanities mentioning his unmentionables that, while I wouldn't be repeating out loud, made me snicker. I wasn't really clear on why Fiona put up with Nicole's cheekiness in her message-taking emails, but I thought Fi secretly enjoyed the break from the constant professionalism she had to endure from everyone else in the industry. Nicole made work *fun*. And she was always polite in front of the clients, at least.

I wrinkled my nose at the message from Woodsy and forwarded it to Fiona.

[Here, you can let Woodsy know what *you're* drinking since I won't be taking that meeting now. (Thanks again, by the way.)] I was so grateful that I didn't need to meet up with that tosspot. Not today, anyway.

Her response was quick in coming, [Gee, thanks. Can't wait to have a few bevvies with that wanker... not. Don't tell him I said that.]

I snorted. *As if I would.*

Deleting that email chain, I moved onto the next one. An update from the insurer on another client's claim. Patrick's car had been vandalised by a gang of pixies, and the assessor had seen the damage now and approved the repairs. I rolled my eyes.

Bet Patrick would add a protection ward to the car once it was back from the shop.

Protection wards cost less than his excess; plus I could guarantee his renewal premium would be increasing if he didn't invest in one. I told him last year to buy a protection ward when he first took out the policy.

But had he listened? No. Of course not. They never did the first time I recommended it. *Oh well, live and learn, I guess.*

I glanced at the clock above my desk. Only half an hour until I could finish for the day. I quickly called Patrick, but it went straight to voicemail. I left a message letting him know to contact the repairer to book his car in at a time that suited him.

Two more emails were updates on claims that didn't require any action from me other than updating the notes in our system, and the next was a client letting us know she'd finally paid her home insurance renewal. I forwarded that one on to accounting. The insurer had been threatening cancellation of the policy for a week now due to non-payment.

The next email made me pause. It was a message from the Australian Insurance Company's state manager advising of a position as an insurance assessor through the independent assessing company, MagicAssess. One of their assessors specialising in magica claims who was based on the Sunshine Coast was seeking an assistant to train up to be a qualified assessor.

My eyes widened at the base pay rate on offer. I knew assessors were well paid, but I had no idea the starting rate for their assistant would be so high. Way more than what I earned as a fully qualified broker.

I'd only ever worked as an insurance broker so I didn't know the intricate details of their work, but what I did know was that an insurance assessor's job was quite different to mine. As a broker, I was just the middleman. I requested quotes from different insurers, arranged cover, and lodged claims on my client's behalf. It involved plenty of sitting at my desk on the phone and responding to emails.

Meanwhile, assessors were a lot more hands on. Their job was to work with the client who was lodging the claim to ensure they were getting the maximum compensation from the insurer. They still wrote reports but they actually went out to the property or vehicle that was involved in the claim and investigated. Sometimes they even worked with the police or fire service to dig into the real reason for the incident. Since magical creatures had revealed themselves to the world a little over three decades ago, their job had gotten a whole heck of a lot trickier.

How do assessors tell if a fire was caused by a human with a match, or by a dragon with a nasty cough?

I scanned the information and, for a moment, imagined what that amount of money would do for my family. I could finally afford to buy a whole new set of tyres for the car and upgrade my wards around the house. Millie could wear new school uniforms that actually fit her. She could go on any school camps she wanted without me having to pick and choose which ones we could afford. And if I did a good job as an assistant and studied hard, maybe one day I could be an assessor myself. Who knew how much I could earn then! Maybe I could take Millie on an overseas holiday to England like we'd always talked about. My heart bloomed at the thought. She'd love that.

I yanked myself back from the daydream abruptly. There was no use imagining the kind of life we could lead with more money. I wouldn't abandon Fiona and the team here. And anyway, the chances of me getting the job were slim to none. I scanned over the rest of the email that detailed the recommended skills the applicants should have, which included working with non-verbal magicas. I didn't have any experience in the role itself, and only had a small amount of knowledge when it came to working with wild magicas. In my late teens, before I had Millie, I'd back-packed around Central and South America with my ex. At one stage, we worked with a small conservation group to save the endangered blue-ringed kraken. Together, we'd scuba dived down into their nest in the Great Blue Hole of Belize and collected their eggs, returning them to the incubator. We'd successfully saved dozens of kraken larvals. Regardless of that experience, the last dot point caught my eye.

Competent in archery and swordsmanship.

I barked a laugh. Were they joking? Had they accidentally copied and pasted that from somewhere else? It wouldn't be the strangest mistake I'd seen in the insurance world, but it did seem particularly odd. In an age of guns and wards, no one used swords and arrows anymore. Did they?

Fiona poked her head around my door. "What are you chuckling about? I'm reading through the latest policy updates from MoonCorp, and it's hell. I need a giggle."

I pointed at my screen. "I was just reading the email from the Australian Insurance Company about the assessor's assistant job."

She shot me a strange look and quirked an eyebrow. "Are you thinking of leaving me, Trix?"

I blushed and looked down. "No, not really. But you know how it is when your imagination gets away from you. I was thinking how nice it would be to have that much money, but the last line of the requirements made me laugh." I quoted it to her.

She snorted in amusement before saying, "Well, insurance assessors do need some basic combat training just in case."

"Just in case? In case of what?"

Fiona shrugged. "It's true that a large part of their job is just interviewing claimants and writing reports. I don't know the precise details since I've never worked in assessing, but I've heard that occasionally, the creature that caused the damage hangs around. Assessors need to be prepared to battle it if necessary."

"Firecrackers! I never even thought of that." I shuddered, my dreams of being an assessor flying out the window. I might have spent my late teens swimming with giant sea creatures but that didn't mean I was still that brave now that I was in my mid-thirties. Age and responsibility had made me risk averse. I had to think about what was best for Millie.

Fiona burst out laughing then. "I'm just imagining you and your insane need to not swear, in the midst of battle, yelping about mother trucking monsters."

I crossed my arms in mock offence and leaned back in my chair. It rolled away from the desk with my movement, putting me off balance and ruining the effect I was going for. I recovered quickly and announced primly, "Just because you're a part of the uncouth youth of today who can't keep the 'F' word out of their mouths, doesn't mean I have to join the ranks. Swearing is the sign of a small mind," I sniffed. "Besides, my cusses are way more fun."

Fi sniggered at me before turning serious. Taking a step closer to my desk, she said, "Just so you know, if you ever did decide to move on, you know I would give you a glowing reference. Don't be afraid to put my number on your résumé." She tossed a glance over her shoulder and lowered her voice. "Though I hope I don't lose my best employee anytime soon."

I blinked in surprise at her declaration. "Thanks, Fi. I really appreciate that."

She shrugged my gratitude off, checked her phone, cursed, and abruptly changed the subject. "By the way, I got your email with the report for Woodsy, thanks, but I haven't had a chance to read through the whole thing yet. Is there anything important I need to bring up with him?

"Nothing urgent, but I included a summary of the major points from the commission reports for you. It's in the second tab on the spreadsheet."

"Oh! You're on the ball. As always. Thanks. Sorry, I didn't even notice the second tab. I've been so focussed on reading through the changes to the MoonCorp policy wording that my brain has turned to mush." She pointed at the door. "Your work here is done. Off you trot."

I glanced at the clock. "But it's not five yet," I countered.

"It's close enough. And I'm the boss. So it's my decision." She winked.

"Are you sure, Fi?" I bit my lip and glanced at my computer. "There's still a few emails I haven't read…"

She waved a hand, sweeping my feeble protests away. "Give them a quick scan if you must. If there's nothing urgent, just sort them out tomorrow." "Okey-dokey then. Thanks, Fi! I owe you."

She shrugged. "All good, lovely. All the best with the teachers tonight!" Fiona gave me a double-thumbs up before returning to her office.

The business was going well; that should cheer Woodsy up enough to avoid him turning sour about not getting to harass me for the evening. The guy couldn't take no for an answer. My nose wrinkled involuntarily as I thought of that sleazeball. I'd rather hang with Garg than that jerk. When you'd rather go on a date with a demon named Gargolegmew than have one drink with a human male, you knew things were pretty dire.

Using the dribble of water that was still left in my bottle, I watered my potted succulent. Unfortunately, I did *not* have a green thumb. Nicole had given the plant to me in the hopes I would manage to keep it alive since they were so hardy. Alas, it seemed I either watered it too much or not enough, and it constantly looked on the verge of giving up its tenacious hold on life.

"Sorry, Heather. You know I try my best." Yes, I'd named my plant. It was a totally normal thing to do. I'd read that plants liked being talked to. I had to try everything I could to keep it away from death's door. I needed at least one win in life.

Chapter Three

I SHUT MY OFFICE door behind me and turned to face the small alcove in the wall beside the door frame. I placed my hand over the blue crystal nestled in the recess. A small surge of light flickered from beneath my palm as the protection ward activated. It would still allow employees with clearance to enter my room but should stop any undesirables from both the magical and mundane community from breaking in.

Walking down the hall towards the front door, I called out a farewell to my colleagues. Tim gave me a friendly wave as I passed his office door. He was a wizard with commercial insurance...quite literally. His mother was a human, but his father was a wizard on the Inter-Magical Community Council. His knowledge of both sides was so helpful to the office. Contrary to the old movies' portrayals of wizards from before the Spark, there were no pointy hats or flowing robes here. He was just an average-looking thirty-something-year-old guy with mousy blond hair and a soft gut.

In contrast, I received a curt nod from Shirlene in response to my farewell. She looked pointedly at her clock, making me flush. I didn't bother explaining that Fi had let me go early. The last thing I needed was to give Shirlene any more proof that I was one of Fi's favourites. Like me, Shirlene was a human but she was in her late fifties. She was good at her job but, like many of the older generation, had struggled with embracing the magical community.

Around thirty-five years ago, shortly before I was born, the magical creatures of our world had revealed themselves to the human race, resulting in what we called the Spark. Even though it had been more than three decades, many older people, and some younger ones with strict family beliefs, hadn't come to terms with accepting magicas as part of our society. I'd grown up with them as part of my life but still saw the frequent exclusion and prejudice from our community.

I shrugged off Shirlene's frostiness; it was par for the course. While she sucked up to Fiona and laughed too loudly at Tim's jokes, she wasn't particularly friendly with either myself or Nicole. Speaking of the wild blonde, I forced myself to hide a snigger behind my hand as I approached her desk from behind. Nicole's desk was the first thing clients saw when they entered Maroochydore Mundane and Magica Insurance Brokers. But when there wasn't anyone around, Nic would often turn music on while she entertained herself playing card games on her computer. I'd never commented on Nicole's pathological need to play solitaire on company time and, so far, neither had Fi. So long as the work got done on time, Fiona wasn't a super strict boss. That's part of the reason we loved working for her. If it wasn't for Woodsy, Shirlene's attitude, and the distinctly average pay rate, it would almost be the perfect job. I stepped behind Nicole's chair and gave her shoulders a quick squeeze.

"Fi has let me off early. I'll see you in the morning!" I announced cheerily.

"Good luck at the interviews tonight! Try not to stress, I'm sure it will all be good news. And make sure you check out the ass on that delicious Mr Jones for me." She waggled her eyebrows suggestively.

I sighed. "I told you *once* that he was good looking. I didn't say he was delicious." I wrinkled my nose. "I'm not hitting on my daughter's vice principal and I am *definitely* not checking out anyone's buttocks, thank you very much! Not even for you."

Nicole leaned back in her chair and sighed dramatically. "He *likes* you." She'd drawled the word *like* as if we were highschoolers ourselves. "You'd better make a move on him before one of the other vultures – I mean mums – do."

I rolled my eyes. "Nic! You know I'm not ready to date again."

"You'll never be ready," she muttered under her breath.

I shot her a glare and opened my mouth to retaliate, but she interrupted with an abrupt change of subject.

"Are we still on for the movies tomorrow night?" she asked with a quirked eyebrow.

I smacked my forehead. "Oh! I almost forgot. But yeah, sure, so long as I can find someone to stay with Millie."

"You know, Millie is probably old enough now to look after herself for a few hours."

I chewed my lip. "She's only fifteen..."

"Precisely. I was making my own meals at ten."

"No offence, Nicole, but maybe your childhood isn't the prime example of child-rearing tips."

Instead of taking offence like some would, Nicole simply burst out laughing. "That's fair!"

I flashed a grin at my friend's laid-back manner before glancing at the time on my phone. "I'd better get going before I end up late picking up Millie from netball practise."

"Oh, yeah! She practises on Thursdays and competes on Saturdays, right? Tell Millie that Aunty Nicole wishes her good luck at the game on the weekend. And if it's looking like the other team will win, tell her to squash some toes. Or break their fingers...whatever's in range."

"Nicole! She can't do that! And she would never."

Nicole gave a nonchalant shrug. "Well, sometimes you've got to step on some toes to get to the top. Weren't you ever told that as a kid?"

"No!"

"Ah, yes. And we've segued neatly back to my dodgy childhood. All right, get going, woman, before you're late – or worse, we take a deep dive into my inner child's trauma." She made an impatient shooing motion with her hands.

I blew her a kiss as I stepped out of the office. It was a warm day for August, but being the tail-end of winter in Queensland, it wasn't too humid yet, thankfully. That would all change in a few months. A breeze blew off the Pacific Ocean and carried the scent of the sea air with it. I breathed deeply, paralysed for a moment as it brought back memories of my time in Belize, before making a beeline for my car. Hopping into my trusty silver Commodore, I rolled the window down, forgoing the air-con this time.

Merging smoothly into the afternoon traffic, I sent a silent thanks to Fi for letting me go early. I'd forgotten about the extra traffic on a Thursday afternoon, with everyone rushing to the shops to take advantage of late-night shopping. I prided myself on being a very capable driver, but you never knew what other dingle-berries were on the road. I kept a close eye on a hatchback in front of me that was weaving across lanes erratically.

I breathed a sigh of relief at the next intersection as they turned right, mounting the kerb as they did so, while I continued straight. I was grateful to have avoided an accident with that particular dingle-berry but still had to give myself a little shake. Anxiety clawed in my gut; life was so uncertain. It could change in the blink of an eye.

Tearing my focus away from the fragility of my mortality, I made my way to the netball courts. Even though the carpark was massive, finding a park here on game day was a talent in itself, but it didn't take me too long to find a spot during the week. Bushland bordered the western perimeter of the Maroochydore Netball Courts, while a six-foot wire fence separated the rest of the grounds from industrial sheds. I walked into the clubhouse and checked the posting. Matilda's team, the Maroochydore Minotaurs, were practising on court four today and would be taking on the Mooloolaba Munchkins on Saturday. Despite their unassuming name, the Munchkins were a strong team. Millie and the girls would be hard-pressed to beat them.

It had been tricky since the world had found out magic was real. Some of the questions the Australian Netball Association had faced had included: could magicas play in human teams? Wouldn't that give an unfair advantage to teams with more magicas than humans? Should they have their own nationally recognised association so only magicas could play against magicas? But that idea came with its own problems; not all the magical creatures were equal. A team made up of winged magicas like fairies would have an advantage over a team of squat, non-winged brownies. Thankfully, the Australian Netball Association had decided to become more inclusive. Magicas could play on human teams under the proviso they weren't allowed to use their magic (including wings), and magicas couldn't make up more than fifty percent of a team. There were also two referees on all games. One ensured the rules of netball were observed while the second was a magica who watched for unauthorised use of magic during the game.

I checked the time on my phone's lock screen; Millie's practise session would finish in ten minutes. As I made to leave the clubhouse, someone called my name. Turning back, I greeted Faith, the aged pixie with bright-pink hair who volunteered her time in the clubhouse's canteen on practise and game days. I double-tapped three fingers in the universal sign of goodwill to magicas. It was akin to a handshake among humans. Faith's eyes sparkled with a youthful mischief that belied her age, the lines of her face crinkling up as she hopped up on a stool behind the canteen so she could see me properly. Waving a plastic bottle filled with a colourful drink that promised to replace all of Millie's lost electrolytes, she beckoned me over.

"Compliments of Miss Ellie. She asked me to give this to you for your Matilda."

My heart swelled at the kindness of Millie's teammate's mother. I cleared my throat loudly, determined not to make a scene. "She already paid for it?" I asked.

Faith nodded.

"That's so sweet of her. I'll have to thank her."

The pixie's expression turned mischievous as she changed the subject. "So...any young men courting you yet, Trix?"

I snorted and rolled my eyes at the familiar question. "If there wasn't a man in my life last week, what makes you think there will be today?"

She grinned, baring her sharp teeth. "Life can change in a flash. And I can sense change is coming for you."

I smiled tightly at the recurring prediction before waving goodbye and rushing down to court four. When I reached the edge of the grass court, Ellie gave me a friendly wave from the sidelines. I went over and thanked her profusely. I owed her big time. Usually Millie caught the bus home from school, but Ellie brought her to netball practise every Thursday while I was at work. Ellie's daughter, Isabella, was one of Millie's best friends, and Ellie's warmth and kindness was prevalent in every one of our interactions. The entire elven family were stunningly beautiful, making some of the school parents feel threatened by their perfection, but I found them to be nothing but wonderful. You'd think they'd be conceited, but I'd never seen the slightest hint of that.

After insisting to Ellie that she let me return the favour someday, I turned back to the court. "Honey!" I called as I spotted my daughter.

At the sound of my voice, Matilda passed the ball back to Isabella, thus completing her ball drill, and turned, her face breaking into a huge grin. "You made it on time!" She rushed over and enveloped me in a hug, her auburn hair smacking me in the face, but I couldn't bring myself to care. While Millie had got her reddish-bronze locks from her father, her brown eyes were all mine.

Had she had another growth spurt? She could almost put her arms over my shoulders instead of the other way around. An unexpected lump lodged itself in my throat. I cleared my throat as I fought to tamp down the unexpected wave of emotion at seeing my girl growing up so fast. We broke apart, and I pushed the multi-coloured drink towards her.

"Thanks, Mum! Rainbow Raspberry is my favourite."

"You can thank Isabella's mum. She bought it for you."

"Aww, Ellie is awesome." She took a long drink and sighed happily before darting over to give Ellie a hug in thanks. With a wave goodbye to her coach and teammates, we began our walk back to the carpark. Changing the subject to distract myself, I said, "Aunty Nicole said to say, 'Good luck on Saturday and step on their toes if you're not winning.'"

Millie's mouth dropped open, aghast at the idea of cheating. "Aunty Nicole! You know I'm not going to do that, right?"

Chuckling, I squeezed her arm affectionately. "I know, sweetheart, but you know Nic. She's incorrigible."

She gave an un-ladylike snort and responded with some typical teenage sass. "That's one way to describe her." Her eyes sparkled with mischief. It was so much fun to see her becoming her own person, making jokes and finding her voice.

Mussing her hair, I laughed with her. Pointing her to the back seat of the sedan, I slid into the driver's seat. "Hop in, little dove. Your formal uniform is in there. Time to get changed and head to your parent-teacher interviews. We don't want to be late."

With the carefree grace of a young person whose back hasn't started aching for no good reason, Millie flung open the back door and swung into the car. She grinned at me in the rear-view mirror and bounced in her seat. "Awesome. I can't wait to find out what they have to say."

"All good things, I hope?"

Affronted, she placed a melodramatic hand over her heart and exclaimed, "Mother! How could you suspect anything else?"

Before putting the car into gear, I held up my hands in surrender. "Okay, okay, no offence meant! I just thought it was a little unusual for your teachers to request a meeting with me about you."

As she switched out of her netball gear and into her school uniform, she said, "They probably want to give me a special award and need to talk to you about the appropriate size of my medal." She pumped her eyebrows. Oh, wait, it was a double-pump. She was just joking around.

Or she was being totally serious. I couldn't remember the code anymore.

Far out. Being a mum was hard.

Chapter Four

As we made our way into Millie's school, I watched her stride through the metal gates.

And I mean I really watched her.

I tended to get so busy with everyday life that I didn't always take the time to notice, but I could see now my little girl was growing up. There had been an awkward scuffle in the back seat of the car as she'd changed into her formal school uniform, but you wouldn't know it now. The vertical blue stripes accentuated her height while the sensible black shoes added an air of importance. She was in Year Ten, with two years left of high school before she had to make a decision on whether to enter the workforce or go to university. I noticed her skirt was still an acceptable length for now. I'd only let the hem out last month, and there wasn't much more fabric left to extend it. I'd have to see if I could find the right size at an op shop because there was no way I could afford the forty dollars the school asked for one skirt. I made a mental note to visit an op shop on the weekend.

Matilda had always been a bright student with mostly As and Bs on her report card, so I hadn't known what to make of it when I'd received the school's letter with two requests for parent-teacher interviews. When I'd booked them in, Millie hadn't seemed worried, so I'd shrugged it off and figured we'd find out tonight as to why the requests had been made.

We headed straight to the school hall where they were conducting the interviews. With a heave, I pushed the heavy glass door open, and we signed in at the fold out table they had set up near the entrance. Maroochydore Magica and Mundane State High School was a medium-sized school. Not so small that she wouldn't get any opportunities but not so large that she'd be lost in the crowd of students.

A few years ago, they'd received a grant to upgrade the hall, and now it was an air-conditioned beauty with soaring ceilings, striking dark wooden beams, and polished timber floors. The senior volunteering at the front desk directed us to Mr Albert Conningsby, Millie's physical education teacher. He was waiting for us on the opposite side of the hall and close to the main stage. Our shoes squeaked as we weaved our way through the other teachers' desks, and the hum of the air-conditioner could barely be heard over the general murmur of the other parents and students attending. Conningsby gave a cheery wave as we sat together in the blue plastic chairs opposite him. The PE teacher was a satyr, his half-goat form making for an extremely agile sportsman. His charming nature made him a hit with all the students and most of the parents as well, even those who weren't fully on-board with supporting the magicas as part of their school community.

We exchanged pleasantries before I leaned forward and said, "As lovely as it is to see you, Mr Conningsby, I'm not entirely sure why Matilda had a requirement for an interview with you tonight. Is something wrong?"

"Just call me Conns; all the kids do." He flashed a cheeky grin. "I knew that would make you wonder, but I promise it's for a good reason. Matilda is a fantastic student." Out of the corner of my eye, I noticed Millie straighten in her chair at his compliment. "I don't have any problems with her in class," he assured me. "This is for an opportunity that's come up. I know Matilda plays netball as one of her extracurricular activities, and I've witnessed her athleticism at school. She's a talented kid. Our senior netball team is down a player, and we have qualified for the State competition. I was hoping that Matilda would try out for the team."

"Oh," was all I managed to get out. Selfishly, all I could think of was the added cost. I slumped back in my chair and turned to look at my daughter.

Millie looked at me with shining eyes. "Oh my gosh, Mum! Can I, please?"

The satyr echoed her in a teasing tone combined with a pleading look, "Can she, Mum?"

My brain whirred. Finally, I managed to stutter one question, "I thought the senior team was for sixteen and seventeen year olds?"

"It is usually. But our centre is down with a badly broken arm for at least eight weeks, and now our reserve has had to fly home to New Zealand due to a family issue. We need to look at replacing both our centre and the reserve as a matter of urgency."

My heart squeezed at the look of hope shining from Millie's eyes. It broke me. The cost of the uniform plus fuel to get her to the extra practise, not to mention the cost of her trip to the State competition, played on my mind. But the look in her eyes made me push those thoughts aside. Or at least, shove them deep into a box to worry about later. I'd figure out a way to save money somewhere. I'd make it work. For my Millie. I desperately wanted to ask about the fees involved. But I'd let tonight be a night of celebration and leave the question of money to a later date when I could talk to Conningsby privately.

I beamed at Matilda. "What a fantastic opportunity. Thank you for thinking of her, Conns. Send me an email with the details of when and where the tryouts are, and we'll be there."

Matilda threw herself at me in a bear hug, unafraid to show her affection in front of her peers. "Thank you, Mama," she whispered in my ear.

I squeezed her hard and kissed her on the forehead, all the while hiding the panic of finding more money. After a few more friendly comments from Conningsby, I realised the next student and his parents were hovering nearby, so we abandoned the desk. As I stood, I managed to knock over my chair, the *clang* echoing through the hall and halting conversations. My face burned as I righted it with a muttered apology before fleeing the scene.

Millie and I hurried over to the refreshments table. The school had laid out a beautiful charcuterie board where the spread of fruit was a larger variety than Millie got in a year. I rarely ate fruit myself simply because it was too expensive. Plus, my body had finished growing, so I figured I probably didn't need it as much as my girl. But free food was always welcome, so I grabbed a plate and piled it up with a slice of glistening red watermelon, some juicy yellow mango pieces, thick wedges of ripe oranges, and a golden piece of honeycomb. Millie followed suit. The other parents around me were mostly fixating on the free cups of coffee and biscuits. As we waited for our next interview, we both ate our fill. While I was biting into a particularly juicy orange, at which point it squirted down my chin, my least favourite person approached.

Marjory.

"Good evening, Beatrix," she simpered.

Marjory was the stuff of nightmares. What I meant by that was, she had a tiny waist, a perky bosom, and legs for days. And don't forget the perfectly styled hair. Think of that porcelain doll your grandmother gave you as a child but you never really liked because its glass eyes creeped you out. Remember her perfectly curled golden locks? Well, that was what the nightmare – I mean, Marjory – looked like. That might sound mean...but only to those who hadn't met her yet. No matter how pretty she looked on the outside, it couldn't hide the ugliness on the inside. And that was the only part that mattered to me.

"Hey Marjory," I garbled a response while frantically seeking out a napkin to remove the orange juice from my face.

She cast a pitying look at my daughter, and rage filled me, heating my cheeks as the juice continued to dribble down my chin. She looked like a not-quite-ripe cherry in her magenta jacket and skirt ensemble. In that moment, I wished I could pop her like one.

Finally finding a napkin, I wiped my face aggressively. "What do you want?" I asked, the tone coming out ruder than I'd intended.

Millie shot me a panicked look. No words were spoken by her, but her eyes said everything. She was friends with Marjory's daughter; plus the insufferable woman was the President of the P&C – the Parents and Citizens Association – so she controlled the distribution of the funding. Millie's eyes were pleading with me to play nice. Lucky for her, I practised doing just that every day when dealing with emotional clients. I reined in my anger, cleared my throat, and pasted my best fake smile on my face. "I do beg your pardon." Sarcasm dripped from my words. "It's been a long day, and you startled me. How can I help you, Marjory?"

She smoothed her already straight pencil skirt and said, "I just wanted to remind you about our fundraiser this weekend. We are still looking for volunteers at the cake stall, and I noticed you haven't nominated yourself for anything this year. I understand how daunting it can be when it's your first time volunteering, but don't forget, the committee is here to help. We'll show you the ropes." She flashed a smile I think she thought was encouraging, but it looked like a predator's smile to me.

I rubbed the back of my neck and shifted my weight. I mainly avoided volunteering so I didn't have to spend any extra time with her. But also, half the time they asked for volunteers, I was either working or taking Millie to a netball game. "When is it again?" I asked, delaying an actual answer.

"We'll be running the stall from eight in the morning until three in the afternoon on Saturday, and we'll need you to bake something to sell. Make sure it has a list of all the ingredients to display, and ensure that it only uses gluten and dairy-free alternatives," came her quick response.

I held up a hand to pause her instructions. Regardless of availability, I literally couldn't afford to buy gluten-free flour and a non-dairy based milk. But I wasn't telling her that. "I'm sorry, Marjory, but Matilda is playing netball on Saturday morning. By the time we finish there, go home and shower, and make it to the fundraiser, you'll be packing up. I'll see whether I'm free for the next one, okay?"

Marjory pursed her lips. "Extracurricular sport isn't the only thing that matters, you know. School spirit is important, and volunteering your time ensures a positive culture is developed."

Culture, schmulture. If someone else had a turn at being President, maybe I could summon a little more team spirit.

Marjory continued, "Especially for families in *your* position. You never know what opportunities Matilda might be presented with if you actually put some effort in to the school." She gave me a pitying smile.

The witch actually thought she was helping! No, she wasn't an actual witch; I was just calling her that so I didn't use a real swear word that started with a "b". To be fair, I was probably being rude to the witches.

"Don't let Matilda fall into the same trap as you did. Married young, no university degree, limited funds. Set her up for success by—"

My blood was boiling. I held my hand up and spoke over her in order to cut her tirade off. "Thank you for your concern, Marjory," I hissed. "We're doing just fine. Matilda has just been invited to try out for the school's senior netball team, so I think it's very important that she continues to hone her skills to ensure she has the best chance of being accepted and representing the school at state level." As petty as it was, it gave me great pleasure to see Marjory's eyes widen. I waved my hand breezily, pretending not to notice. "It's time for our next interview, so I'll have to leave you. Good luck on Saturday, Marjory!" I smiled innocently, gripped Millie's arm, and steered her away from the hell beast.

"Mum," Millie whispered out of the corner of her mouth, "you're holding me too tight."

My hand immediately released her, and I groaned at my thoughtlessness. It wasn't fair to take my anger out on anyone else, let alone my Millie. "I'm sorry! Are you okay?"

She giggled. "I'm fine. I just didn't want to lose feeling in my fingers." Millie stopped walking towards her drama teacher and grabbed my hand, forcing me to turn and look at her. She peered into my eyes, studying me closely before cocking her head. "You genuinely don't like her." She was always an observant child. "I don't think I've ever known you to actually not like someone."

"I'm sorry," I repeated. "I don't know why, but Marjory really gets under my skin. But that's my issue. You treat her how you find her, okay?"

Millie pulled me into a one-armed hug. "You don't need to apologise for your feelings," she murmured.

My lips quirked up at hearing her feed me the line I usually gave her. A voice cleared their throat nearby. Katie Snow, the drama teacher, stood and held out her hand with a smile. I returned her grin and shook her hand. I liked Mrs Snow. Although, she could show Nicole a thing or two about excessive energy levels, and that was saying something. We sat down, and she went on to tell me about an absolutely fabulous – her words, not mine – dramatic arts workshop she thought Millie would benefit greatly from. A visiting representative from some elite performing arts school was running a week-long workshop in October, and Millie was on her list of three students from the school that she wanted to attend.

I don't know if she saw the fear in my eyes when she told me the price or if the teachers knew more than they let on, but she went on to say there was a grant that was available for eligible secondary students to attend specialist art workshops. She promised to send the information about both the workshop and the grant through to my email. Millie was bouncing with excitement by the time we finished, Mrs Snow matching her energy.

As for me? I was ready for a nap.

I thanked Mrs Snow for thinking of Millie and escaped the hall as soon as I could, dodging the Vice Principal, Mr Jones, as I did. Sure, he was handsome, but I didn't like the arrogant attitude that came with the good looks.

I kept my face impassive as we exited the hall, but a tumult of emotions raged inside me. I was so bloody proud of Millie. And I was so happy I could be here for her. But it was bittersweet. Back when I was in high school, I'd had similar opportunities offered to me over the years. But, unlike Millie, I'd had no one in my corner. By the time I hit my senior year, I'd stopped bothering to tell my mum because I knew we'd be gone before I had a chance to attend whatever workshop or event was being offered. She had drifted through life, moving towns at least once a year, dragging me along with her. I'd taken myself to school events, and whenever I was questioned about my mother's whereabouts, I'd had to come up with an excuse for her absence. My teachers must have thought she was a very sickly woman. I refused to let Millie's dreams be crushed like mine were.

Now, of course, I realised that my mother probably had some deep-rooted mental health issues. I still held a lot of resentment towards her for not letting me be a kid and for not trying to help herself. Being a single mother was hard, I knew that now, but she never talked about my father and never opened up to me about her life's challenges. Even now, whenever we spoke, she refused to answer any of my questions that went deeper than what she had been up to in the past six months.

I tamped down the turmoil inside and sucked in a deep breath. Turning to Matilda, I beamed. "What wonderful offers, my girl! I'm so proud of you!" I pulled her into a tight hug, and she squeezed me back.

Upon being released, she did a celebratory dance – or what I liked to call a 'Millie-special'. Her feet spread, her knees bowed out, and she windmilled her arms while yelling in a high-pitched voice, "Yew!"

What was a yew, anyway? I'd always thought it was a European tree. Apparently, I'd been wrong. And I hadn't just been wrong, I'd been wrong with a heavy-handed dose of eye-rolling in my direction when I'd originally suggested that to her. I now knew it was, in fact, an exclamation of excitement.

I grinned at her exuberance. I still had no idea where the money would come from, but we'd figure it out. Maybe I could get a second job stacking shelves at the supermarket at night? I didn't really have anything to sell second-hand that would fetch any money. Even my car was basic and wouldn't be worth more than a couple grand. I wouldn't be able to replace it for that price, and I really didn't want to sell it and rely solely on public transport. I'd have to reach out to my ex to see if he could chip in some extra money for Millie's extracurricular fees, but last I'd heard, he was fairly skint as well. Chris was a good father. But he'd been an average husband.

For a second, my brain suggested selling photos of my feet online or whatever else was *hot* right now. I grimaced internally and shoved that idea away until I became truly desperate.

I was only ninety-five percent desperate so far; no need to do anything too crazy.

Yet.

Chapter Five

"Come on, little dove. We're getting pizza to celebrate!" Our local pizza shop had a loyalty program for its regular customers, and I had enough credits built up to claim a free pizza. Takeaway was rare in our house, but Millie deserved to stuff her face with the cheesiest of pizzas after having received such high accolades from her teachers.

We stood in line behind an older couple at the tiny pizzeria. It might be small, but Terry the gnome made the best pizza in Maroochydore, and no one could convince me otherwise. Through the internal window, I could see Terry working the ovens with his daughter assisting him. They were both no higher than my belly button; the shop had been custom-designed to make all the benches and cooking equipment to their height. I'd have to duck my head if I went into the kitchen.

Once the couple had finished placing their order and wandered over to sit down on the bench seat behind us, the teenage boy serving gave us a friendly smile and waved us up to the counter. I noticed a blush creeping up Millie's cheeks as she stared at him. She hid her awkwardness by tucking her hair behind her ears and studiously analysing the menu above his head. Even though we always ordered the same pizza. Every time. I suppressed my smile at her attempt to brush off her embarrassment.

I'm glad Millie's biggest problem is wondering whether the boy thinks she's cute.

When I opened my mouth to order, the bell over the door tinkled and a flurry of wind rushed in with the person entering. A peculiar feeling prickled over my spine. I closed my mouth and frowned, turning my head to see who had entered. A beautiful woman with an emerald sheen to her skin and vibrant purple eyes hurried to the counter. Her hair was wild with leaves knotted through it. A forest druid. My eyebrows raised of their own volition; it was rare to see a druid in the city.

She stood next to us and said brusquely, "Human, I must insist I go next."

Millie cocked her head and looked at me, curious to see my reaction. She knew I had a pet hate of rudeness, including people cutting in front of me. It didn't matter whether I was in the line at a takeaway shop or driving on the highway. But something unsettled me about this druid. An undercurrent of danger carried in the air around her.

I had Millie to think of, so I took a step back and waved her forward. "That's fine. Please go ahead."

I saw my daughter's look of surprise and heard the older man sitting behind us muttering to his wife about how this kind of rudeness would never have been tolerated in their day. He also said something about how we would all regret not just wiping magicas out now while we still had a chance of winning. At his last comment, I shot a glare his way, and he ducked his head, suddenly engrossed in twisting his wedding ring around his finger.

Meanwhile, the druid gave her order to the boy – an eggplant and seaweed covered pizza with bird-of-paradise sauce. The kid frowned and explained that wasn't on their menu. The woman became visually agitated, snapping a twig out of her hair, and barked, "Just give the order to your boss."

He jumped back at her snarl and rushed into the kitchen, speaking quickly with Terry. The gnome nodded and shooed the boy back out the front while he prepared her order. I turned to the woman, who stood there staring into the kitchen intently as she shifted her weight from foot to foot.

The prickling sensation hadn't left me but I couldn't ignore her obvious distress, so I asked, "Are you all right? You seem...upset."

The druid looked at me then, and I immediately regretted having engaged her attention. Time stood still as her vivid eyes bored into mine.

The scent of a rainforest after a storm washed over me while the sensation of dirt squeezed between my toes.

Birds chirped, wolves howled, and a roar that could only belong to a dragon filled my ears.

A peculiar heaviness pressed on my head while the images of thousands of fauna and flora flashed in my mind's eye. Pure contentment settled around me like a cloak, wrapping around the very core of my being.

The druid broke the connection, and the abrupt loss of her power made my soul feel raw and my lungs ache. The sense of peace faded and I felt as if my heart had been shaken all about inside my chest and then abandoned in a space that was now too big for it. After the onslaught had passed, an unexpected weakness made my knees shake and left me reeling. I gripped the counter for support and closed my eyes. My heart was racing, and my breathing came in short pants.

"Mum, are you okay?" Millie asked. Her voice echoed in my ears as if it were coming from a long way away. Her hand gripped my arm, acting as a tether for me, pulling me back to earth. She shook me. "What's happening?" A note of panic was creeping into her voice. I hated how I'd been the one who'd put it there.

I squeezed her hand and whispered hoarsely, "I'm okay."

The druid was still standing there, her head cocked while she considered me with a puzzled expression. Almost afraid of what would happen, I straightened and stared back at her defiantly. The sensation of drowning in the earth's delights didn't return.

My daughter looked between the two of us. "What just happened, Mum?" she repeated.

I hesitated. I didn't really know how to answer her. Plus, if I tried to explain the sensations that had just overwhelmed my senses in front of the other humans, the druid might be accused of attacking my mind. A big no-no by the laws of the Inter-Magical Community Council. I kissed Millie on the forehead. "Just a weird dizzy spell, love. I'm fine now."

Her answering scowl meant she didn't believe me, but I pasted a cheerful smile on my face anyway, in the hopes it would ease her concern.

"I'm Falendael," the druid said and stuck out her hand. Confusion haunted her expression as I shook her hand.

With difficulty, I forced myself to appear relaxed. "I'm Trix, and this is my daughter Matilda."

"Thank you for letting me cut in. Please allow me to pay for your order."

I gulped. "You don't need to do that." We might be broke, but I hated accepting charity.

"I want to. I was rude before. I am sorry for all that. Please allow me to make things right."

Glancing at Millie, who shrugged her acceptance of Falendael's offer, I said, "It's really not necessary, but thank you. We appreciate that."

Lucky us; we'd get to use our freebie another night.

I placed our order of a cheesy garlic bread, a meatlovers pizza, and a supreme, while Falendael pushed some cash across the counter. Terry exited the kitchens then with a pizza box, and the druid's lithe form walked over to him. I said walked, but really, I should probably have said danced. I'd never seen a creature move so gracefully. She knelt in front of him and whispered a few words. He frowned and glanced at me. He muttered an answer back, and I heard him use my full name. She stood abruptly. Passing him a circular glass vial of green liquid, she accepted the pizza box and, casting one last searching look my way, swiftly exited the pizzeria and immediately disappeared into the growing dusk.

I gave myself a shake and grabbed Terry's attention before he disappeared. "What was that all about?" I asked him.

He grinned widely, his eyes disappearing into his crinkles. "Oh, you know how some customers are. Falendael is a big deal where she hails from and insists on a special order and paying in the currency of exotic ingredients that are hard to come by on the Sunny Coast." He waved a hand dismissively but faltered when I cocked a disbelieving eyebrow.

"Mate. Come on. You know that's not what I'm asking. I heard you give her my name. Why?"

He wrung his hands. "I'm sorry, Trix. Perhaps that was wrong of me. I didn't think anything of it until I saw the way she looked at you. It's not always a good idea to capture the attention of a druid, especially with the power of that one." He shifted uncomfortably as I stared at him.

"What the heck, Terry?" I ground out between my teeth. Worry pressed down on me, but I tried not to make a big deal of it in front of Millie.

"Sorry, Trix!" he mumbled and wiped his hands nervously on his apron. "I need to get back to the kitchen, but I'm sure it will be fine." He nodded, the panic not quite leaving his eyes as he tried to convince himself as well as me. "It will all be fine," he repeated and disappeared back into the miniature kitchen.

Placing a hand on my arm, Millie tugged me away as I stared after the gnome. "Mum?" she couldn't hide the tremble in her voice at the strange turn of events.

I loosed a frustrated huff and nodded my head slightly towards the older gentleman, who was suspiciously quiet as his fingers stopped twisting his ring; he was doing a poor job of hiding his eavesdropping. Since we were still waiting for our order, I stepped outside to claim a little more privacy.

The door swung shut behind us, and Millie grabbed my hand. "Mum, what just happened?" Her eyes shone as fear of the unknown gripped her.

I rubbed my eyes, suddenly feeling very tired. "To be honest, I don't really know myself."

"What happened with that druid? With Falendael? She stared at you for ages until you looked like you were going to pass out. Then her personality totally flipped, and she was super nice. And why did Terry apologise?"

"I don't know!" I glanced around to make sure no one was listening and lowered my voice. "The druid... Somehow she" —I entwined my hands together into a ball in front of me— "inserted all these images and sounds and smells in my head. It wasn't an attack," I hurried to explain, "although I'm sure some people would try to say it was. It was sort of...like..." I stammered as I tried to find the right words. "Like a massive info dump. But the most beautiful info dump you could imagine." I sighed and rubbed my heart, missing the strange sense of peace that had come with it.

"That's..." Millie hesitated. "I mean, yeah, nah. That's uber weird."

"I'll be fine. Let's just grab the pizza and get home, okay?" I rubbed my head as pain spiked unexpectedly. "I've got a little headache, that's all. I'll take some paracetamol and then we can just watch reality TV to celebrate. Today has been a big day. I'm sure I'm just overtired." I offered a weak smile as the headache steadily grew.

Millie hesitated, not entirely convinced by my excuse. The older couple exited the shop then, pizza box in hand, so we re-entered the pizzeria and waited for the smiling teenage boy to pass us our order. This time, Millie didn't show any sign of blushing at his dimpled grin. She kept a watchful eye on me all night as I tried my best to ignore the worsening pain in my head that the painkillers couldn't touch. I did my best to make a big deal out of her terrific new opportunities, but I wasn't fooling anyone. Millie joined in on my attempts to overdramatise the excitement. But she was pretending as much as me. We had always had each other. Through thick and thin, we'd always been together for the past decade. But with my sudden onset of what was turning into a killer migraine, the idea that I was mortal and things could change in a heartbeat was scary for both of us.

We both called an early night. It wasn't until I got in the shower and turned the heat up as much as I could stand it, that I let the stress of the day catch up to me. I felt utterly overwhelmed as I stood under the running water. I had no idea where I'd find the extra money, the headache continued to pound in my skull, and the ache in my chest remained from the loss of the druid's connection. I still didn't understand what had happened at the pizzeria and had no idea where to find answers. Finally, I let myself break down and cried until I had no more tears left to shed.

Chapter Six

After inhaling her breakfast of the cheapest no-name brand of wheat cereal I could find, which was slathered in milk and sugar, Millie rushed to the bathroom to straighten her hair. It probably shouldn't but her shift in priorities still surprised me. She'd never been worried about makeup or hairstyles until the past few months, and I wasn't sure if it was a natural progression as she matured, if there was pressure from the other girls in her grade, or if her sudden interest in boys was to blame.

As I finished my own bowl of cereal, I popped another couple of painkillers. My headache had eased since last night but was still niggling at the back of my skull. Rinsing out the bowl in the sink, I stared vacantly into our front yard. I debated with myself as to whether I should be sitting Millie down for a discussion about not giving into peer pressure or if that would come across as controlling. I chewed my lip as I pondered her change in behaviour. It wasn't hurting anyone, and I hadn't seen any sign of problematic relationships, but kids could be cruel. Plus, I didn't trust Millie to tell me her problems when she had a knack of seeing the toll my own problems had on me. She'd rather hide her worries than add to mine.

She'd learned that from me.

Resolving to make time on the weekend for a deep and meaningful – or a D&M as she called them – I stacked the dishwasher and set it going, then got dressed myself. Glancing at my phone, I jolted when I saw the time.

"Millie! We're going to be late! Let's go, let's go, let's go!"

"Coming!" came the distant reply.

I grabbed my brown leather handbag, tossed my phone in it, and snatched the keys off the hook. I stepped outside in my bare feet, knowing my work shoes were still in my car. They lived on the floor of the passenger seat of my Commodore where I took them off each time I got home. A whisper of a sound reached my ears, and I jerked to the side just as a grey bird swooped past my head.

"What the flippity-flapjack!" I squealed and stumbled away from the attacking creature. Frantically, I swung my head from side to side, seeking my avian assailant. It was banking over a power pole on the opposite side of the street when I spotted it. I gaped as it flew back towards me, wondering what I'd done to offend the bird.

Instead of aiming for my head again, it landed on the roof of my car. It wasn't just any old bird though; it was a tawny frogmouth. People often called them owls, but they were actually more closely related to the nightjar family. Their mottled silver, black, and brown feathers gave them a knack for blending in with the bark of native trees. It wasn't totally uncommon to see them in suburban areas, but it was rare during the daytime.

I shook my head, confused. How did I know all that? I wasn't an expert on birds. Those weren't facts I remembered learning. I thought about the druid's info dump from the night before.

What did she do to me?

The sound of the tawny frogmouth's talons scratching the paint on the roof of my car made me wince.

"What are you doing, mate?" I tried to reprimand the animal, but my voice came out more like a squeak.

Studying it, I wondered if it was a shifter or some other sort of magica that only resembled the native bird. It didn't have the tell-tale blue ring around its pupils that shifters usually had, and I didn't know of any magica that looked like a tawny frogmouth.

"What do you want?" I asked and immediately felt foolish for talking to the wild bird.

She —and don't ask me how I knew it was a she; I just did— cocked her head at me before stamping her feet on the roof of my car again. I groaned for the sake of my poor paint.

"Please stop doing that," I moaned.

She immediately dived off the car and flew to the ground. I flinched at her response to my request but then dismissed the idea. It was just a coincidence; she couldn't possibly understand me. She'd probably gotten a fright from my voice. She side-stepped closer to my feet, and I froze at her proximity. Grasping the leg of my slacks with her beak, she tugged. Bobbing her head once, she croaked her species' strange *whump-whump* call.

A voice in my head said, "*Stay.*"

I shook my head and backed away from the tawny frogmouth. "Nope. Nup. This is too weird." Was I losing my mind? Having an over-friendly bird accost me was one thing, but hearing voices in my head was next level. Stress was doing a number on me. "Go home."

The grey bird gave me a melancholy look before she flew off. How the heckin' heck I knew it was a melancholy look beats me. I stared after her, wondering what on earth I had just witnessed. Millie rushed out then, slamming the front door behind her and slinging her school bag over her shoulder, distracting me from the weirdest encounter of my week. She flung herself into the passenger seat.

"Mum! What're you waiting for? Let's go!"

I pushed the image of the tawny frogmouth from my mind and hopped into my car. Checking the time on the dash, I sighed. "We missed the bus. I'll have to drive you all the way to school this morning."

Leaving the sleepy suburb of Maroochydore behind, we made good time until we got closer to Millie's school. The traffic slowed to a crawl as we approached the drop-off zone. As usual, I ducked onto a side street before we reached the stop-drop-go sign.

Millie leaned over and kissed my cheek and, with a cheerful wave, exited the sedan and met her friends on the corner. I headed straight for work; it would take anywhere between ten to twenty minutes depending on traffic. Either way, I'd still be there before my nine o'clock start time. As I drove along the side streets, doing my best to avoid the busier areas, something shiny flashed on the road in front of me. I frowned and slowed my vehicle, scanning the grey bitumen for the object that had caught my eye. My steering wheel suddenly started shuddering, and my car rattled.

"What the—?" I swiftly pulled over to the kerb, pulled on my work flats, and opened my door. When I walked around to the passenger side of the car, it quickly became obvious what the problem was. My hands flew to my mouth as I stared at the flat tyre. I examined it and found a large wedge of metal stuck in the rubber. I took a few deep breaths as I tried not to have a meltdown. I couldn't afford this. Last time I checked, one tyre cost about a quarter of my weekly wage. Not good. Tears pricked my eyes at the new expense dumped in my lap.

I pinched the bridge of my nose and took a slow breath in, counting to five as I did. Blowing out the air, I repeated the action a few more times and felt the tightness in my chest easing slightly. There was no point in panicking. One step at a time. Just focus on doing the next thing.

I opened the passenger door and reached into my handbag to grab my mobile. I called Fiona to let her know I would be late into work. As always, she was understanding. After I'd hung up, I opened the boot and pulled out the jack and began the process of changing the flat. I'd grown up without a father, and my mother wasn't exactly a handywoman. It was times like this that I was thankful for my relationship with my ex, Chris. He might have decided he didn't love me anymore, but before the heartbreak, he'd taken the time to teach me the basics of being independent. I was grateful to him for having sat me down multiple times to teach me about changing tyres, motor oil, and lightbulbs. I worked quickly, the growing heat of the morning causing sweat to roll down my back. I didn't have any spare clothes to change into, so hopefully blasting the car's air-con and a healthy dose of deodorant would cover any smell.

After dropping the jack and tightening the nuts on the spare tyre, I grunted as I heaved the flat tyre into the boot of my car. My back would not be happy tomorrow.

Slamming the boot, I fell into my seat and cranked the air-con. Cold air enveloped me, and I sighed in relief. The last thing I needed was to add a speeding ticket to my growing list of bills, so I drove to work as fast as I could without breaking any limits. Tearing into the nearest available carpark to my work, I ran to the ticket machine. I let out a hiss of frustration. A sign on it announced it was out of order.

An actual swear word was on the tip of my tongue, but I ground my teeth together. Racing back to my car, I found a scrap of paper in my glovebox and scribbled a note to say the machine was out of order when I went to pay for my day's parking. I popped it on my dashboard, locked the car, and ran to my office. I hurried through the front door, the air-conditioning blasting a rush of cold air over my shoulders as I entered.

Nicole flashed me a grin over her desk and queried, "Coffee? I reckon you need one after the morning you've had. Fi told me what happened."

As much I might want a latte, there was no way I could afford one. I kept my face neutral even though inside I was squirming at the idea that I couldn't afford a six-dollar coffee, let alone a new tyre. "Nah, I'm fine. I had a coffee at home this morning, and you know how I get if I have more than one a day."

Nicole raised an eyebrow but didn't say anything. She stood up and flitted down the hall to ask our colleagues if they wanted a coffee from Bards and Beans. I followed her at a more sedate pace, offering a good morning to Shirlene and Tim as I walked past their doors. Shirlene glowered at me, showcasing her offence at my late arrival. A shiver ran down my spine. Shirlene's barely concealed anger was more potent than usual. Shirlene tended to either talk over me in meetings or simply ignore me unless I asked her a direct question, but she seemed particularly outraged this morning. I shrugged her attitude off; if Fiona was okay with me arriving late, Shirlene would just have to deal with it. I rolled my eyes at Nicole as she walked back past me to head to the popular café. Fiona always got a dirty chai, so Nicole hadn't bothered to ask her for her order.

Conscious of the time, I scurried to my desk, pulled out my chair and turned on my computer. In my haste, I somehow managed to smash my ankle into my desk leg; I bit my tongue as a tirade of expletives threatened to burst forth. After taking a few deep breaths to calm the spike of pain, I pulled my water bottle out of my handbag and placed it carefully on my desk, praying for no more spills today, before shoving the leather bag into its home in the bottom drawer.

As my computer whirred to life, Fi popped her head around my door. "Oh, good, you made it! You okay?"

"A bit hot and somewhat flustered, but I'm here now." I flashed a wry grin.

Fi walked all the way into my office then. Today, she was wearing a form-fitting sleeveless dress in lilac. Guess that was the pros of being the boss; you could wear whatever you wanted. "I'm glad. Flat tyres are the worst." She opened her mouth to say something else when her mobile rang. She groaned in frustration as she pulled it out of her pocket.

Where does she find all these women's clothes with pockets?

"I've got to have a serious chat with you, but it will have to wait. I need to take this and my nine-thirty will be here any minute." She answered her phone before I could seek comfort that the serious talk wasn't actually a proper 'serious talk' and gave me a small wave before disappearing down the hall.

An icy sensation swept through my body at her suggestion that, 'we need to talk.' The last time someone had said that to me, my whole world had imploded and I'd become a single mother in the space of an afternoon. I shook my head to clear the unwelcome thoughts. Fi was always appreciative of my work, and the sales figures were good. Okay, I was a little late today but that was out of my control. There was no way she was firing me. I probably needed to see a therapist to work through my abandonment issues, but I couldn't afford one. I forced myself to focus on reviewing my schedule for the day.

Everything would be fine. I was sure of it.

If I told myself often enough, maybe one day I would believe it.

Chapter Seven

Mrs Hinschen settled herself into the chair opposite my desk. Unlike Gargolegmew, Mrs Hinschen was all human. Grey hair was coiffed stylishly around her heart-shaped face, where wrinkles had begun to claim their place. She smiled sweetly at me as I placed a printed out copy of her house renewal in front of her.

"Before we begin, can I get you anything, Mrs Hinschen? Tea, coffee, water?"

"Oh, no thank you, dear. I just had a coffee. I met my daughter for brunch at that cafe down the road and thought I'd pop in since I had to cancel my appointment yesterday. I hope you don't mind?"

"Not at all!" I flashed her a genuine smile. I'd taken over the management of this elderly woman's policies last year and had found her charming from day one. I could never be cross with her. "Was your brunch at the café opposite the supermarket? Bards and Beans?"

She nodded enthusiastically. "That's the one! I just adore the cute little waiters, and their coffee is divine."

I flinched internally at her use of the term "cute" for the fairies who worked there. Hopefully she hadn't used that vaguely offensive word in front of them. Quickly scanning her hair and clothing, I decided she must have kept her opinions to herself since there were no tangles in her hair or inappropriate notes stuck to her pastel-pink blouse. Fairies might have grown used to being called cute by humans, but they made sure they pulled pranks on anyone who dared use the term. I debated whether to mention the faux pas to Mrs Hinschen. She probably should be educated, but I didn't think it would be professional of her insurance broker to be the one to teach her.

Clearing my throat, I turned the print-out of her policy to page one. "Mrs Hinschen—"

She frowned and held a hand up to stop me. "I keep telling you to call me Jane, Beatrix."

My lips quirked up, and I gave an acquiescent bob of my head. "Very well, Jane. And you can call me Trix. I've looked over your policy and just wanted to confirm that none of your contact details or the details of your home have changed in the past year?"

"Nothing's changed, dear, no."

"You haven't added anything to your home that would warrant increasing the building sum insured? Things like a shed, a pool, or renovating the interior would qualify."

She laughed, a surprisingly loud guffaw in relation to the stature of the woman. "Oh goodness, no. It's just me in the house. Mr Hinschen left this world quite a few years ago now, before I brought this property. There's no shed, I never learnt to swim, and I rather like the old cottage feel, so haven't bothered with any upgrades. I fear these modern houses are so heartless. There's no warmth about them whatsoever."

"I'm inclined to agree with you there," I said conversationally as I made a note on the computer. "What about your contents? You've only got them insured for the minimum allowed amount. Are you sure that would cover the replacement of everything if you lost it all in a house fire?"

"God forbid that should ever happen!" she cried. Her hands fluttered over her chest.

I started at her sudden outburst but recovered myself, quickly placating her. "I'm sure it won't, Jane, but it's my job to make sure you are protected in the unlikely event of the worst-case scenario. I also should mention that if you have any valuables, such as jewellery, firearms, artwork, or antiques, that are worth over five thousand dollars, we will need to note them as a specified valuable under your contents." After eight years working in domestic insurance, I could spout my script in my sleep.

Mrs Hinschen pursed her lips and stared out my window. After a beat, she shot me a sheepish look and mumbled, "Well, I do have a Winchester rifle worth six thousand dollars that I should probably note as one of my valuables then."

I'm sure my eyebrows nearly disappeared into my hair. "Oh!" Struggling to school my face into some semblance of normality, I cleared my throat for the second time in ten minutes. I hadn't expected this sweet old woman to say yes to owning an expensive firearm. Looks could be deceiving. "Okay. Yes, that will need to be noted. I'll need you to send me the full details of the weapon along with its serial number. Do you have a license for it, and does it stay locked in a gun safe when not in use?"

"Yes, of course! I'm very passionate about firearm safety. So was my Howard. We used to work at the local rifle range, you know, Beatrix."

"No, I did not," I murmured as I ignored the unabbreviated use of my first name and made notes on my monitor. I tried to assimilate the idea of the sweet and stylish Jane wielding a rifle and found myself struggling. This appointment was not going down the way I'd expected.

Once I'd updated Jane's home and contents insurance and bid her farewell, the rest of the day flew past. There was a steady stream of phone calls, another appointment with a client, and an hour-long webinar on updated industry guidelines.

Yawn.

By the time I had a chance to seek out Fiona for 'the chat', she was nowhere to be found. I asked Nic where she'd disappeared to.

"Oh! Fi got called out for a renewal meeting by the Forrests. She probably won't make it back before five."

The Forrests were a family of elves and one of our biggest commercial clients. Ellie from netball was the daughter of one of the owners. They ran a chain of cafes, and their annual premiums were close to fifty grand. Fi had been chasing a meeting with them for weeks to discuss any changes to their policies before renewal came around next month. She would have dropped everything to make sure she could meet them today. I was pleased for her because I knew it had been stressing her out, but it didn't help my own stress levels, knowing I wouldn't get to find out what she wanted to talk to me about before the weekend.

I chewed a nail as I scanned through my emails. After updating a few claims' notes, I rolled my chair away from my desk, stood, and stretched before making my way to our kitchenette. Boiling the jug, I made myself a cup of instant coffee and grabbed a ginger biscuit from the communal stash of snacks. Fi was a great boss and asked Nic to keep it stocked for us. At the sound of rustling packets, Nic joined me at the bench.

Leaning against the counter, my best friend raised an eyebrow at me. "Thought you only had one coffee a day?"

I poked my tongue out at her. "I need it today, all right?"

She smirked and twisted one of her rings around her fingers. "Hey, are we still on for the movies tonight?" Nicole asked before stuffing two chocolate biscuits into her mouth at once.

I sighed wistfully. Between Millie's new extracurricular activities and then the tyre this morning, there was no way I could afford to go to the movies. Nic was my best friend and would offer to pay for my ticket in a heartbeat, but she'd already done that last time we went together. I didn't want to make a habit of it. I just wished I could shout her for a change. I didn't want her to worry about me any more than she already did.

"Actually," I said slowly as I washed my hands at the sink, "I thought it would be fun to have a movie night at home instead? We could cook popcorn all together, have some soft drinks with Millie—" Nicole snorted loudly at the idea of drinking a non-alcoholic beverage on a Friday night "—and have a movie marathon?"

Nic hesitated a beat too long, and I had a sneaking suspicion that she knew why I had made the suggestion but didn't want to embarrass me by discussing finances at work. She gave a nonchalant shrug and said, "Sounds good to me. The popcorn at the cinema is stupidly overpriced anyway. Plus, somehow it always smells like feet in there. But, fair warning, I'm bringing two bottles of wine."

I sniggered. "I'll make up the spare bed then."

We heard the front door open and the murmur of voices. Nic flashed me a smile before darting back to her post. I wandered back to my desk with my drink. I heard Shirlene greet the couple who had just arrived and invite them into her office.

With most of my work caught up on, I unlocked my phone and searched for night-fill or weekend jobs in Maroochydore. As I scrolled through the list of casual jobs available, I reluctantly favourited the offers from local supermarkets seeking staff, as well as the cafés and pubs looking for waiters. The thought of filling shelves with groceries for other people or serving alcohol to drunks left me with a bad taste in my mouth. It wasn't what I wanted for my life, but what choice did I have? Getting a second job meant I could pay the ever-increasing pile of bills, but I'd run the risk of missing out on Millie's games on Saturday mornings.

The insurance assessing job popped back into my mind. Drumming my fingers against the desk, I hesitated. With a sigh, I brought the email back up on my computer and reread it. The money on offer was very tempting. But it was a full-time position. Leaving Fi and the team would be so hard. But what if Fi's serious talk was in fact to tell me she had to let me go? I needed to have a back-up plan for a full-time position. I sighed again. Even if I applied with Fi's promised reference, I probably wouldn't get it anyway. Before I could change my mind, I forwarded the information to my private email address. Just in case I decided to apply on the weekend.

I also reviewed the app on my phone that I used to budget. We weren't subscribed to any streaming services or entertainment apps, so there was no savings to be made there. Working in insurance meant I kept a close eye on any new insurers in the market and changed my policy for my car every time renewal came around if I could find a more competitive premium. Unfortunately, we couldn't afford contents or life insurance.

The protection wards I'd put on the house and the car were all but depleted. How did that saying go? A doctor is his own worst patient. If I was my own client, I'd be giving myself a serious talking-to. If things didn't turn around soon, I'd have to start looking for a cheaper place to rent. The thought turned my stomach. I loathed the idea of uprooting. Even though it was only a rental, I loved our little home and the memories that Millie and I had made there.

There was one other option, one that I hated to consider. But desperate times and all that.

I could ask my mother for help.

Chapter Eight

I FOUND SOMETHING NEW to stress about when I returned to my car to find the dreaded slip of paper tucked under my windscreen wiper. A parking fine. Glaring at it, I bit back a real curse. You could bet your bottom dollar I'd be contesting it since the meter was broken when I parked. Hopefully I could get it waived but the added stress to an already stressful day didn't help my mood. Knowing that Nicole was coming over for a movie marathon was the only thing that helped keep my panic about my financial situation at bay on the drive home.

I decided to put off calling my mother until the morning. Or Sunday. Or maybe I'd wait until next week. The idea of asking her for help irked me, but I might not have another choice. When we last spoke in March, she mentioned that she'd received a windfall. At the time, she'd offered to share it with me, but I'd declined. I hadn't bothered to press for details of where the money came from. Whether she had found herself a sugar daddy or an illegal side hustle, I didn't really care. That was her business and if she didn't want to share that with me that was her prerogative. But if she was willing to share it to help Millie get ahead, then I'd swallow my pride and ask her for assistance. After pulling into my driveway, I checked my letterbox. There were two letters, one from the power company and the other from my real estate agent.

Dread pooled in my gut. At least one of those letters was a bill.

I opened the electricity one first. Thankfully, the figure was just below our usual monthly fee, and I had allowed for it in my budgeting. I relaxed a little. The real estate agent usually sent out a notice of inspection by letter, but I'd already received a letter a couple weeks ago with an inspection date for next month. Frowning, I slid the lonely piece of paper out of the envelope. I forced my eyes to focus on the individual words even while my heart sank as I read each one.

They were increasing our rent by fifty dollars a week.

Mother-freaking-trucker.

That was the final nail in the coffin. What was I going to do? I couldn't afford that. I was already living week to week. Pay day was next week, and I only had forty-three dollars in my account as of right now. That would be... I did a quick calculation in my head... two thousand, six hundred extra dollars per year.

I *really* couldn't afford that. Not on top of the replacement tyre. Plus Millie's new opportunities at school. Never mind even thinking about the upcoming car insurance renewal and the fact my protection wards were fading fast. And I only had a simple alarm ward. It wasn't even a proper boundary ward that would stop would-be thieves from entering the property.

I scrubbed my hands over my face. Even with the increase, the rent was still on the cheaper end for this suburb. My landlord had been kind to me for a long time. There was no way I could find another rental for less than this price in Maroochydore. Which would mean I'd have to uproot us from our home. If our new rental was too far away, Millie might be forced to change schools...I couldn't do that to her. I knew what it was like having to make friends in a new school as a teenager. It was hard. I couldn't put her through that too.

As I pinched the bridge of my nose, despair threatened to engulf me. My darling friend chose that moment to pull into my drive. Gulping deep breaths, I managed to cover my panic as Nic hauled out two full bags of takeaway from my favourite Thai restaurant. That was lucky; guess I didn't need to break out the two-minute noodles, after all.

We watched some leather-clad assassin with a smoking hot bod save the world while we dug into our dinner. Soon after the meal Millie excused herself, claiming she needed her sleep in preparation for her netball game in the morning. I reckon she was trying to give Nic and

I space to have a D&M if we needed it. Once I had downed my third glass of wine, and I could hear Millie's shower running, I broke down to my best friend. I told her all the worries that plagued me; from the growing pile of bills, to the strange encounters with the druid and the tawny frogmouth. Darling Nic held me as I sobbed into her shoulder. I was ridiculously thankful to have a friend like her, and I told her so, which then resulted in both of us having a blub together.

My emotional outburst resulted in a switch from watching action movies to romcoms. We all knew there would be a happily-ever-after in the end, but it didn't mean we couldn't enjoy the journey getting there. However, the male lead hadn't yet managed to convince his housekeeper of his love in Portuguese before the two of us passed out on the couch sometime before midnight.

My alcohol-induced kip made me believe we were all on a cruise together with the waves rolling the ship around while someone tapped on my porthole asking for a chocolate éclair. I jerked awake to realise the sound of tapping wasn't just in my dream. Blearily, I looked around, trying to figure out where the sound was coming from. The kitchen window. Carefully, I removed Nic's foot from off my lap and went to investigate.

In my head, I channelled that sexy assassin we watched earlier as I crept towards the tap-tap-tap in stealth mode. But after my third crash into furniture, I figured maybe I wasn't being so sneaky after all. I sighed and straightened, attempting to walk straight. Which also proved difficult. This was why I didn't normally drink. It wasn't just because I couldn't afford the habit.

The tapping sounded again. I was getting close. The alcohol numbed any rational feelings of fear I might have normally felt as I moved towards the sound.

Oh no.

This was how people in horror movies usually wound up dead.

That realisation didn't stop my feet from moving closer to the window. A nearby streetlamp offered its feeble glow, creating strange shadows in my yard. I peered through the window pane, adrenaline finally making an appearance, causing my heart to race and my breath to fog up the glass. Something small and grey popped up in front of my face, and I let out a strangled screech.

"No need to yell. It's just me." The voice in my head was back.

I peered through the glass, blinking furiously in an effort to make my eyes focus on the grey creature sitting on my sill. It was the tawny frogmouth. "It's you!" I hissed.

"Yes, me. I noticed you didn't listen to my earlier suggestion to stay put. Might have saved you a flat tyre if you had." The bird fluffed itself up.

"You know about my flat? And how did you know it was going to happen?"

"I occasionally receive premonitions."

"Like, you can see the future?" I snorted in disbelief. *"Riiigght,"* I drew the word out. That wine had really done a number on me. I believed I was having a conversation with a psychic tawny frogmouth. That was a bit wild even for my imagination.

"I can!" Her tone was indignant. *"I'm trying to help you, Trix."*

I squinted at the bird in suspicion. "Why are you trying to help me? And, for that matter, how do you know my name?"

She bobbed her head. *"I know a lot of things about you."*

"That doesn't sound stalkerish at all." I stumbled over the "ish" sound, slurring my words.

She croaked a raspy noise in what I assumed was her version of a laugh.

I crossed my arms with a *humph*. "All righty, Miss Know-It-All, you know my name, but you haven't told me yours," I probed her.

The tawny frogmouth hesitated before saying, *"You used to call me Froggy."*

"Why does every sentence out of your mouth...or mind or whatever just raise more questions? What kind of name is Froggy? Scratch that. What do you mean, I 'used to'?"

She studied me with her yellow eyes and opened her beak in what looked like a smile. *"You knew me when you were a child."* Her tone was matter of fact, as if it was obvious.

Gobsmacked, I simply stared at her.

She shrugged her wings and explained, *"You were only young. You didn't have much of an imagination when it came to names."*

"Yeah, nah. Are you being serious right now? I think I would remember having a tawny frogmouth for a friend."

"You wouldn't remember if your memory was wiped."

I snorted. "That's not possible. No one can wipe memories."

"Some magicas can. They don't share that information with the humans lest their powers be abused."

I hesitated. What Froggy said made some sort of sense. I shook my head, trying to clear it. The alcohol didn't help my attempts, and the shaking only exacerbated the pounding in my head. "Why are you sharing it with me then?"

The bird shifted uncomfortably. *"I can't tell you that."*

"Wait a sec. Are you trying to tell me a magica wiped my mind?"

"Can't tell you that either."

A lengthy pause stretched between us as we considered each other. Eventually, I said, "This is the weirdest dream I've had in a long time."

"It's not a dream."

With a snicker, I gestured at the bird on the windowsill. "Since when do humans speak to tawny frogmouths?"

She fluffed up her feathers unhappily and sighed. *"I wish I could explain."*

"Me too," I quipped and laughed at my asinine joke. Drunk me was funny.

Apparently, Froggy didn't agree. With a frosty glare, she announced, *"If you don't think this conversation is real, there's no point in continuing. I'll return when you're a bit more lucid."*

On silent wings, she abandoned my window and disappeared into the darkness.

A pang of sadness struck me in the chest as she left me. Stumbling back down my hallway, I made a stop at the bathroom and grabbed some painkillers. Throwing myself onto my bed, I stared at the ceiling for a long time. I had just about convinced myself that it definitely, actually, for-sure, one hundred percent had been a dream when I finally fell back asleep.

Millie bounced around, making us all breakfast while Nic and I dragged our bleary-eyed-selves off our respective beds. Or couch, in Nic's case. I silently handed my friend some painkillers before setting to making us both some coffee. Millie set a plate full of toast on the dining table, and I thanked the universe for giving me a daughter with the foresight to offer simple carbs to us two hungover misfits.

As I set the coffee mug in front of Nic, she took a massive bite of toast before flashing both of us a grin which included chunks of crust imbedded between her teeth. She rasped out, "Think I'll keep you lot around. You know the way to a girl's heart." She waved the half-chewed buttery slice of toast around, crumbs dropping over the wooden dining table.

Millie shook a finger at Nicole. "Now, look here, I know your head is hurting, but that doesn't mean you get to make a mess." She pointed at the crumbs. "You'll be wiping the table down once you're finished."

Nicole dropped her head sheepishly and muttered, "Yes, Miss." In a stage whisper, she grumped to me, "She didn't used to be this bossy! Now she's fifteen she reckons she runs the joint." She winked at Millie who sniggered and threw the damp dishcloth at Nic's head.

Looking at them both, I sighed happily. This was my family. Matilda by blood and Nicole by choice.

With a screwed-up face, Nic poked her tongue at me. "Ugh. You look like you're having a sappy moment." She held her hands over her ears with a look of mock horror on her face. "Nup! Don't wanna hear how much you love me. I know you do. How could you not? I am pretty fabulous."

"And surprisingly quick at recovering from a hangover," I observed drily.

"Gimme carbs and coffee and I'm fine," she declared before sucking a stray drip of melted butter off her hand. Keeping her eyes averted, Nic feigned a casual air and commented, "So I noticed that letter from the real estate."

Millie looked at me, confused. "What letter?"

I hadn't bothered to tell her. She'd start telling me she didn't want to do the workshop or something and then both of us would be sacrificing everything and no one would be happy. There was no point in stressing her out with my money troubles.

I glared daggers at Nic for bringing it up, but she continued as if she didn't notice. "Bloody idiots, always upping rent as soon as they get the chance. Mine just went up last month too. So rude. Look how nice you keep this place! You'd think they'd want to keep you happy since you look after their house so well."

My brows pulled together. She seemed to be rambling. *Where on Earth is she going with this?*

"*Anywhooo...* I had a thought, and...stop me if I'm overstepping here..." She paused, and I noticed a tightness around her eyes that wasn't usually there. She sucked in a breath and plunged on, "I thought that maybe I could move in with you two? I could rent the third bedroom. That way we can share the costs, and it will ease the strain on everyone's pocket." Nic finally swung her eyes up to meet mine. Her lips quirked up in a grin, and she added, "We could say we're a couple, so I'm not technically in breach of sub-renting or whatever the term is." She waggled her eyebrows suggestively.

I burst out laughing. And it wasn't just because of Nic's ridiculous facial acrobatics. The pressure that had been pushing down on me since I'd received that letter yesterday had suddenly eased. I felt like I could breathe again.

Before I confirmed it, I looked at Millie. "What are your thoughts, little dove?"

She wore a huge grin. "I'm not sure that I'm one hundred percent on board with the mess this one creates wherever she goes, but I'm definitely keen to have a cool aunty as a housemate."

Nic poked her tongue at Millie and said, "I'll have you know, I'm actually quite the domestic goddess." She flipped her hair dramatically over her shoulder and added, "Just so we're clear, becoming a couple was a joke. I love lesbians, but I ain't one. Give me the male form any day." She made an obscene gesture, indicating what she might like to do to the male form and I whipped my hand over Millie's eyes.

"Mum!" she complained.

"Okay, so there might be some teething issues while we figure out each other's boundaries, but I think that's a wonderful idea." I beamed at my friend, relief making me giddy. "Thank you so much, Nic. You are, quite literally, a lifesaver."

My friend smirked and gave a nonchalant shrug. "I know."

Her sharing the cost of rent wouldn't solve all our problems, but at least we could keep a roof over our heads.

Chapter Nine

"Seriously, good luck today. Win, lose, or draw, I'm so proud of you," I said as we arrived at the netball courts, and I pulled Millie into a hug.

Her nervous energy softened, and she leaned into my arms, curling her own around my back. "Thanks, Mum." She jogged ahead of me to check the noticeboard at the clubhouse to confirm her court number.

I'd found one of the last carparks in the place, but that meant I was stuck way up the back of the parking lot. With a sigh, I began the long trek towards the courts. They were all outdoor courts, but four were asphalt and six were grass. Before I made it to the clubhouse, Millie was already jogging towards the grass courts. She held up one hand with her fingers splayed. Court five it was. Following her at a much more sedate pace, I sucked in a deep breath, inhaling the smell of the weekly sausage sizzle run by the club. There was something about having sausages and onion on buttered bread with barbecue sauce cooked by somebody else that just tasted so much better than when you did it at home. I debated giving in to my craving. But even though it was only a few dollars, I simply couldn't afford to get in the habit of eating out.

Five dollars here, a couple of dollars there, and all of a sudden, I couldn't afford this month's electricity bill. Sitting down on the grass near the edge of court five, I watched Millie start her stretches for a few seconds before opening my handbag. She'd be warming up for a little while before the game started so I may as well amuse myself. With a sad little sigh, I pulled out a romance novel with an impossibly attractive businessman on the front along with a packet of plain biscuits I'd packed. What a depressing analogy for my life.

I put my book away once the game started. It was exciting, as far as netball games go. The Minotaurs and Munchkins were tied at half-time. But Millie's team pulled ahead in the last quarter thanks to a foul by the fairy on the Munchkins team who tried to get away with using her glamour to distract the Minotaurs' goal keeper. When the whistle sounded, ending the game, Millie cheered along with her team. After a massive group hug, they all shook hands with the Munchkins, congratulating them on a good game. With one final team cheer, Millie ran towards me, a grin stretching her face.

As her feet hit the white line that marked the edge of the court, a screech ripped through the air. The general hubbub of the players and parents died immediately as we all stopped what we were doing and sought the origin of the unearthly sound. The shriek sounded again. It was coming from the bushland that bordered the western side of the courts.

A general murmuring started up again as people speculated on what it could be.

A voice behind me muttered, "That sounds like a griffin. And an angry one at that."

"Someone, call the police!"

Ellie appeared beside me, concern marring her beautiful face. "What's the point? They won't help. I'm calling Altan." She had her phone at her ear in a matter of seconds.

"Who's Altan?" I asked and grabbed Millie, holding her tight at my side as I scanned the dense bush. Large gum trees, taller than the clubhouse, dotted the scrublands, while thick undergrowth made it impossible to see between them.

Ellie didn't reply to me, instead speaking quickly to the person on the other end of her phone. She ended the brief conversation with an urgent, "I don't care how much it costs. We need you here now!"

Before I could ask her again for an explanation, a magica crashed out of the shrubbery. Its sharp beak, shaggy mane, and feathered wings were obvious even at this distance. A wild griffin. My adrenaline spiked and a wave of fear crashed over me. The griffin made a beeline for the courts, half flying, half loping, not getting more than a metre off the ground as he charged towards us. The sight of the wild magica resulted in a panicked rush to the carpark. Magicas and humans alike were shoving each other aside to get to the perceived safety of their cars. Frantically, I mentally ran through my knowledge of griffins. Somehow, I knew that they pursued people who ran from them but were less likely to hunt those who froze. But I had no idea how to fight them.

Gritting my teeth, I pushed Millie behind me.

"What do we do, Mum?" The terror in Millie's voice made the pressure in my chest that much worse. My own fear had my heart racing, but knowing she was petrified, and I had no way to fix it, was the worst feeling in the world. So I lied.

"Everything will be okay, little dove. Just stay close to me and don't run. You'll only attract its attention." I glanced at Ellie who was gripping Isabella as tightly as I was Millie. "Any other ideas, Ellie?"

My friend replied, "I read somewhere that griffins can be contained within an iron cage, and they don't like water."

Sucks to be us. I didn't have a cage hidden in my handbag and there were no nearby bodies of water to dump the magica in. Guess our only option for now was to stay frozen and hope it chased someone else. I exhaled loudly. "Right. Do you have a weapon? Or any iron?"

Ellie's mouth was set in a grim line as she shook her head. Guess we were waiting for a rescue.

The magica roared again and bounded towards the clubhouse, taking a swipe at Faith, who was shoving a teen into the building. The elderly pixie screamed and leapt away, somehow avoiding the sharp claws. I automatically took a step towards her. I was torn. She needed help, but I couldn't abandon Millie.

One of the dads who was closest to Faith grabbed the clubhouse fire hose and pointed it at the creature, turning it on full blast. The griffin howled and leapt away from the stream of water, standing just out of range and snarling. The distraction gave Faith time to scramble away and into the clubhouse herself.

I looked at the carpark to see if we could run while the griffin's attention was elsewhere. But no such luck. There was a traffic jam at the entrance to the courts, thanks to three cars colliding in their hurry to escape. I groaned. This was not looking good. The only other safe place I could see was the clubhouse. But the griffin was between us and the building. The magica's tail whipped back and forth and he stretched his wings out wide, looking twice the size. I shivered involuntarily. The griffin was a formidable predator. Padding away from the clubhouse, he scented the air, swinging his head from side to side as he did so. His sickly green eyes swept over us, and locked onto his next target.

Me.

The griffin loped toward court five, his front talons tearing up the earth with each stride.

Oh, heck. This wasn't going to end well. Desperately, I looked around for anything I could use as a weapon. Maybe my handbag was heavy enough to swing at its head and knock it out. Unlikely, but it was the only idea I had. Hefting my bag into one hand, I widened my stance, ready to do everything I could to defend Millie.

A flash of light in my periphery signalled the opening of a portal beside us. It wasn't the dark violet of a Hellscape portal, but the pleasant sky blue of a teleportation portal that operated within the Earth's plane. Yeesh. Those things were expensive.

A man stepped through the portal and I glanced at Ellie. Was this the man she called for help? Altan?

Not a man, I corrected myself. *A sphinx.*

I hadn't dealt with sphinxes much as they weren't common in the tropics, preferring to stick to cooler climates. Sphinxes looked mostly human aside from their tail and feline ears. Although most of his face had human features, the sphinx's cat-like ears that poked through his dark hair on the side of his head were pinned, and his amber eyes were glaring daggers at the griffin. My gaze swept over his humanoid figure, ignoring the way his black, form-fitting outfit hugged his body. There was no time for ogling, only action. I just hoped he knew how to use the sword strapped to his waist.

"Altan!" Ellie cried. "Thank the Goddess that you're here!"

He gave her a nod before darting towards the beast.

The griffin roared his displeasure and raised his talon, ready to shred the sphinx. But Altan easily flitted out of the way and threw something at the magica. A puff of orange smoke drifted off his coat and the creature screamed. Whatever Altan had done seemed to have enraged the beast, not subdued him. Altan unsheathed his sword but the griffin dashed away from him before he could put it to use. The sphinx cursed, and the griffin raced towards us, intent on engaging with me. Ellie and I stood shoulder-to-shoulder, ready to protect our girls. I lifted my handbag, praying it would slow down those lethal talons a tiny bit. I might not have any special abilities or combat experience, but I'd do whatever I had to do to save Millie. There was no way I was going down without a fight.

The griffin skidded to a stop in front of us, his musky scent overpowering. He reared back on his haunches and shrieked, his taloned front legs clawing the air. As he came back to earth, he swept his right wing forward. Right towards my elven friend.

"Look out!" I screamed and shoved Ellie to the ground. The heavy wing of the griffin narrowly avoided her but took me out instead. It hit me in the gut, sending me flying a few metres where I landed with a *whump.*

My mouth hung open as I tried to breathe, all the air gone from my lungs. Turning my head, I watched helplessly as Millie raised her fists and screamed her anger and fear at the magica's face. Panic engulfed me as the eagle eyes bore down on her and he opened his beak.

Scrambling desperately to try and get back on my feet, but unable to make a sound due to the lack of oxygen in my lungs, I mouthed the word, "No!"

The sphinx suddenly reappeared, slicing the tip of the griffin's lion tail off, causing the creature to whirl around as he screamed in pain. The griffin snaked his head forward toward the sphinx and snapped his beak, only missing Altan by an inch. Altan used that moment to smack the griffin on the head.

I frowned. That didn't seem like a smart move. In fact, I'd go so far as to say that bopping a griffin on the noggin was borderline suicidal.

I was immediately proven wrong. Whatever it was that Altan had clasped in his hand when he hit the griffin, exploded on contact. Altan jumped away from the griffin, and an iron cage shimmered into existence, enclosing the wild magica. Screeching, the griffin threw himself against the bars as they solidified, the metal rattling as his body connected.

The griffin was captured.

We all froze for a second as it took a minute for reality to sink in. We were safe. Millie ran over to me as I finally managed to drag in a ragged breath. "Mum! Are you okay?"

"Fine. You?" I croaked out, using her offered arm to stand up. Pulling her into a hug, I thanked whichever angel that was watching over us today. I fully comprehended how lucky our escape was. I'd be having nightmares about that magica standing over Millie for weeks.

"I'm okay. The others are too." Millie kept an arm around my waist as we shuffled over to where our saviour was talking to my elven friend.

Ellie immediately introduced me to Altan. I double-tapped three fingers on my chest and said, "You saved my girl. Thank you."

The sphinx shrugged without meeting my eyes. "It's no problem." He had a foreign accent but I couldn't place it. "It's a part of my job to handle magicas like that. Strange that he was in such a built-up area though." He stared off into the distance and rubbed his chin, still not looking at me.

A spark of annoyance ignited inside me when he didn't meet my gaze but I shut it down. He'd just saved my kid. He could afford to have rudimentary manners. Why did I take his disinterest so personally? I shook off the strange surge of irritation. "What kind of work do you do?"

When Altan didn't immediately respond, Ellie chimed in, explaining, "Altan is an insurance assessor. My husband creates beads, and Altan often buys them from us for his work."

Huh. If that's the skillset of an assessor, maybe I should reconsider applying for the assistant's job.

"Was it a bead you used to create the iron cage?"

"Yes." His minimalist answers were giving me the...well, needless to say, I found them very frustrating.

"Look, I really appreciate it. I wish I knew how to handle a situation like that. We were in big trouble before you arrived. Thank you for saving us."

He blinked slowly, turning his head to meet my gaze. A different kind of spark erupted in my chest as his almond-shaped eyes held mine. He inclined his head slightly before clearing his throat. "I must go now. I need to arrange transport for the griffin to a secure location for wild magicas. He needs medical attention and he won't get it while I'm here —how do you Australians say it?— chinwagging with you."

Without any further discussion, the sphinx pulled out his phone, turned on his heel and strode away.

Minus his lack of manners, the sphinx had some serious skills. I didn't know precisely how I was going to do it, but I promised myself, I would never feel that helpless again.

Chapter Ten

The adrenaline that had been keeping me going abandoned me, leaving me trembling. I sagged against Millie.

"Here, drink this," Ellie said, and passed me a bottle of some sort of bright purple drink from her bag.

I didn't have the energy to politely decline her generosity, so I guzzled half the bottle. Once I felt like I wasn't about to keel over anymore, I tried to hand it back.

Ellie shook her head and said, "You saved me, Trix."

"What? No I didn't. That was all Altan."

"He got rid of the griffin in the end, but it was you who moved me out of harm's way."

I snorted. "You mean, I shoved you to the ground."

She grinned, "Hey, it got the job done." Clasping my hands in hers, she added, "Let me thank you properly. Come for dinner tonight."

"Oh no, I wouldn't want to intrude."

"You're not intruding. I want you to come. And Isabella was planning on inviting Millie for a sleepover anyway."

I glanced at our girls who were chattering about the attack. It would probably do Millie good to spend time with a friend to recover from the fear of the day. "Oh, all right then. I'll come for dinner, and I'm sure Millie would love a sleepover. I didn't bring any spare clothes for her though. We'll have to duck home first."

"That's no problem at all," Ellie replied with a gentle smile. "I can't wait!"

I told the girls about Ellie's invitation, and they both squealed in excitement. Grabbing Millie, we raced home. While helping her pack her overnight bag, I asked Millie how she was feeling after the griffin attack. She quickly assured me that she was fine and I remembered how I used to feel invincible when I was her age too.

Dive with giant krakens? No problem.

Jump on a unicorn bareback? Sounds fun.

Fight a wild griffin? Well, I might have had some qualms about that one, but probably would have given it a shot.

Things were different for me now. But at least Millie felt unflustered now the danger was over. Leaving her to shower and straighten her hair, I quickly chucked a load of clothes, including her sweaty netball uniform, into the washing machine. As I finished the one chore I wanted done before we went visiting, I realised I hadn't asked Ellie if she wanted me to bring a plate of food. Panicking, I looked through the pantry and fridge to see what I had.

Millie came into the kitchen then and asked, "Mum, are you ready?"

I shot her a look with thinly-veiled desperation in my eyes. "We don't have any decent food to share!"

She cocked her head, then shrugged. "I don't think they're expecting us to bring anything."

"Maybe not, but it's polite to bring a plate whenever you go to someone else's for dinner," I said stubbornly, refusing to risk making a social faux pas, especially with the elves.

She twirled the signet ring I'd got her for her last birthday around her finger while she pondered. "Hey," she suddenly exclaimed, making me jump. "You make really good pinwheels. Everybody always loves them. Why don't we do that?"

Rechecking the pantry, I shoved some boxes out of the way so I could look into the back corners. I swear it was like a black hole in there. I'd think I didn't have any baking powder, buy some more, then lo and behold, the next day I'd randomly find two more hidden away behind the cereal. I blew out a frustrated huff.

"No tomato paste. We could use normal tomato sauce, I suppose." Then I opened the freezer again. "No puff pastry. Another day perhaps, but it won't be today." I drummed my fingers on my chin. "I guess a plate of basic finger food would be better than nothing?"

I grabbed the lone cucumber and some carrots from the crisper and pulled out a fresh box of crackers from the pantry. After placing all of those on the kitchen bench, I turned back and grabbed one unopened glass jar of basil pesto and one of sundried tomatoes. Fiona had given me both of them last month as a thank you for sorting out a big client's claim. As much as I enjoyed the taste, they weren't on my standard shopping list; usually I could never afford them. Crouching down, I opened the cupboard door and pulled out the nicest serving plate I had. It was circular with an abstract blue and yellow design and was something I'd bought for myself from a garage sale last year.

Lifting the large plate onto the bench, I asked Millie, "Can you please set up the crackers on one side of this for me?" She set to work while I began slicing the vegetables. I also cubed the last of the cheese from my fridge and tried to arrange it nicely on the plate. It was no fine dining, but at least I had something to offer our hosts.

Leaving Millie to cover it with cling wrap, I showered swiftly and headed back into my bedroom to get dressed.

Staring into my wardrobe, I chewed my lip. What the heck did I wear? How fancy did I need to look?

I shook my head. No need to overthink this. I'd just wear what was comfortable. I grabbed my favourite bell-bottom denim jeans and a simple black fitted tee with a V-neckline. I also grabbed my grey knit sweater in case it was cooler than expected. Standing in front of the mirrored wardrobe door, I brushed out my dark hair, noting how strands of it shone violet when it caught the artificial light just right. I let it curl loosely over my shoulders but snapped a spare hair tie around my wrist in case I got annoyed with it being in my face throughout the course of the evening. I paused and stared at my reflection for a moment longer than usual. My brows creased.

I barely recognise myself.

It wasn't that I looked different, exactly. But my life had veered off track and taken a path unlike the one I had planned when I finished high school. The woman in the mirror was not who I had expected to be. Travelling the world, helping magicas, learning foreign languages, and tackling new adventures with my husband, Chris, was what I had anticipated.

But with the unexpected pregnancy when I was nineteen, we moved back to Australia to give our daughter a normal life. When Chris got a job as an investigative journalist and decided his work was more important than family, it set me on a brand-new path of singledom and solo parenting. My throat suddenly felt tight. I coughed and gave myself a mental shake. Maybe it was time to find the remnants of my old self and stitch me back together.

A quick application of eye liner, mascara, and a muted cherry lipstick was all the make-up I bothered with. It was more than my usual choice of no make-up at all. It only took me twenty minutes to get myself ready.

Racing to the car, the two of us headed to Ellie's place. We'd been there twice before but both times I hadn't gone inside the house. It was only fifteen minutes away, and as we slowed down in front of the mailbox, I was once again struck by the beautiful property. They had one of the nicest houses on one of the nicest streets, one suburb over from us. There was a thick hedge lining the boundary, so we pulled up on the grey slate driveway and parked behind a sleek black European-looking sports car. The manicured lawns wrapped around the house, and a circular water feature was the centre of attention in the front yard. From what I could see of the outside, the property would have to be at least four times the size of my rental. The building itself was modern yet still classic. Rendered concrete painted white with lots of stylised flowing lines that the elves were so well known for.

Half a dozen fruit trees had been planted strategically near the house to shield the front windows from prying eyes. At a glance, I could see the trees were lemon and lime trees in alternating order. My eyes slid over them towards the front door before I whipped my head back around. The trees weren't fruiting. How did I instinctively know which ones were lemons and which were limes? I certainly didn't consider myself an expert on citrus trees. Weird. I scowled at the trees as if it were their fault that I knew which was which.

As we walked up to the entrance, past the parked car, I whistled low under my breath. Now that was a nice car. I couldn't even bear to look back at my shabby little sedan. The paint on my car's roof was beginning to fade, and the spare tyre seemed to be judging me, accusing me of neglect. Millie darted ahead and rang the doorbell beside the massive front door. I followed at a more sedate pace with the plate of nibbles clasped tightly in my arms. No need to play fast and loose with my one nice thing.

Ellie opened the door with a smile, looking stunning in a simple silver dress. Her brown hair was pulled up into an elegant twist on the top of her head. My shoulders automatically hunched over in an effort to hide myself. I was so underdressed.

"Come in, come in." She ushered us forward. Upon seeing my plate of food, she placed a hand over her heart. "Oh, Trix, I didn't expect you to bring anything; that is so generous. Thank you!"

"It's not much," I mumbled.

"It's everything," she replied sweetly and gave me a peck on the cheek.

I flushed at her show of sincere gratitude. If it were anyone else, I would have said they were lying to be polite. But not Ellie. She was the most honest and kind person I'd ever met. When I stepped through the front door, I couldn't stop a small gasp from escaping my lips as I took in the elves' house. The furnishings were minimal, but all were stylish and fitted the feel of the house impeccably. Even the air temperature was perfect.

A few metres ahead of us a door opened, and Isabella poked her head out. Millie quickly disappeared, joining her friend in her bedroom. Ellie gently took my elbow and guided me down the hallway where a light-coloured wooden panelled feature on the wall led us into a huge open plan living-dining-kitchen space. My jaw dropped. A shining crystal chandelier hung over the centre of the sunken lounge. A mirror took up most of the wall in front of the spacious grey sofa, and I'd bet my bottom dollar it was one of those fancy televisions that could be set to look like a mirror when it wasn't in use.

Dragging my eyes away from the breathtaking lounge room, I turned to the kitchen. Marble counter tops greeted me, and I bit back a groan of longing as I stared around my dream kitchen. All the fittings in the kitchen were matte black, even the double sink. A bold statement but in this space, it worked beautifully.

Ellie drew the plate of nibbles out of my hands and set it on one of the countertops. I stood awkwardly beside the stylish elf, wondering what to do with myself.

"Do you need a hand with anything?" I blurted out.

"You're such a sweetheart. No, no, I'm fine. Thank you though." She glanced behind us, towards the pantry door of the kitchen. "My brother is joining us for dinner, and he has claimed the right to preparing the meal himself."

"That's lovely." Touching the elf's arm, I said, "Ellie, if this is a family thing, I can just go. I don't need to be here. I really do feel like I'm intruding."

"Trix." Ellie seized my hands and clasped them tightly in hers. Holding my gaze, she said, "You saved my bacon today. You put yourself in harm's way for my sake. Me. An elf. And I'm not inviting you over out of some warped sense of duty. I genuinely would love for you to join us for dinner. I'm not sure if you realise, but I don't have many human friends. Most humans don't go out of their way to befriend elves. Whereas you" —she paused to take a breath— "you are always so kind to all of us and never treat me any differently to your human friends. I truly appreciate you."

Flabbergasted, I stared at her. "But you're the one that keeps picking up *my* kid for netball practise. I feel indebted to you."

"Oh, Trix." She giggled, a tinkling sound. "That's what friends are for. To help each other. And you are bringing me so much joy by joining us for dinner. We are friends, yes?"

"Yeah, we are—"

"Friends join each other for dinner, yes?"

"Well, yes, but—"

"No buts," she interrupted me. "Come meet my brother. Then we'll go find my husband."

Chapter Eleven

Ellie led me through her kitchen and opened the pantry's double doors. That's how I found out it was actually a butler's pantry.

Because who doesn't need an entire room for a pantry, am I right? There was a second fridge tucked away to the left, and the door to the fridge was open. A man was bent over, rummaging through the crisper. My first impression was of tight buttocks filling out a pair of charcoal grey trousers.

"Perry," Ellie called softly. "My friend, Trix, has arrived."

I tore my eyes away from the elf's impressive physique as he stood. A buttoned up white shirt was stretched tight over what looked to be an extremely lean, yet muscled torso. His sleeves were rolled up to his elbows.

What was it about rolled up sleeves that was so attractive on a man?

Meeting his eyes, I prayed that the blush wasn't showing on my cheeks as I held out my hand. He wiped his cold hands on the front of his pants before grasping mine.

"Hi, Trix." Perry offered a warm smile, a dimple showing in his cheek. "Got any new tricks?"

I winced internally but returned his cheeky grin. "Only a couple," I replied sardonically. "And certainly not any that I'm telling you about."

How does one be sassy in a flirtatious way? Too sassy and I just sound rude, not sassy enough and nobody laughs.

It was a fine line to tread, and I didn't really know where the court was, let alone the specific line.

His lips twisted and he apologised, raking a hand through his hair. "That was a bit lame, wasn't it? You probably get that line all the time."

"Only every other day," I quipped.

He chuckled. "Well, it's very nice to meet you even if I'm embarrassing myself. I heard that I owe you a great debt."

My head swivelled between him and Ellie. "What...what do you mean?"

"You're the great defender, aren't you? Ellie told me all about how you saved her life today."

My cheeks blazed and I trained my eyes on the floor. "She's exaggerating the story a lot. I literally just pushed her into the dirt so the griffin's wing didn't wallop her. It wasn't much. It was Altan that saved the day. He got rid of the griffin right as it was about to attack Millie and Isabella."

"Don't be so humble," admonished Ellie. "I would be nursing a very sore head if you hadn't intervened when you did. And you wound up taking the hit instead of me! How are your ribs anyway?"

"A little tender," I admitted. "But nothing's broken."

Perry shook his head in admiration. "I'd love to chat more but I've got to keep cooking. How about we talk more over dinner?"

"No problemo." I gave an awkward thumbs up.

Who even says problemo? I can't do this.

I coughed to cover my embarrassment and added, "Hey, before I go, I just asked Ellie, who said no, but I'll ask you too— do you need a hand with anything?"

"Don't be silly. I've got it handled. Thanks though! You two go enjoy yourselves." He winked and turned back to the fridge.

We left him to it, and Ellie insisted on giving me a tour of her home. I soon came to realise that each piece of furniture had been lovingly hand-picked by her. She'd styled the space in a way that rang of nature. There were indoor plants dotted in all the rooms, lots of natural light, and all the furniture had flowing lines and organic shapes. Ellie was a calming presence. Stylish yet down-to-earth. She even asked my opinion on some of the artwork dotted around the walls. I didn't have much knowledge of art, but she still engaged with my clumsy attempts at explaining why I liked them.

Eventually, she took me out to the shed and introduced me to her husband, Vic. Ellie explained they all had elven names but had adopted more human sounding nicknames. Her husband's real name was Vicarus, her real name was Elleriah, and her brother's name was Periadonus. Since Isabella had been born on Earth after the Spark, her name was Isabella from birth.

We chatted to Vic in his shed for some time. He also thanked me profusely for saving his wife's life and, once again, I had to correct Ellie's exaggerations. Mercifully, I was able to redirect the conversation quite quickly by asking about his work. Unlike the usual contents of a man cave, there were hundreds of colourful jars lining the walls and a giant metal table in the centre of the workspace, covered in scientific-looking instruments.

It turned out Vic was one of the original creators of beads. From what I understood, beads were generally used by law enforcement to give them protection against spells or magicas. And, after today, I now knew they were used by insurance assessors too. Vic was obviously passionate about his work as he spoke with animated expressions about the chemical composition of mixing science and magic so it would protect a non-magic user, as well. I only understood maybe a third of what he was saying, but I listened in rapt attention all the same.

After getting a detailed breakdown of how a tiny bead could house an entire cage, I directed my next question to Ellie. "When you called Altan for help today, I heard you say something about not caring about the cost. If you don't mind me asking, what was that about?"

With a glance at her husband, Ellie explained, "We were in immediate danger. I don't know anyone better qualified than Altan to remove a wild magica. But he needed to get to us in a matter of seconds, and he spends his weekends up in Maleny. That's at least forty minutes away from the netball courts. We would have been killed before he arrived if he had travelled by car. So I told him I'd reimburse him to use a company teleportation bead that he had on hand."

I winced. "I've heard those are really expensive."

She nodded. "Around a quarter of a million dollars."

I froze at the insane price tag. "Ellie," I whispered, "I could never afford to give you any money towards that."

She snorted. "And I would never expect you to. We can afford it. And don't forget, I wasn't only asking Altan to save you. I would have paid that even if it was just me and Isabella there. You and Millie just happened to be with us."

Vic nodded sagely. "You can't put a price on life." He launched into an explanation of how portal beads worked, thoroughly confusing me as he discussed physics and alchemy.

After listening to Vic wax lyrical on beads for another twenty minutes, Ellie interrupted him to say it was time for dinner. As he finished locking up his shed and his precious beads, she stole forward and gave him a quick kiss. He grabbed her waist and embraced her, swinging her around as he returned the kiss. She laughed breathlessly. I ducked my head and looked away. They were obviously still very much in love. While I was happy for them, I couldn't help but feel a pang in my own heart. It had been years since my divorce, and I'd yet to find another special someone to share my life with.

I gave myself a shake. At least I had Millie. That was all that mattered now.

Vic led our little trio back into the house, towards the dining table, holding Ellie's hand the entire way. Our shoes clicked against the white tiles, and the scent of sautéed garlic smacked me in the face, making my mouth water. A rich brown piece of wood had been varnished to make a custom tabletop, and gold upholstered chairs surrounded it, continuing the feeling of warmth. A sage-green table runner ran down the centre of the table, upon which sat an ornate crystal vase with an artfully arranged bouquet of flowers.

The table was already set, and I noticed my plate of nibbles was proudly displayed right in the middle. I couldn't help but feel my simple dish looked out of place. The two girls ran in then, giggling as they pulled out their chairs. Perry arrived too, loaded up with ceramic bowls of various dishes.

As he filled the table with his cooking efforts, Ellie grabbed my arm, suddenly stricken. "I am so sorry. I never even asked about your diet! Our family are all vegetarians. However, I do know most humans enjoy meat, but I didn't even think to check with you! I'll ask Perry to cook you and Millie something else."

"No, no," I countered, gesturing to the assorted dishes laid out before us. "This is wonderful! To be honest" —I rubbed the back of my neck ruefully— "I've always wanted to cook more vegetable-based dishes. But I was never taught, and I haven't made the time to learn."

Ellie raised one elegant eyebrow and shot me a sly smile. "I'm sure if you asked nicely, Perry would be more than happy to give you some tips. He might even share some family recipes if you play your cards right." She winked.

I snorted at her insinuation that the sophisticated Perry would ever choose to date me. I'm sure he was a lovely elf, but people like him didn't get with people like me. We all took our seats and dug in, leaving the table silent for a few minutes. That was a sign of a good meal in my book.

Surprisingly, my simple plate of nibbles emptied quickly, but I felt like that was the elven family's way of making me feel like it was a valuable contribution. While I may not agree with them, I appreciated the intent.

The slivers of carrot sautéed in the garlic butter I'd smelled earlier were delicious. The roasted cauliflower and cheese sauce was moreish. But when I bit into Perry's roast vegetable salad, I couldn't stop a moan from escaping past my lips. It was the best thing I'd ever eaten. Roasted pumpkin and beetroot formed the base with fresh spinach leaves, crumbled goat's cheese, and lightly toasted pine nuts to top it off. The balsamic glaze drizzled over the salad gave it a beautiful balance of sweetness and acidity.

I pointed my fork at it and, with my mouth still full, said, "Thish ish ah-maaashing!"

Perry grinned in response.

Millie simply looked horrified that I'd spoken with food in my mouth in front of others.

As the inhaling of food slowed, Perry asked me about my job. When I told him I was an insurance broker, there was a familiar pause. Most people assumed my profession to be dull, so I anticipated the conversation to move on to other topics quickly as usual. Perry surprised me and asked for more details.

"Well. I actually have quite a few amusing stories when it comes to insurance. I know, I know, that's probably not what you expect. But I promise, it's not all boring. A few months ago, I received a claim form from a client after they'd hit a kangaroo with their car. On the form, there's a question of who is responsible for the accident. They'd written that the responsible party was God." There was a moment of confused silence around the table. "Since it was the kangaroo that He made that jumped out in front of the vehicle." Everyone chuckled at that, and I felt myself relax into the conversation.

The evening passed quickly, and I didn't embarrass myself too badly. Not by my standards anyway. Being a teenager, Millie might have something to say about my conduct later. I ferried the empty dishes to the kitchen and loaded the dishwasher, but the adrenaline-fueled day finally caught up with me and by nine o'clock, I was exhausted. So, I said my goodbyes, giving my daughter a big cuddle before I left. Whispering in her ear, I reminded her to help with the breakfast dishes in the morning.

As I took my empty plate with me towards the front door, Ellie said, "I'll drop Matilda home around lunch time tomorrow, okay?"

"Perfect," I agreed. "But if anything happens and you need to change your plans, just call me, okay? I don't have any commitments, so can come back here if you need me to."

With one last peck on the cheek from Ellie, I exited the house. Jeepers, it was a bit colder out here than inside. Hurrying to the promised warmth of my car, I shot another admiring glance towards the sports car. It must be Perry's. Perhaps he was also involved in the family business.

I heard the front door open and shut behind me, and I turned around, thinking Millie must have forgotten something. But it was Perry who'd followed me. While the nearest streetlamp couldn't filter through the thick boundary hedges, the moon was bright enough for me to recognise him.

He said, "I really enjoyed talking to you tonight, Trix."

The guy was speaking to me like I was an interesting person. Alarm bells were ringing in my head so loudly that it made it hard to think. Adrenaline spiked through my body.

What the flippity-flapjack do I say now? "Yeah, me too." What the heck was that? Was I telling him I enjoyed talking to myself? Crackers, I felt so awkward.

"Maybe we could catch up another time?" He cocked his head, his face half hidden in shadow. "And maybe next time I won't make a joke about your name." He smiled sweetly in apology.

"Yeah, sure," I said automatically, still not sure how to talk to the poor guy.

The elf leaned forward and gave me a gentle kiss on the cheek. Blood rushed to my head, and I'm fairly sure I stopped breathing. And apparently my brain completely stopped working as my plate slipped through my fingers. Thankfully, Perry was too quick for gravity. He snatched it out of the air and returned the plate to my waiting hands. He stared at me for a long moment, his body closer to mine than it was before.

Oh my gosh. I was not expecting this.

There was nothing for me to do other than yelp a goodnight and throw myself into my car before anything *else* happened. How I didn't break my nice plate when I threw it on the passenger seat, I'll never know.

My heart rate didn't return to normal until long after I got home and hopped straight into a scalding hot shower. As I blasted the water over myself, I reviewed the evening. I hadn't dated since my ex had broken my heart. This morning, I'd woken up with no plans to change my relationship status in the near future. Nic kept going on (and on and on) about getting back out there. But after tonight, it had me thinking…maybe she was right.

Perry was sweet. He could cook. I was friends with his sister.

A girl could do a lot worse.

After a solid twenty minutes in the shower, I made up my mind.

If Perry was being anything more than polite and actually asked me on a date, I would start knocking down the walls from around my heart, and say yes.

Chapter Twelve

THE NEXT DAY FELT weird waking up without my daughter in the house. She rarely spent a night away from me. Since her dad worked as an investigative journalist and travelled all around the world, he rarely had Millie overnight. Whenever he was in town, he'd make the effort to take her out for a meal, but I didn't know if he even had a permanent house.

I got up and began working through the chore list. In my frazzled state after I got home from dinner last night, I'd forgotten to do anything about the wet washing. Pulling it out of the washing machine and into a basket, I hung it on the clothesline straightaway. Dredging up some chuck steak from out of my freezer, I set it on the sink to defrost. No fancy cuts for me, just whatever was on special at the butchers.

Speaking of money, I needed to hit the op shops and grab Millie her new school skirt. It shouldn't be too hard to find a navy skirt in her size. Racing out, I was lucky enough to locate one in the first op shop I went to. Ignoring the packed shelves of random items that were once someone's trash and were now patiently waiting to become someone else's treasure, along with the dozens of rows of second-hand clothing, I paid my four dollars and headed home again. Grabbing my vacuum, I plugged it into the wall and started my most hated chore. If only I could afford to buy one of those little robot vacuums to clean for me, I'd be the happiest woman alive.

While my hands were busy vacuuming, my mind was free to wander. The worry about money was constant but it wasn't what occupied my thoughts today. I couldn't help but mull over yesterday's attack. I had been useless when that griffin came at me. And it nearly got Millie. I shuddered. If it hadn't been for the sphinx swooping into the rescue...

It didn't bear thinking about. I hated how helpless I'd been. The email about the insurance assessing job popped into my mind once again.

Competent in archery and swordsmanship.

If I could learn to fight like Altan, I would never need to feel this crushing sense of inadequacy ever again. Maybe I should apply to be the insurance assessor's assistant after all.

The morning heated up, causing me to work up a sweat as I finished the vacuuming. I debated turning the air conditioning on but didn't feel like being faced with a massive power bill before we even made it to summer. As my skin grew stickier, Fiona's comment about needing to talk resurfaced. A sick feeling of dread sat in the pit of my stomach as I wondered if I still had a job. How could I afford anything if I lost my position? Panic over the weekly rental payment, the need for a new tyre, and Millie's extra school expenses fought for my attention.

I needed a distraction. I was going to head into a full-blown panic attack if I wasn't careful. Throwing caution to the wind, I updated my résumé and applied for the job before I could talk myself out of it. If I could learn how to fight and earn an amazing wage while I did that, it was a win-win. Obviously, there was some risk involved, but as I saw yesterday, risk was a part of life. At least if I got trained up, I would be prepared for any other lemons life decided to throw at me.

I sighed. I probably wouldn't get the position anyway. But at least I was taking action. Two baskets of unfolded washing sitting on the couch caught my attention, waiting to be taken care of, so I turned on some trash TV. It wasn't exactly educational, but at least it got my mind off of everything.

After eating a simple jam sandwich for lunch, I grabbed the washing off the line. I loathed housework. But I would admit that it was a satisfying feeling when the house was tidy. I enjoyed the end result even if I didn't like the journey getting there.

Glancing outside, I figured I'd better tidy up the garden a little bit. The real estate had booked an inspection in a couple of weeks, so I better make sure both the inside and outside looked spick and span. I grabbed my gardening gloves and a plastic bucket along with my wide-brimmed hat and sunnies. There were a few large fruit trees hugging my wooden boundary fence that were still clinging to life. Surrounding them were a mountain of weeds.

There used to be some flowers hidden in there somewhere, but I wasn't entirely sure where they were anymore. Here's hoping I remembered what their leaves looked like so they didn't get tossed with the weeds. Staring at my own personal jungle, I sighed. I knew I had to start somewhere. But starting a job this big was always a challenge. Grumbling to myself, I knelt down at the front corner of the garden bed and began the arduous task.

I did manage to recognise one of the flowering plants' leaves. A spider lily, if I recalled correctly. The usually green leaves had wilted and were lying flat and brown on the earth.

"I'm sorry, buddy," I apologised to the plant. Poor thing had no hope with me trying to look after it. "When I'm done here, I'll come back and water you, I promise."

At the sound of some rustling, I looked over my shoulder before turning back. I paused. Was it just me or did the spider lily's leaves look a little more green now? I shook my head. I might believe in talking to plants to help them grow but there was no way that would work in the space of a few seconds. I had to be imagining things.

I kept weeding. Even though it was extremely dry, the soil was quite loose, which made my job easier. Every time I filled a bucket with weeds, I took it over to my compost corner. Again, not something that I did a very good job of maintaining, but I tried. I entered the shade of my orange tree and continued tugging out the unwanted plants that had claimed the space.

A prickle of unease crept over me, and the hairs on the back of my neck rose. Someone was watching me.

I stopped what I was doing and whipped my head up, studying the tree branches above me. Two big yellow eyes stared back at me, and I nearly keeled over from the shock.

"You!" I pointed an accusing finger at the tawny frogmouth.

The bird blended in perfectly with the tree, its mottled feathers looking like bark. It stared at me and blinked slowly. I must have been hallucinating the other day when I'd thought it had talked to me. Actually, that was twice now if I included our chat after my drinking session on Friday evening. Once could be passed off as stress-induced hallucinations. The second time, maybe I'd just had too much to drink. This was the third time I'd seen the bird, and so far it wasn't speaking. It probably wasn't even the same tawny frogmouth.

Relief coursed through me at its silence. Maybe I wasn't losing my mind after all.

"You're not crazy," came the now familiar voice in my head.

"Oh, come on!" I shouted at it. I had no excuse as to why it would be happening today. Might as well accept it. Changing my worry from the fact I could talk to birds and onto what the bird was saying, I demanded, "Don't tell me you can read my thoughts too?"

"Of course not. Only the ones you send me. But you're an open book. I can figure out what you're thinking pretty easily. I promise you're not insane. You've just had your powers returned to you finally. But not your memories, it seems."

"What the heck does that mean?"

"Can't say." She shrugged her wings apologetically.

"What do you mean, Mrs Know-It-All?"

"It's Froggy. And if I could tell you, I would, I swear it. But many years ago, I took an Everlasting Oath. I am unable to reveal your history until you discover it for yourself. However, I made no promise not to speak to you since they thought we'd never be able to communicate in this way again."

"Who's the mysterious 'they'?"

She gave an unhappy sigh. *"Can't say."*

"Well, you're not very helpful, are you?" I grumbled.

"I'm trying to be."

"Look, my life is hard enough without you coming along and making me look like an insane person talking to an owl." Froggy opened her beak to correct me, but I jumped in before she could, "I'm sorry! You're not an owl!" I flung the words out, exasperation getting the best of me. "I know! And that's another thing. I don't know why I know you're related to the nightjar family or why I could tell the difference between lime and lemon trees last night, but I know. I have all these random facts about creatures and plants in my head now. It's like I swallowed an encyclopedia."

Ugh. Might be showing my age there. Kids these days probably had no idea what encyclopedias were since the internet answered all their questions.

A car door shutting nearby broke the uncomfortable silence that stretched between me and the bird.

Froggy's head swivelled towards the sound. *"Your daughter has returned. It seems you need more time to process your new powers. You won't see me, but I'll be around. Just call out for me when you're ready to talk."* She flew away.

I bit my lip as guilt gnawed my insides. Froggy only wanted to help me. She was acting within the limits of her... What had she called it? Her Everlasting Oath. I should have asked her what that was.

Well, it was too late now.

With a groan, I pushed myself to my feet, dusting off my knees and removing my gloves. The sound of young people running into the house made me smile. The silence had been deafening. As cheesy as it sounded, my girl filled my life with light and laughter. I was lucky to have her.

I returned to the slightly cooler interior of my brick house and greeted Millie, Isabella, and Ellie before grabbing a glass of water for myself and my guests. Millie and Isa gushed about the fun they had had at the beach this morning before showing me the new clothes they'd bought at Sunshine Plaza. I listened quietly, content to bask in their enthusiasm.

Once the girls had disappeared into Millie's room, I turned to Ellie. "Thank you for giving her such a nice time." Conflicted for a moment, I decided to ignore my shame and open up to the elf who had laid claim to my friendship. "I would normally like to give you some money for the clothes you bought her, but I'm a bit strapped at the moment." I watched her carefully, a part of me wondering if she'd reject our friendship when she found out precisely how poor I was.

"Oh, Trix. Thank you for the offer, but I would never expect that from you." She hesitated for a second and shifted her weight before continuing, "I guessed that things weren't going great for you financially. You do a good job of hiding it though; Millie is so beautifully cared for. So I figured it would be nice to ease some of the pressure off you. I hope you don't mind?"

My brows pulled together as I analysed her words. Part of me was thankful for her generosity, but another part threw me into a shame spiral.

I was a charity case for the affluent elven family, wasn't I?

I couldn't even afford to buy my daughter new clothes. Based on previous experience, I knew my poker face was awful, so I turned away to hide the ugly emotions. I knew they weren't fair, but I couldn't help it. Ellie turned me around and wrapped her arms around me in a tender hug.

"Don't be mad," the elf soothed as she rubbed circles on my back.

I jerked in surprise. I wasn't used to being touched affectionately aside from my daughter's hugs.

"You're such a good mum. I only want to help. Please let me."

Unbidden, tears blurred my vision and escaped down my cheeks. I tried so hard to be a good mum. It was nice to hear I wasn't a complete failure. More tears fell.

"Sorry," I mumbled into Ellie's shirt, which was now rather damp.

"Don't apologise, sweetie. I didn't mean to make you feel bad. Look at me." She pulled away and tipped my chin up, forcing me to meet her gaze. "I don't know your history. But it seems to me that we both have a lack of support. I'm lucky to have Vic, and we're well off, yes. But I have no friends. Like I said last night, humans are not always kind to elves. But you are. If my situation can improve yours by me occasionally spending money on you or your daughter, then I consider that a win for both of us."

I grabbed the roll of paper towel off the kitchen bench and ripped off a piece to blow my nose. "I'm sorry. I feel like I'm being ungrateful. But I just can't shake the sense of our friendship being one-sided. You're giving me so much, and all I can give you is my time."

She stroked my hair, tucking the wayward strands behind my ear. "Time is the most precious gift of all. Money comes and goes. But your friendship means more than you know."

Chapter Thirteen

It was finally Monday morning. I swear to God and whoever else was listening, if Fi didn't talk to me straight away, I was going to block out an hour in her calendar myself to have this chat. My nerves couldn't handle any more waiting. To my relief and, at the same time, anxiety, Fi called me into her office as soon as I'd dumped my handbag in mine.

"Do you have time for that chat now?" she asked.

"Yes, of course," I blurted out, my words running together in my nervousness. I smiled at her, but it felt like a grimace on my face, my skin on my cheeks pulling too tight. Shutting the door behind me, Fi gestured to a chair.

She never ever shut her door.

Oh, feathers and fur. This couldn't be good.

I sat down but couldn't stop my knee from incessantly bouncing. If I kept this up, I could probably start competing in the highland dancing competition I'd seen advertised on the local noticeboard.

Fi walked back around behind her desk and pushed a takeaway coffee cup over to me. She must have already been over to Bards and Beans this morning and bought me a coffee herself. She rarely did that. What did it mean?

My brain flicked up a gear and went into overdrive.

This is it. There's bad news coming. I just know it.

All I could hear was my heart thumping in my ears, and my fingers felt cold. Too cold. Meanwhile, my cheeks were too hot. Ice prickled along my skin as I started hyperventilating.

Fi raised an eyebrow and smirked. "Jesus, Trix, calm down. I have a proposal for you." She leaned forward and wrapped her fingers around her takeaway cup as she stared at me intently.

"A proposal?" I stammered as my breath hitched. "You mean you're not going to fire me?"

She burst out laughing. "Why would you think that? You daft woman!" she exclaimed. "You're my best worker."

Relief flooded my body and I sagged in the chair.

"No, silly," she said with a chuckle. "Look, cards on the table. I know you are struggling with the cost of living right now. I talked to Woodsy, and we can't offer you a pay rise for another six months. But I can get you a work phone and a fuel card, and you can work from home one day a week, if you want." Her eyes were intense as she stared at me, gauging my reaction.

"Oh, Fi, that is so generous. Thank you!" While my mouth spouted gratitude, my brain tried to calculate how much money it would save me in the long run.

Fi glanced at the closed door and tapped her long fingernails against the desk. "Or..."

My head swivelled between her and the door. "Or what?"

She sighed unhappily, her mouth twisting into a grimace. "I can't say I was surprised, but I'm still sad."

"What's going on, Fi? Why are you sad?"

She still wouldn't meet my eyes, instead studying her nails. "I got a phone call this morning from MagicAssess."

I froze. *No way. There's no way I got shortlisted for the job.*

"They were asking what I thought of you as an employee. As promised, I gave you the best reference I've ever given anyone. They are desperate for workers and are willing to train new employees on the job." She finally met my eyes. "So, it looks like you've got the position. I told the assessor to come into the office this morning to do the final interview."

"Wha—" I shook my head. All of my comfort bubbles were popping very loudly around me. Rubbing my temples, I closed my eyes and whispered, "I applied on a whim. I don't know if I actually want the job, Fi."

She gave a wry chuckle. "As much as I hate to lose you, I think it's a smart choice. There's more flexibility in your hours, better perks, and the wage is...exorbitant." Reaching her hand over the desk, Fi clasped mine and said, "I know it's scary. And of course I don't want to lose you. But you need to think of what's best for you, Trix. And I think this might be it." Leaning back in her chair, she folded her hands behind her head and said, "Of course, if you want to stay here and accept my offer of a phone and fuel card, I won't say no."

Weighing up my options, I couldn't help but remember my feeling of helplessness on Saturday. The only way to fight that would be to train in some form of combat. If I got the assessing job, I'd get the training and hands-on experience, and be paid handsomely for my efforts. As scary as it was to consider starting a new job, the idea of living the rest of my life hoping that someone would save me when trouble came knocking was scarier.

A murmur of voices interrupted us from the front desk, followed by Nic's cheery voice directing someone down the hallway. A brief knock preceded the door to Fiona's office opening.

The sphinx appeared then, all six-scowling-feet of him.

I leapt to my feet and pointed at him. "You!" I exclaimed.

At my shout, his teeth bared slightly and he pinned his ears. "Yes. It's me. Hello, Beatrix."

Fi looked between us. "You've met?"

"He saved Millie's life on Saturday when a griffin attacked at her netball game," I muttered.

Altan's tail curled into a question mark and he spoke slowly. "Yes, that's right. And that's where I discovered her incompetence when handling attacking magicas. I must admit, I was very surprised to see your résumé in my inbox."

Fiona glared at him. "Altan. No need to be rude. Your company is desperate. I will praise Trix's work ethic and her willingness to learn all day until the hippogryphs come to roost. So kindly, piss off with your attitude, and be grateful you have someone who is willing to work with *you*."

My mouth hung open at Fi's tirade, and even Altan looked a little taken aback. His amber eyes struck me again with their intensity. I jutted my jaw out and held his gaze, refusing to be cowed by his animosity.

Well, just because he was rude, didn't mean both of us should be. I performed the magica greeting before holding my hand out and pasting on a smile. "Nice to formally meet you, sir. My name is Beatrix Greenstone, but everyone calls me Trix."

After a short hesitation, the sphinx extended his own hand and grasped mine in a firm handshake. Warmth immediately transferred into mine, and a strange tingle at his contact made me gulp. His palm was smooth to the touch, and his complexion was fairly pale, contrasting with his dark brown hair.

I realised too late that he was waiting for me to release his hand. I blushed and dropped his hand like I'd been scalded. So much for my strong first impression. Well, technically it was my second, but I didn't want to count Saturday.

"So, Trix." His voice wrapped around my one-syllable moniker like a caress, his accent doing strange things to my body. "Why do you prefer Trix? Beatrix is a fine name."

I flinched but forced myself to take a deep breath. Raising my eyes to capture his, I smiled apologetically. "I'm afraid we need to become better acquainted before I can share that with you."

He gave a muted huff. I couldn't figure out whether he thought I was amusing or frustrating. "Fine. Based on your résumé and what I saw on Saturday, I am struggling to understand your reasoning for applying. Can you please explain to me why I should be saddled with you?"

I cleared my throat and straightened my spine, while anger made my cheeks flame. "No one is saddling anyone with anything," I hissed. "I realise I'm not qualified in the assessing sector. But I have eight years' experience as an insurance broker. I'm committed to doing the best flipping job I possibly can in whatever work I do. And, as you so kindly pointed out, I was useless on Saturday. I want to learn how to protect myself and others so I am never put in a position where I'm helpless ever again."

He blinked, his amber eyes intense. "Your reasoning does you credit. I will say that while you were, indeed, useless in combat on Saturday, you thought on your feet, and you put yourself in harm's way to protect a civilian. I can teach you how to fight. What I can't teach are protective instincts and intuition. And you already have them." He laced his fingers together and nodded slowly. "It will take time to bring you up to scratch. Probably a lot of time," he conceded with a heavy sigh. "But I will teach you." He inclined his head graciously.

Anger flared in my gut at his arrogance and I gritted my teeth. Taking a steadying breath, I couldn't keep the snarky edge entirely out of my voice when I said, "Before any of us commit to anything, I'd like to point out that you haven't properly introduced yourself to me yet. I don't even know your last name." I clipped my mouth shut as my brain caught up with my words. Embarrassment made heat prickle across my arms.

Since when was I confrontational?

Merriment danced in Fiona's eyes as she watched us spar verbally, and I could see her holding back a chuckle. At least someone was having fun. I had no idea where this barely contained attitude had appeared from. Technically, Ellie had already told me his name on the weekend, and, if he was slated to be my new boss, I should definitely shut my trap.

Why wouldn't my mouth cooperate? Why was I caught up on this tiny issue of manners?

The sphinx swivelled back to me. His gaze swept from my toes to the top of my head, seeming to take in so much more than just my physical appearance. I wilted under his keen assessment, all my prior bravado dissipating as swiftly as it had appeared. He stepped into my personal space, bringing his body far closer than I was comfortable with. We weren't touching, but the heat from him pressed against my skin like a physical caress.

"My name," he spoke slowly, giving each word an unexpected weight, "is Altan Lozano. You may call me Altan or sir."

A shiver ran down my spine. "Understood, sir." I tried for haughty indifference, but it ended up coming out as more of a breathy whisper. Talk about embarrassing.

He looked deep into my eyes, and I glowered back, refusing to lose the staring match. Electricity prickled against my skin, and a mounting pressure grew between us. Fiona cleared her throat then, and the spell was broken. We quickly stepped apart and faced her.

Thank the wolf's moon that ordeal was over. I really needed to get my breathing under control. It was certainly not any sort of attraction that I was feeling. Definitely not. And certainly not one with my new boss. This was just a weird reaction my body was having to all the changes going on in my life and had nothing to do with the fact his voice sounded like honey.

Fiona sat down and swept imaginary specks of dust off her desk while trying to hide her smile. "All righty. Let's get down to brass tacks." Out of the corner of my eye, I saw Altan's ear flick, but he remained silent. She gestured to the chairs and waited for us both to sit.

Altan tugged a black leather bag off his shoulder that I hadn't noticed until now and pulled out some paperwork, placing it on the desk between us. He tapped it lightly without looking at me. "Your contract."

Before I could reach for it, Fi snatched it away and started perusing it. After a moment, she said, "Obviously, Trix will need to review this before she commits to anything. And she has the right to change any terms she doesn't agree with." She raised a sculpted eyebrow at Altan.

He crossed his arms and said, "I thought you were just her reference?"

Fi glared at him.

He gave a self-important sniff and raised his chin. Eventually, he bowed his head in surrender. "She may make some changes to the contract. Provided they are within reason," he added, and his eyes flickered to me briefly.

Leaning forward and clasping her hands together, Fi gave him a stern glare. "Okay, assuming that the contract is acceptable and you agree to any adjustments, Trix will work out her four weeks' notice here before she starts with you."

He mimicked her posture but spoke softly. Somehow that made what he had to say seem even more important. I found myself leaning forward to listen more intently. "I need her as soon as possible. Why else do you think I was called over from London?"

Weird. His accent didn't really sound very British.

He continued, "Australia doesn't have enough insurance assessors to keep up with the claims being filed. Your country has taken too long to accept wards as the first defence against damage to property. The number of insurance claims have tripled in the past five years, and as you don't have an appropriate training system for assessors, they keep dying on the job." His words had quickened, and he was hissing in aggravation by the end of his monologue.

"Um, sorry to interrupt. What's this about dying on the job?" I folded my arms tightly against my chest to hide the sudden trembling.

He waved his hand dismissively without looking at me. "You'll be fine. I'll be training you, therefore you will be competent. Follow my instructions, and you won't die."

"Cool, thanks, that totally makes me feel better." I slouched down in my chair with a huff.

He ignored me.

Fi spread her hands wide. "No need to get pissy with me, Altan. I know there are no assessors. That's why I recommended Trix. But rules are rules. She's been working with me for eight years, so she needs to work out her notice. But I want to help you. Both of you. How does it sound if she finishes her work here early two days a week in order to fit in more training with you? What about three o'clock on Mondays and Wednesdays? That way she'll be more prepared to enter the field when she goes full-time with you."

Altan's lips pressed into a thin line. He gave a curt nod. "That is acceptable." Rummaging through his bag, he presented a business card to me. "Review the contract and let me know of any changes you need. I'll meet you here at three this afternoon."

I opened my mouth to tell him I hadn't agreed to anything yet, but the sphinx was already leaving. He exited the office as swiftly as he'd entered, his tail curling around the door handle and shutting it with a crisp click behind him.

After we heard the front office door close, the tense silence was broken by Fiona letting out a low whistle. "What was that?" she exclaimed. "Talk about tension!"

I chuckled weakly. "Yeah, he doesn't seem to like me very much, does he?"

Fi snorted. "Sure, we'll continue to live in your favourite world of total oblivion. What's new?" she muttered.

Shooting her a glare, I chose to ignore her jibes. Glancing back at the door where he'd disappeared, I asked Fi, "Do you think he meant that I'm starting training this afternoon?"

"He doesn't waste any time, does he?" she mused, another smile playing across her lips.

I gulped, his mention of assessors dying on the job playing on my mind. No wonder the pay rate was so high. "Fi…" I began but bit my lip. I tried again. "I don't know if—"

She held up a hand. "Don't want to hear it. I've got a good feeling about this."

"What about Matilda? Assessors travel for work. Millie isn't old enough to be left alone at home for one night, let alone multiple."

"Isn't she fifteen now?"

"Well, yes, but I never leave her alone."

Fiona shook her head as if to clear it. "Don't worry about that. We'll figure this out together, Trix. You can't stop living your life because of fear of the unknown or because logistics get a little tricky." She drummed her fingers on the table as she thought. "What if you rented a room to someone you trust who could care for Millie while you're away?"

"Nic did actually just make the suggestion of moving in with us," I mumbled.

Spreading her hands wide, she grinned. "Well, there's your solution."

Frowning, I picked up the contract. "Let me look at this first. Then I'll decide."

She nodded and relaxed back in her chair, seeming satisfied with my answer. "Go back to your desk, read through the contract, then send me your official resignation by email, noting the days we've agreed for you to finish early. No more new clients or claims for you. Let Nic know to put them through to Shirlene. I'm going to talk to Nicole about whether she wants to leave reception and study so she can take over managing our domestic clients. If she says yes, then I only need to find a receptionist. And I had four résumés emailed through last month alone without even advertising a job. I doubt trwe'll have a problem getting someone to do the admin role." Fi stood and came around her desk before pulling me up into a hug. "I'm going to miss you. But this is the start of something big. I can feel it."

Chapter Fourteen

"So what's on the cards for this afternoon?" I asked cheerily, determined to crack a smile from the sphinx. He was already waiting in the reception area when I clocked off at three. Nic's eyebrows got a workout as she tried to surreptitiously figure out where I was going with the hot magica.

I mouthed the word, "Later," to her before ignoring the rest of her inappropriate hand gestures that were hidden behind her desk.

The tip of his tail twitched, but he simply said, "The library."

"The library?"

"Yes. You know, it's the place where people go to borrow books and read them and perhaps even learn something in the process."

I harrumphed and crossed my arms defensively over my chest. "I read." There was no need to tell him it was usually soppy romance books involving overprotective billionaires and the like. I thought I caught a glimpse of a smirk, but the expression disappeared too fast for me to be sure. "Allow me to extend my question. What are we going to the library for?" My words were polite but my tone was sarcastic.

Oh no, sassy Trix was back. I wish she'd take a holiday. This was exhausting.

Altan rolled his eyes and led the way towards the carpark. I followed diligently. He answered my sarcasm with his own. "I already told you. To try and learn something. Specifically about insurance assessing. This country's training system for assessors is woefully behind the times. But I will attempt to give you a brief review of the history of your new job, and we'll see if your library has any appropriate texts on magical creatures and a summary of the most common beads."

"Why?" I asked, genuinely curious, and nearly smacked into his back when he stopped.

He finally met my eyes. His mouth was gaping. I had a feeling I was about to get a lecture.

"Why?" Incredulity coated his tone. "Because my job —which is going to be your new job— is to find the truth. And when magic is involved, the truth can get a little muddled. Can you tell me the difference between a wyvern's scorch marks and scorch marks from a fire lit by mundane means?"

I shook my head mutely.

"Can you tell me the two signs to discern if a bead has been used in the past twenty-four hours?"

I crossed my arms defensively. This was becoming a habit when I was around him.

"Did you hear about the partial collapse of the Queensland State Museum in the nineties?"

I shook my head again. At the time, I would have been learning my times tables, not keeping up with current events.

"Initially, they thought it was caused by an earthquake. But it was, in fact, taken down by a dark witch. The only reason they figured it out was because someone noticed the sinkhole was perfectly symmetrical and had a black tar residue at the site of her casting. How can you do your job if you don't know about these things?"

I ducked my head and moved past him. "I understand," I said sullenly. "My magical knowledge is lacking. We better get started then."

In silence, we walked the two blocks to the local library, where the silence continued. Not that I minded. The quiet hush and the scent of paper was always comforting. I made a mental note to bring Millie here more often. Ignoring the self-service desk that told you in which section you could find what titles, Altan spent the first hour combing the shelves for specific texts. I sat on a comfortable couch reading *A Complete History of the Spark*. While I had lived through it, I had only been a toddler, so wasn't really aware of the details of the event. I also was supremely useless at retaining dates, so had decided at a very young age that I was not interested in learning about history. My lack of knowledge regarding such a huge event irked Altan to no end. I'll admit, I did feel a little guilty for not having made the time to learn.

Thirty-five years ago, the Spark had ripped a hole in the curtain between our planes of existence and magicas had poured onto Earth. I already knew there had been stigma surrounding the newly discovered magical creatures but hadn't realised it had almost led to a world war. Someone called Star Song had come in and saved the day, putting a stop to the conflict and then creating a Council that represented the needs of both magicas and humans. I smirked. Star Song sounded like a sixties superhero.

When Altan stopped by my armchair and dropped another tome on the table in front of me, I asked, "So can I call you Alt? Or maybe you'd prefer Tan?" I joked. He looked at me in open-mouthed horror as I butchered his name.

He sputtered, "My name is sacred. You cannot ruin it in such a fashion."

I laughed. "Don't you know Aussies shorten everything? Brisbane becomes Brissie, or BrisVegas if you're feeling spicy. Afternoon becomes arvo; service station becomes servo. Goodness, even my daughter's name! Her name is Matilda, but everyone calls her Millie."

"But Matilda is a beautiful name. Why would you shorten it?"

I bristled a little at his accusatory tone. "I never said it wasn't." I shrugged. "It's just what we do."

He sniffed in reproach. "Be that as it may, please ensure you leave my name out of your strange customs."

"Fair enough." I shot him a curious look. "By the way, you mentioned you were from London. But your accent doesn't really sound English?"

His ear flicked. "I've lived in many countries throughout my lifetime."

"That didn't answer my question. You don't need to give me your life story if you don't want. But I would appreciate it if, as my colleague and trainer, you would share some information with me so I can get to know you a little better. To foster trust, you need to offer some of your own trust up for sacrifice first." I offered him a friendly smile.

After a long pause during which he examined me, he said, "My most recent home was London for two years. I have spent decades travelling around Europe. But I spent my formative years in Wales, England, then Greece. Does that answer your question?"

"Yes, thank you."

"Your turn."

I cocked my head. "My turn? For what?"

"I offered up some personal information as a sign of trust. Now it's your turn to trust me."

I opened and closed my mouth a couple of times. How did you summarise your life in a few short sentences?

"When I finished high school, my boyfriend, Chris, and I travelled around Central and South America. We worked with a small conservation group to save the endangered blue-ringed kraken. When I was nineteen, I fell pregnant with Matilda and came back to Australia and married Chris. We separated soon after my daughter started school. I got a job with Fi and have now been an insurance broker for eight years."

"And your upbringing?"

"My mother raised me alone. I never knew my father, and my mum refused to talk about him. She was quite...scatterbrained when I was growing up. I sort of wound up looking after both of us. Now she flits around the world, never really settling down. She's supposed to be coming for a visit in a couple months, but who knows." I shrugged, trying not to let my pain show on my face.

Oh no, was that sympathy I spied in Altan's eyes? Good grief, I had overshared, hadn't I?

"Sorry," he murmured, casting his gaze to the blue-carpeted floor.

I cleared my throat. "It's all good. At the end of the day, my life has led me to having the most amazing relationship with my beautiful daughter. I wouldn't change it for the world." I leaned forward then and pinned the sphinx with a fierce look. "Altan, there's something I need to say. I haven't reviewed the entire contract yet, but I need you to know, my daughter comes first, okay? If she is sick, I'll be with her. If she is getting an award or competing at a major competition, I'd like to request the time off to be there for her. I am her mother. If she's struggling, I'm in her corner every single time. If it comes down to a choice between the job or Millie's health, mental or physical, she's going to win. If that's a problem, I need to know now."

His eyes softened. "That is a commendable attitude. Of course. She is your priority. I understand and will do everything in my power to ensure that your needs are met. Your contract also has an excellent life insurance policy attached to it, so there's no need to worry about Millie if the worst ever happened. Which it won't," he assured me firmly, "because I'm in charge of your training."

Something in my chest eased, and I nodded my thanks. Without another word, he disappeared back into the stacks while I returned to my attempts to commit the Spark history lesson to memory. After another ten minutes of struggling to absorb the information, I distracted myself by scanning through the contents page, wondering if I could find any information on humans communicating with tawny frogmouths. There was nothing that stuck out to me in the chapter headings. I'd have to ask the librarian to run a search for me.

With a furtive glance towards the library shelves, I slipped my phone out of my handbag, feeling like a wayward school student. I quickly texted Nic, briefly explaining the job offer and why I had finished early. She responded immediately with a bucket load of emojis. I snickered to myself.

Altan's voice called from the stacks, "That doesn't sound like studying."

The librarian shushed him immediately.

A wicked smile curled my lips. Served the interfering drongo right.

Chapter Fifteen

Walking into work on Tuesday morning was surreal. Knowing I had a specific end date at which point I would no longer walk through these doors was daunting.

The morning flew by as I began the slow process of following up claims and responding to unread emails so that there wouldn't be a huge workload for whoever took over my portfolio. After eating my lunch at my desk, I typed up an email to my clients to make them aware of my end date. The idea of starting a new job after being here for eight years was petrifying. But not as petrifying as seeing my daughter staring down a wild griffin and not being able to save her.

I rinsed my plate in the kitchenette's sink before filling a cup with water and taking it back to my office. Usually, I was awful at remembering to water Heather, so I congratulated myself on the fact it had been less than a week. As I approached the plant, my mouth dropped open and I froze. She looked perfect. The succulent hadn't looked this good since Nic had first given her to me.

"Heather! You look fantastic! How in the cockatoo's crest did this happen?" Maybe talking to her had finally worked. How strange.

Before I had time to ponder on my first plant that had not only survived but seemed to be thriving, Nic burst into my office.

"Trix!" she screeched.

I leapt to my feet. "What? What's wrong?"

She waved a piece of paper in front of my nose, a grin splitting her face. "Fi just offered to pay for me to do my training to become a proper insurance broker!"

I grabbed her hands and joined in with her impromptu celebration dance. "I'm so happy for you!"

"By the way, have you spoken to your real estate yet? I was serious about what we spoke about on Saturday. If you're still okay with me moving in, I'm there. This way we both save money on rent. Plus, if your new job takes you out of town, then you've always got someone at home to take care of Matilda."

"I've been meaning to ask you precisely that question. If I do need to travel for work, can I rely on you to care for Millie while I'm gone? Take her to the bus stop in the morning, pick her up from netball practise, take her to her game on the weekend?" I wrung my hands. "I know it's a lot to ask."

"Absolutely. I can do that."

"She's my baby," I reminded her. "To be fair, I'm probably excessively overprotective. Are you sure you're okay to take on the responsibility of caring for a minor plus dealing with my nagging?"

Placing her hand over her heart, Nic turned solemn. "I will take care of Millie like she was my own."

I only hesitated for a second before accepting her declaration. "I trust you."

The next three weeks flew by. At first, work was chaotic as we all adjusted into our new roles. Guilt pecked at my heart when I felt like I wasn't taking on my fair share of the workload, and Shirlene sent me dirty looks and snarky comments every time I had to pass a new client onto her.

Meanwhile, Tim regaled me with stories of his uncle's friend who was also an assessor. The friend was still alive, so that gave me some hope, but some of the stories he shared scared the beejeebus out of me. Between the tales of hospital visits from third-degree burns after a dragon attack while assessing arson, and a scare where he'd thought he was turning into a werewolf were enough to make me question my decision. Turned out it had actually been a nip from a kangaroo when they'd been assessing a break-in at a zoo. When it had got infected, and he'd turned feverish, he'd assumed he'd been bitten by the werewolf and had run down the highway naked, screaming about the moon. He was retired now and lived in a psych ward.

Not sure how Tim figured that story was a good one to share with me.

I spent a portion of my final days at Maroochydore Mundane and Magica Insurance Brokers training Nic. I showed her how to perform basic transactions on our system so she could still make changes to home and car insurance policies while also doing her study. I spoke to my real estate and had Nic added to the lease, at which point she started moving boxes into the spare room.

The rest of the time Altan punished me.

I mean, trained. Altan trained me.

If I wasn't reading thick tomes on the minuscule difference between the footprint of a normal emu and a deadly kapamu (there was a fourth toe that only hit the ground every third stride due to the nature of their bone structure), then he made me run.

I was not a runner. Never had been, never planned on being one. Altan was determined to change all that. We started off with a kilometre because that was all I could manage. As it was, I was gasping like a fish out of water after that effort. Then, given we only met for training two nights a week, he insisted that I made a habit of jogging a minimum of five days a week. Which I loathed. However, Millie had fun joining me since she already exercised for netball. At least one of us was enjoying ourselves.

On the weekends, I was exhausted. I dragged myself to Millie's netball games on Saturday mornings, which remained griffin-free, thank goodness. Then I spent the rest of the time laying on the couch and watching TV while trying to recover from the week's efforts. The good news was I finally caught up on current events, like the fact that the Big Mango in Bowen had been stolen, and the women's national netball team, the Australian Diamonds, had won a big international competition. The bad news was my muscles stiffened during those days of inactivity, making Mondays feel like I'd been portalled to the Hellscape. In the third week, Altan added in weights training. And I'd thought running was bad.

I didn't tell him because I didn't want another lecture, but that first week of weights training, I only managed three jogs. My poor broken body was protesting too much from the added exercises. I wasn't twenty anymore. If he was going to demand that I hold weights while doing squats followed up by a leg press and then a stair climb, that was his fault for expecting too much of me.

I had been a single mother with a full-time office job for almost eight years; it's not like I had time to go to the gym.

He could go suck it.

Chapter Sixteen

"Venus flytrap!" I screamed as a fireball sailed towards my head. I instinctively dropped to the ground and began rolling around like a tortoise stuck on its shell, certain the scent of burning hair meant my braid had caught fire.

Pausing my panic-stricken flailing when no pain emerged, I looked around from my position on the floor. The fireball had hit the wall of the empty hall that Altan had hired and harmlessly fizzled into ash on the carpet.

Altan studied his nails nonchalantly, refusing to meet my glare. "Well," he muttered, "your reflexes aren't as bad as I expected. So that's something, I suppose."

"Why don't you just grab an actual flamethrower out of your arsenal? Here you are, wasting time and money on throwing tiny magical fireball beads at me. Let's go the whole hog. Flamethrower for the win. Do a proper job, why don't you?" I was babbling hysterically as I patted my hair gingerly while the scent of burning still filled my nostrils.

He rolled his eyes. "You're so dramatic. What happens if we're on a job and a wyvern throws a fireball at you? Are you going to flail around caterwauling while he finishes the job? Or are you going to throw one of the beads I gave you and stun him?"

I stood up, hands on hips, and gaped at him incredulously. He made it sound so easy. But you try thinking on your feet when a wall of flame is on course to melt off your face and let me know how well your brain functions. Something of my thoughts must have shown on my face because Altan sighed and put the next fireball bead back into his pocket.

"Here," was all he said before pulling something small from his top pocket and lobbing it towards me.

I screamed and fell backward, anticipating another attack, and landed spectacularly on my buttocks. Luckily, I had gained a bit of padding there after having Millie. The innocuous green ball he'd lobbed at me sat innocently on the floor beside my foot.

A frustrated huff came from the sphinx's direction. "It's a healing bead. To keep on hand in case your scalp actually does get singed." I glared at him, still clutching the end of my braid. "That brings me to the first lesson. Expect the unexpected."

"Gee, that's original." I rolled my eyes.

"The saying might be boringly predictable, but it's life-threateningly accurate. When I was younger, one of my first assessing jobs was a claim where there was a fire. The fire department had determined it was an accident caused by a gas stove. When I was investigating, I found out the owner had pissed off a fire sprite. Do you know how I found out? The hard way." He pulled up his sleeve and flashed the inside of his forearm. A white scar marred his flesh.

My eyes widened. "What hap—"

"Use your imagination," he spat out. He pulled his sleeve back down and turned away. His shoulders moved as he took some deep breaths. When he faced me again, the mask was back. "Lesson two. Be prepared."

"Isn't that basically the same as lesson one?"

He tossed me a scathing look. "No. You'll need to pay more attention than that to nuanced conversation if you have any hope of being a competent assessor. Being prepared means making sure you always have access to your armour, weapons, and tools."

"So bring a hammer with me?"

Altan rolled his eyes. "If you think it would help, sure. But no, when I say tools, I mean the tools you need to survive. In this case, starting off with a standard issue of beads from Caroline would be a good start. Basic wards to shield you from physical attacks, healing beads, and offensive spells like fire attacks." He ticked them off on his fingers. "As you progress in your training and experiences, I will consider giving you access to more powerful beads."

"Who's Caroline? And why can't I have access now?"

"You'll meet Caroline next week when I take you to Head Office in Brisbane. She takes care of everyone's armour fittings and ensures their bead kits are always fully stocked. As to why you can't have more powerful beads right away, you know what they say — the tool is only as good as the wielder. If I gave you a subtler spell, you might use it in a situation where it doesn't help or even makes it worse. Plus, the more advanced the spell, the more it costs the company. No." He shook his head vigorously. "We can't have you sending MagicAssess bankrupt."

I grumbled for the next hour as he made me run sprints across the hall and climb a rope attached to the centre beam of the ceiling. Whenever I slowed down, he threw beads called bee stings at me that exploded on impact and stung my legs. That was one way to inspire motivation, I guess. I was certain I was dying by the end of it. When he finally gave in, I tumbled to the floor and drew in rasping breaths as I tried to convince my pounding heart rate to slow.

Altan crossed his arms and stared down at me.

"Haven't you..." I paused to suck in air. "Punished me...enough? Why...are you...still making me...run?"

The sphinx narrowed his eyes. "To keep you alive. Don't think this is going to stop, Trix. You need to get fit and stay fit. Even when we're on a case, I expect you to be jogging every day. Take up training in some form of martial arts, if you want. What if a harpy comes at you? Once they lock onto their prey, there is no escaping them. You either kill it or you run until it collapses from exhaustion. Anatomically, harpies are built similarly to your smaller native birds. If you read the book I gave you on Monday, you would know this already."

My blank look turned bashful when he correctly assumed that I hadn't gotten around to reading about avian magicas. Which I really should. It might have something in there about talking to tawny frog-mouths.

"They burn calories fast. It is possible to escape their talons by outlasting them, but if you aren't fit enough to do that, you wind up dead. Do you want to die, Trix?"

"No," I huffed out.

"Good. Then keep running like your life depends on it. Because it does."

"Do you realise..." My breathing was slowly returning to normal, but my words were still breathy. "That you don't exactly..." I sucked in a deep breath. "Inspire people to want this job?"

He leaned against the wall, tilted his head back, and closed his eyes. "You are extremely trying," he murmured. The only physical sign of his aggravation was his tail sweeping against the floor. With a sigh, he opened his eyes and directed his amber gaze towards me. "This isn't a cushy office job, no. I don't want some jock coming in, all guns blazing, thinking he's going to be a hero. You need to be compassionate with clients, calm under pressure, and not too proud to run if you meet an enemy you can't beat. You need to be able to take instructions and also work independently. We're often dealing with magicas, so, yes, sometimes you need to be creative. It's a lot to take in. I understand. You won't be perfect on your first go. But my job is to show you how to do your job and stay safe. I wish someone would create an actual academy for assessors to train them all properly." He shrugged. "Since no one has bothered, I'm stuck trying to impart as much knowledge as I can to you so you can eventually become a decent assessor. And not die."

I pushed myself off the floor and said, "I get it. I understand why you're doing all this. I know I'm not the finest physical specimen out there, and I'm as clumsy as a new-born foal. But I want you to know, I am trying."

The sphinx's ear flicked, and he cocked his head. "I see you. I just hope it's not too little too late."

"What do you mean?"

"Next week, you will officially be my full-time assistant. As I mentioned, on Monday we will travel to HO to get you outfitted. I'm waiting on further details, but it looks like we lost an assessor this week. Initial reports suggest she was drowned by a rogue mermaid. Therefore, it is likely we will be taking on a larger workload than anticipated. I had hoped to give you a few days to find your feet and train you some more, but we may have to dive straight into a claim on your first week."

"Did you know her? The assessor?"

"A little," his response was clipped, and he turned away from me.

"I'm sorry for your loss."

He shrugged, keeping his face hidden. "You get used to it."

"How many assessors are there in Queensland?" I asked softly.

"Ten." His shoulders tensed. "Sorry, nine now. Plus you."

Resolve overtook the doubt I'd been fighting for the past four weeks. "I'm not going anywhere, Altan. I'm going to be the best bloody assistant you've ever had. And I'm not planning on dying anytime soon."

The sphinx snuck a look over his shoulder, a small smile playing on his lips. "That's a good attitude to have. Just be careful you don't get cocky."

I shook my head. "Not cocky. Confident. And I trust you to prepare mc for the work."

Altan froze at my comment. Clearing his throat, he mumbled a gruff, "Good," and stalked off to pack the empty bead casings into his bag so Ellie's husband could refill them.

Confusing emotions filled my belly with bubbles. If it was anyone other than Altan, I'd say he felt chuffed by me declaring my trust in him. But he didn't care about what I thought.

Did he?

CHAPTER SEVENTEEN

Tʜɪs ᴡᴀs ɪᴛ. Mʏ last day at Maroochydore Mundane and Magica Insurance Brokers.

Eight years of walking through these doors and this was the day it ended. I was already on the cusp of crying before Fiona began her speech, and that sent me over the edge. It was a beautiful afternoon tea with my colleagues and even Shirlene managed a brittle, "Good luck."

"Wonders never cease," I whispered to Nic.

Fi proudly presented me with a gift basket that the office had contributed to. A bottle of my favourite wine, some more of that delicious basil pesto she'd given me, an engraved pen, and a voucher for a spa day that was large enough for multiple treatments left me in a puddle of tears. Fiona also insisted that I finish an hour early today, ignoring my protests. There were hugs all around, and even though Nic was moving in, I still clung to her as I sobbed. I'd miss seeing her at work. Having a workmate that actually cared about you was severely underrated.

Once everyone had returned to their respective offices, I pulled out the contract from Altan. This was it. No going back now. I re-read my amendments to ensure I hadn't forgotten anything, initialled the changes, and signed the last page. Scanning it in, I checked the business card he'd given me and emailed him a copy. Then I packed up my few personal items from my office desk into a box, making sure I kept Heather's leaves from getting crushed, and looked one last time at my almost empty inbox. I read the couple of emails that had arrived with claim updates and quickly updated the notes in the system.

Scanning the room to double-check that I hadn't forgotten anything, I bit my lip, trying not to cry again. There had already been enough tears today. For the last time, I exited my office and activated the protection ward. The familiar light flashed beneath my palm. Readjusting my one-handed-hold on my box of personal effects, I said my final goodbyes and walked out the office doors.

And almost dropped my box.

Altan appeared out of nowhere, scaring the daylights out of me. He instinctively grabbed the box, his fingers grazing my ribs as he did so. That same weird energy I'd felt on the first day I'd met him tingled through my body, making me hyper aware of him.

"Sorry to startle you," he said, making sure I had a secure grip on the box before letting go.

My cheeks heated, and I started prattling in a falsetto voice, "That's fine! Wow, your reflexes are super-fast. I didn't even see you coming! We just had my goodbye party. Look at the lovely gifts everyone got me. And this is my plant. I call her Heather. Do you think it's weird to name a plant?" I forced myself to stop, hoping he wouldn't judge me too harshly for my nervous chattering.

You know what? Who cares if he does? I'm my own woman. Screw him. I can natter on as much as I want, thank you very much.

He frowned. "Are you okay?"

All my unjustified outrage fizzled out then, and I nodded meekly, then jerked my head towards the front doors. "Last day. Goodbyes. Just a lot of emotion, you know?"

Altan's tail caressed my shoulder briefly, and I shivered at the light contact. "I understand. I was hoping to catch you before you left. I'm going to need that signed contract from you now."

"I already emailed it through to you."

"Oh. When?"

"This afternoon."

"I haven't been in my office."

"I figured that since you're here, but you should be able to pull it up on your phone." I tilted my head, curious as to why he chose not to get email notifications on his work phone.

He scrunched up his nose at that. "I don't like phones."

"Okay," I replied slowly. "That doesn't tell me why you can't check your emails?"

"I don't have my emails on my phone. I use it for its intended purpose." At the sight of my cocked eyebrow, he added, "For phone calls. That's it."

"Do you mean to tell me you don't take selfies?" I asked, half-joking.

He shook his head with pursed lips and slipped his mobile out of his shirt pocket.

"You use a flip phone?" My eyes widened in incredulity. "Are you serious?" How had I not noticed that before?

Altan's tail flicked, and his ears pinned when he glared at me. "You humans are addicted to your technology. This does the job."

I couldn't help myself. I burst out laughing.

He glared at me for a while before relenting, a ghost of a smile on his lips. With a few more gasps, I finally got myself under control.

"I like your laugh. It is a very—" He paused as he searched for the right word. "Pleasing sound."

Heat rose to my cheeks once again. "Oh, um, thanks." Shifting my box under my arm, I pulled out the contract. "Since you can't check your emails until you're back at your desk, here's the hard copy of my contract."

Plucking it from my hands, he skimmed over my requested amendments, which were all to do with having the freedom to disengage from a job and come home to Matilda if she became unwell or injured. "Do you mind if I take this? I need to sign it and set you up in the system."

I agreed but asked, "I thought you didn't need it until Monday?"

He rubbed a hand over his face. "That leads me to my next question. Are you available on Sunday?"

"Sunday?" I frowned. "I might be. Why?"

"I need to take you to Head Office early. You need a uniform and your beads. The boss wants us to fly to Bowen on Monday to begin work."

"Bowen!" I screeched. "Monday?" I'd never been to Bowen, but I knew it was up north. Somewhere between Mackay and Townsville?

"That's what I said."

Nic came running out of the office at the sound of my yelling and skidded to a halt when she saw Altan. Her head whipped back and forth between us, and she asked, "Are you okay, Trix?"

"Yeah. But Nic? Looks like I might need to invoke a babysitting request earlier than planned."

"Oh, true? I'm sure it will be fine. When do you need me?"

"I need to take Trix to Brisbane for the day on Sunday to arrange her uniform and weapons, then we will fly to Proserpine Airport on Monday for a job in Bowen."

She pumped her eyebrows. "Oh, I see. So I guess you two will have to stay somewhere together in Brisbane on Sunday night too, hmm?" She kept her tone innocent, but I knew what she was insinuating.

So while trying to look like I wasn't moving my top half and using my box of personal effects as a visual barrier, I stepped on her foot.

A tiny squeak sneaked past her lips, but she rolled her eyes and conceded defeat.

"No," Altan said, seemingly oblivious to our childish antics. "We will be flying out from the Brisbane airport on Monday afternoon. There is no need to stay in Brisbane overnight. I'll pick you up from your house at seven on Sunday morning to visit Caroline and return you in the afternoon. Then we will drive down to the airport late Monday morning." With a flick of his ear, he amended his request. "If that is agreeable to both of you?"

"It's a date!" Nic proclaimed.

I muffled a groan. "Not a date. It's for work," I hissed at her.

She stuck her tongue out at me. "Fine. Yes, I have no plans other than unpacking boxes on Sunday, so am available to keep an eye on Millie. I will be there for her during the week for drop-off and pick-up. I will cook food and wash her uniforms. You can rely on me. I will await further instructions." She saluted and marched back into the office without another word.

Altan stared after her. "She is most peculiar."

"That she is," I muttered.

"I'll see you Sunday morning then, yes?"

"All righty, sounds like a plan. Do you want me to text you my address?"

He waved the contract papers. "Your address will be in here, yes?"

"Oh, of course. My number is in there too. Just call me if anything changes, okay?"

"Can do." He smiled then, utterly disarming me. His eyes sparkled, and the sudden warmth in his gaze threw me onto the back foot.

What is this man doing to me?

Chapter Eighteen

Dressed all in black, Altan cut an imposing figure as he argued on his mobile outside my house on Sunday morning. When he snapped his flip phone shut, I bit my tongue to avoid mocking him about using the archaic technology.

With a final wave to Millie and Nic, I slid into the passenger seat of Altan's fancy black car. Immediately, I was grateful for my tights and long-sleeved shirt. Thanks to the air conditioning blasting out of the vents, the interior was ice-cold. Glancing over at Altan, I couldn't help but admire the way his turtleneck hugged his body in all the right ways.

I seriously needed to get a new hobby that didn't involve ogling my boss.

Switching my focus to his car, I winced. I was too afraid to touch anything on the dash of Altan's car. The flawless leather interior and modern accessories looked like they were just waiting for me to break them or, at the very least, smudge them. I sat on my hands instead, hoping I'd last the drive to Brisbane without destroying something somehow.

"What's the plan?" I asked as he pulled away from the curb.

"Caroline can't get in until late morning since it's her day off as well. So I thought it would be a good day to introduce you to archery and hand-to-hand combat. We begin this morning."

"I beg your pardon? What did you say we are doing?" My voice grew high-pitched at the unexpected change of plans. I knew weapons would eventually form a part of my training, but I didn't expect it to happen today. A thrill swept through me at the thought of learning how to fight. Whether that thrill was one of excitement or fear, I couldn't quite decide.

Altan swung his gaze to meet mine. "Have I taught you nothing?"

"You've taught me plenty," I muttered.

"Rule one." He waited.

I sighed, blowing a tendril of hair out of my face, and parroted his lesson, "Expect the unexpected."

"Precisely." Altan scowled at me as if to make sure I was taking him seriously. "You need to be versed in all aspects of fighting. We've been working on your endurance and strength as well as the study of magicas. But sometimes, you won't be able to escape. That's when you need to know how to fight."

"Can you please watch the road while you lecture me?" My hand automatically hovered near the steering wheel, anxiously waiting to correct our trajectory.

He scoffed. "I am an excellent driver. You needn't fear for your safety when I am behind the wheel."

"Said every overconfident teen driver ever."

"Fine. I'll stop talking."

"Fine."

"Fine."

Silence reigned in the car. It stretched on as we sped down the Bruce Highway, Altan keeping his eyes fixed on the road. I sighed loudly in an attempt to break the tension. The sphinx didn't react.

I tried to coax him out of his stubborn silence by asking him, "So...where exactly is Head Office anyway?"

"Brisbane City."

I waited, but no further information was forthcoming. Another idea to draw him out of his sullen mood sparked in my mind. I asked him, "What's black and white and red all over."

He looked at me and raised an eyebrow before returning his eyes to the road. "So...that's your version of a riddle. Are you serious?"

"It's a good one! And it's funny when you know the answer."

He snorted. "It might be amusing to children. That has to be one of the simplest riddles to ever exist. You'll need to do better than that."

"Fine, consider that my homework this week. But my question is, do you know the answer?"

He rolled his eyes before answering primly, "It's a newspaper."

I clapped slowly and, with a sarcastic curl to my lips, said, "Got it in one! Because it's actually *read*, not *red*."

A soft chuckle escaped his lips, and I froze at the sound.

It was...nice.

More than nice. A sudden need to be the reason he laughed every day filled my thoughts. I pushed it away. He was my boss. It was perfectly normal to feel a need to please him due to my work ethic. What wasn't normal was to want to bring him joy beyond that. I squashed the thoughts and blurted out the next sentence in a hurry to stop the erratic beating of my heart. "Okay, so we're heading to Brisbane City for uniforms with Caroline. But whereabouts are we going for combat training?"

The ice had thawed. He replied, "Same building. While there isn't any sort of academy for new assessors, MagicAssess do have an entire floor dedicated to training."

"What's it like?"

"You'll see."

Once again, I found myself on my back, staring at the ceiling.

Altan had easily swept my feet from beneath me for the third time since we'd arrived at the training floor in Head Office. I was going to be well acquainted with the grey tiled ceiling by the time I finished here.

"This is ridiculous," I groaned, rubbing my buttocks as I dragged myself back to my feet. I was going to have some bruises tomorrow.

"This is necessary." The sphinx stood still, waiting patiently for me to rise. I scowled at him. There wasn't a hair out of place, and his clothes remained unrumpled. "Again." He shifted back into his fighting stance, waiting for me to engage once more.

"I know I have some natural cushioning." I was already panting while he looked cool as a cucumber. "But do you think I could get some extra padding? Like a mat? Or some sort of puffy armour?"

"Don't be preposterous. And don't forget to breathe," he advised as he easily blocked my attempted punch with his forearm.

I howled when I made contact with him and clutched my poor hand to my chest. Gritting my teeth, I hissed, "I am rubbish at this."

"Yes, you are," he stated matter-of-factly.

"That's not helpful."

"Everyone starts out rubbish when they're learning. The key is to keep trying."

"But it hurts!"

"Life hurts."

"You are just full of pearls of wisdom today, aren't you?" I snarled and shook my hand out, doing my best to ignore the pain. Scowling at him, I circled, trying to find an opening as we talked. He'd given me a run-down of hand-to-hand techniques before we began the session, and corrected me as we sparred, but I continued to fail.

"Keep your hands up. No, higher. Good. Thumbs on the outside. Move your feet a little further apart to keep your centre of gravity lower."

I obeyed. A tiny part of me was sorry for Altan for having to teach me. I was naturally clumsy, and inexperienced to boot. It had to make his job extra hard. At the same time, I was glad I was finally learning. There was no way I would let any magica threaten my girl ever again. I just needed to practise more.

In the space of one second, Altan's tail had swung through the air and wrapped around my forearm, pulling me towards him. He spun me as I stumbled forward, until my back was held against his chest. His arms wrapped around my torso, effectively trapping me, and his foot was wedged between mine, his leg pressing lightly in between my calves.

"Don't ever forget," he said lightly, his breath tickling my ear, "that you are fighting magicas. We all have different abilities and bodies to you, and we will use them to our advantage."

His tail was still wrapped around my arm, the fur like satin against my skin. One of his hands sat just below my bra-line, a hairs breadth away from touching my breasts. I gulped. It had been a long time since I'd been held like this by anyone. Admittedly, my body wasn't usually bruised and battered from that same person trying to teach me how to throw a punch, but I'd take what I could get. My overactive imagination set off a daydream sequence that involved lots of petting and kissing. Heat rushed to my cheeks and my breathing accelerated.

Imagine how embarrassing it would be if I hyperventilated in the training room of my new job because I couldn't control my raging hormones. At least there weren't any witnesses.

"You've forgotten to breathe again," he murmured, his voice husky. The sphinx pressed me even closer against his chest. That didn't help my situation at all. I could feel *everything*. And that stupid electricity had returned, making the hairs on the back of my neck rise. He whispered in my ear, "Your enemies will use whatever weakness they can find. What's lesson one?"

Lesson one? Blimey. How could he expect me to think right now? Was it something about wearing armour? I couldn't think when the scent of sandalwood and leather was overwhelming my senses.

"Too slow," he purred, his voice sounding like honey, his peculiar accent even more pronounced.

And then he dropped me.

Sweeping his foot across my legs, he knocked me over easily but kept hold of my arm with his tail, softening my fall.

"You! I... That wasn't... Not fair!"

The drongo was grinning. I was going to kill him.

Instead of fearing the murder in my eyes, the sphinx turned his back on me and walked away.

Mate, if I swore, he'd be copping a tongue lashing right now.

"I'll never go easy on you, Trix," he called over his shoulder. "So if you ever land a hit on me, you'll know you earned it."

Grumbling under my breath, I scrambled to my feet and begrudgingly followed him, wondering what else was in store.

Pressing his hand to a purple crystal on the wall, he waited for it to flash before sliding open the massive white concertina doors. My mouth dropped open. It was like that moment in the movies when someone showed the main character his weapons arsenal. Hundreds of guns, bows, swords, and knives were mounted on the walls behind the doors. I had no idea there were that many different types of weapons.

There were rifles, shotguns, and pistols of varying sizes and colours. Crossbows, longbows, and other bows that I didn't have a name for. There were short swords, long swords, curved swords. Knives with two blades, knives that looked like needles. What was I supposed to do with all this?

"This is the assessors' arsenal. Once you're properly set up in the system, you will have access to this locker without needing me to unlock it. You can practise with any of these in the training room and just need to sign out whatever weapons you choose for your assignments. It is unfortunate that we are unable to spend more time on your combat training before we leave tomorrow." He shrugged. "It is what it is, and we'll have to make do with the training I can offer."

"Am I...am I training with these today?" I asked.

"Yes. I think we'll stick with a crossbow and leave the compounds and recurves for another day." He rubbed a hand over his chin. "We'll try out some of these swords and see which suits you best."

"Swords?" I squeaked.

"Certain magicas like komadas dragons have a particular type of armour that is difficult to penetrate with bullets or arrows. But they have one scale on their underbelly that's softer around the edges. If you can get close enough to it without being ripped apart by their teeth or crushed by their coils, you can slip your sword between the plates and hit one of their hearts." As he spoke, he picked up a short knife off its pedestal, flipped it into the air, and caught it easily.

"One of?"

"Yes, komadas have three hearts. But you only need a direct hit on one of them to end their life."

He carefully picked up a sword and handed it to me hilt first. "This is a spatha. A shorter sword so it won't be too heavy for you. You won't have the same range or heavy-hitting effect like a broadsword, but at least you'll be able to swing it." His brows creased, and he fingered the hilt of a curved blade. "The other option we have is this one."

"Is that a scimitar?" I asked.

"Not every curved blade is a scimitar." Amusement lit up his eyes as he plucked it off the wall and handed it to me.

I held both blades in my hands, weighing them up. Raising the oddly shaped sword to my eyeline, I asked, "Is it a mini-scythe?"

"No. In some countries, it is called a shotel. But this isn't a regular shotel. The length of this blade is shorter, wider, and lighter. Traditionally, it was used for hooking mounted opponents and forcing them down to your level. It can work well against unique magicas." He cocked his head as he studied my stance. "We'll do some drills with both blades and see how they feel for you. At the end of the day, you need to be comfortable with your choice. As your skill improves, your weapon will feel like an extension of your body." He took the swords away. Grabbing a crossbow off the rack, he tested its weight before handing it to me. "All right, Trix. Let's see how you go."

Pressing a hidden button behind one of the weapons, he opened a drawer I hadn't noticed and pulled out a few bolts. That was the limit of my knowledge when it came to anything to do with archery. The lesson went as well as you could imagine. Only three of my shots hit the target, and after I was disarmed ten times with the shotel and eight times with the spatha, Altan called it quits.

"We have a lot to work on," he said with a grim look in his eyes. "I want you to keep running every day, gradually increasing the distance, and when we have down-time between claims, we will spend more time on improving your skillset."

I was bent over, my hands on my knees, sucking in air. "You giving up on me?" I managed to gasp out.

"Nope. I never will. But I know that if I keep pushing you, I won't have a functioning partner for this claim."

The claim. The claim that I was supposed to be assessing tomorrow. His words sent me into a panic. If I couldn't even manage to land a punch on my boss, how was I supposed to fight magicas? Doubt reared its ugly head and overtook all my previous bravado.

What if I failed? What if I wasn't good enough? I could die. I would leave Millie behind to fend for herself. How could I be so selfish? I could hope that a claim for a missing landmark would be a simple one to ease me into my new role. I could hope that there wouldn't be too many magicas attacking us on the job. But as I saw at the netball game, nothing was certain. I had to be prepared. But I also had to trust Altan. If he said that was enough for today, then I had to accept that. He swore he'd train me well enough to keep me safe, and I had to believe him.

Unaware of my internal ruminations, Altan glanced at the watch on his wrist. "Caroline should be here by now anyway. Let's go." Leaving me to recover my breath, he returned the shotel to its place on the wall before sliding the spatha into a leather scabbard. He packed it, the crossbow, and some bolts into a duffel bag before closing the concertina doors, locking them again with the crystal. He easily slung the bag over his shoulder and strode across the room, not waiting to see if I was following.

I was still panting as we exited the training room. Something told me I would be back in there and silently cursing Altan's name again soon enough.

CHAPTER NINETEEN

ALTAN WAVED A HAND towards the young pixie in front of me. "This is Caroline. She'll be issuing your uniforms and supplies for our trip." He checked his watch. "I have a previous commitment I need to attend. I'll pick you up around two o'clock, and we'll head back to the Sunshine Coast."

He strode away without a backwards glance. I stared at his retreating back for a long moment before giving myself an internal shake. Turning away from the sight of his taut derriere, I smiled at the pixie and tapped three fingers against my heart.

The green-haired pixie flashed a grin and returned the gesture. "Hey, girl!" She bounced on the balls of her feet, looking like she might begin dancing at any moment. "Come with me, and let's get you sorted."

I followed the pixie down a hall before turning right. She then went down an escalator, across a foyer, into another hall, then turned left. With all the off-white walls and charcoal-grey laminate flooring, everything blurred together, and it was at that point I stopped trying to keep my bearings. I blindly followed her until she stopped at a tiny bright blue door. She opened it and darted through, reaching back to hold it open for me.

Ducking down to avoid hitting my head on the doorframe, I did not expect to see the massive room when I straightened up again. Cupboards and drawers lined three of the walls while the fourth wall was covered in mirrors. A plain brown table sat in the far corner with piles of cardboard boxes sitting on top. I'm certain my eyes have never widened so much as I tried to take it all in.

"Wow."

"Welcome to my happy place." Caroline did a small pirouette. She looked even tinier when compared to the huge room.

"How do you reach the top cupboards? No disrespect meant, but they're taller than me, let alone you."

"You'll find that a lot of the time, my answer will be the same. It's all magic." She waved a hand through the air, and the cupboards rearranged themselves as if they were on a vertical carousel. The drawers that had been closest to the roof were now at eye level. Rubbing her hands together, she said, "Right. Let's get you decked out. Now stand still. The tape doesn't like it when you move."

Before I could ask her what she meant, she snapped her fingers. To my left, a drawer opened and a sewing tape measure flew out it and sailed through the air, floating to a stop in front of my face. The tiny metal tab at the end seemed to study me, nodding up and down a couple of times before it rushed to wrap around my waist where it squeezed firmly.

"Frilled-neck lizards!" I squealed.

It pulled tighter, reprimanding me for my outburst.

Caroline poked her head out from where she was digging through a cupboard on my right, "What the hell was that? Frilled-neck lizards?"

Gritting my teeth, I muttered, "I don't like to swear."

"You're a weirdo." She snorted. "Just let the tape do its job. It won't hurt you."

I nodded silently at her reassurance and waited while the tape raced over my body, pausing as it took my measurements. It was all over in a few minutes, and the tape fluttered over to Caroline, hovering next to her ear as if it were sharing a secret only she could decipher.

"Thanks, champ," she said, and it took me a moment to realise she was speaking to the tape. She blew a kiss in its direction. In response, it curled into the shape of a love heart before gliding back into a drawer and disappearing from view.

Sad really, that this experience was not one of the weirdest moments of my past few weeks. Maybe top ten though.

"Sorry," said Caroline, walking towards me with some sort of shiny purple outfit on a coat hanger. "Sometimes I forget that humans aren't used to magic if they don't usually work alongside magicas."

"I mean, I worked with a wizard at my old job. But the most I saw him do was things like reheating his coffee without using the microwave. I don't recall him taking control of an inanimate object like that."

"Oh, the tape isn't inanimate."

I stared at her.

The pixie laughed, her vibrant green fringe falling into her eyes. "It's an old type of magic. The tape isn't living exactly, but it does have a mind of its own." She grinned at the bemused expression on my face. "The good news is, no need to try on dozens of outfits. It knows your body now and will always give you the right sized clothes." She held out the hanger with what looked like a thin wetsuit.

Finally gaining control over my voice again, I asked, "What is this?"

"Your armour."

"What, is it armour against ants? That's way too thin to protect me! You do remember I'm a human, right? We wear skinsuits filled with blood and goop. We break easy. This won't stop a bee sting, let alone a magica intent on nibbling my bones for breakfast!"

"Looks can be deceiving. Put it on."

I sighed and looked around for the changing rooms. "If you say so. Where do I get dressed?"

Caroline crossed her arms and gave a wicked grin. "Here is fine." Rolling her eyes at my look of horror, she turned around and face the opposite way. "This better?"

I blushed. Didn't look like I had a choice. Some women might not mind getting changed in front of each other, but I hadn't been put in this position very often. Having Millie young meant I hadn't had many of the usual experiences that most twenty-somethings enjoyed. And apparently, that included accepting partial nudity in front of strangers. I wasn't a prude; I was just uncomfortable.

With a muttered, "Fine," I stripped off my tights and shirt, pulling the slippery full-body onesie over my sports bra and underwear. I hadn't worn anything this form-fitting in years. I cringed at my soft middle, wondering how many more weeks of training with Altan it would take for my non-existent abs to consider the possibility of firming up. I zipped up the back as far as I could and said, "Can I get some help, please?"

Turning back around, Caroline zipped me up the rest of the way. "Spin," she commanded, twirling her finger.

Never before had I responded so quickly to someone half my size. I liked Caroline, but she scared me a little.

She scrutinised me as I turned. "Fits you like a glove. Like I said it would. This armour will limit the impact of brute force, blades, and teeth."

She punched my hip to prove her point. I barely felt it. But then again, she was tiny. I still wasn't convinced a bigger opponent wouldn't crush me. "Are you sure? It doesn't feel like armour. How would it hold up against a griffin's talons?"

Caroline looked at me like I was stupid. "Trust me. You'll be fine. Do you need a further demonstration?"

I shrugged non-committedly. "I mean, I trust you Caroline, but I'm just worried, you know? It's my life we're talking about. My kid needs me. I have to survive." An unexpected lump appeared in my throat. What would happen to Matilda if I died on the job? Altan insisted I would be fine if I followed his instructions, but I wasn't a very good student. Doubt hit me again and I wondered if this was all a terrible mistake.

The pixie sighed before striding over to her table, pawing through a drawer. Before I could ask her what she was doing, she spun around and threw a knife at me. I screamed and jumped backwards. Which did not help me to avoid the blade at all. The knife struck my gut before clattering to the floor. I grabbed my stomach, waiting for the pain to hit. But there was nothing.

Looking down, I waited to see the blossom of blood sprouting from between my fingers. When I removed my hand, I was amazed to find the fabric wasn't even damaged. "What did you do that for?" I exclaimed, glaring at her with accusation in my eyes.

She snorted and marched back to me before picking up the knife off the floor. "You wanted proof that you'd be safe. You weren't about to take my word for it. Now you know. The armour is awesome. So stop freaking out, would you?" She lifted my arms, checking the fit across my chest and added, "This armour has been designed to move with your body, to be wearable under civilian clothes if you're undercover, and to keep you safe." She grabbed my arm and drew my attention to an innocuous button on the top of my shoulder. I had to tilt my head awkwardly to see it. "When activated, this button here adds an additional layer of protection. It's located here in case you are ever restrained and are being attacked. You should still be able to reach it by tapping your head to your shoulder." She gestured for me to tap it, so like the good little student I was, I followed her instructions.

Plated armour sprung up over my torso, shoulders, wrists, and thighs. "Mother trucker!" I squeaked in shock. Placing a hand over my racing heart, I looked at the sniggering Caroline with wide eyes. "You couldn't have warned me?"

"It's more fun this way."

"Fun for whom?" I grumbled.

"You're a jumpy little thing, aren't you? We'll have to train that out of you. This is good practise. What's Altan's favourite saying again? Expect the unexpected."

Ignoring her comments on my skittishness, I ran my hands over the plates, perplexed. "How the heck does it do that? It's so light. And there weren't any grooves that the armour could have come out of."

She shrugged. "Simple answer is magic."

"Sure, sure. Cool. Okay." I wasn't okay. But I could pretend. It was one thing to live alongside magicas and chat to them about insurance. It was quite another to see their magic at work. I was beginning to realise what a sheltered life I'd been living. "How do I get it to go back?" I asked her.

She grinned, baring her pointed teeth. "Easy. Just tap twice."

With a light double-tap, the plates disappeared and I was wearing the shiny purple wetsuit thing again. "That's amazing," I breathed.

"Just wait until the day it saves your life. You'll love it even more." She unzipped me and said, "You can get changed again, if you like." She bustled over to the desk, returned the knife to the drawer, and began pulling things out of the boxes. I stripped down and changed into my civilian clothes as she continued talking. "Now, I've also got your office uniforms here. It's just a grey blouse and navy slacks that you can wear whenever you have a mundane task to attend to that requires you to look professional. Also, I've asked the IT department to set you up in our system. We're still waiting on your passcodes and identification badge, so make sure you stick with Altan until those arrive. With his clearance, you can get in just about anywhere. However, I have your standard-issue bead kit, a phone, and a tablet for you." She made a pile of them and added two office uniforms.

Approaching the desk cautiously in case she had any other weapons hidden around, I asked, "If you can make me a magic uniform, why can't you magic me up an ID badge?" I folded up my armour, the slippery fabric belying its strength, and placed it beside her pile.

Raking her slender fingers through her bob cut, Caroline said, "It's complicated. But the short answer is, the badges are made using a process that combines technology and magic to try to stop any would-be thieves from easily forging them and breaking into HO. It takes time." She held out the phone and tablet.

"Huh. Well, there you go. Makes sense." I accepted the proffered items and tucked the uniforms under my arm. Caroline showed me how to unlock the phone and tablet and how to attach the bead kit to the belt loop on my hip.

"There's one thing you need to do on this assignment." She pulled up an app on the tablet. "This app allows you to journal your days. Make notes of who you speak to, any calls Altan makes, any actions that need to be taken. Et cetera, et cetera." Caroline paused and looked at me.

"Okay, great. Just hit the plus button on the top," I said as I tapped it and scanned the screen. "Then write notes and then hit the 'Done' button, yeah?" She nodded. "Seems pretty intuitive."

"Thank the Gods!" the pixie gushed. "I'm so glad you'll actually use it." She leaned forward and whispered, "If we weren't so overwhelmed with work, he'd be getting a reprimand."

"Who? Why?"

"Altan, of course! He's stuck in the dark ages. No idea why, but that sphinx detests all technology. He flat out refuses to log anything in the app." She rolled her eyes. "He turns in a handwritten report for all his claims. It has been so hard to schedule jobs and get updates when he won't use our reporting app. But he's the best assessor in Australia. The company's hands are tied. They have to work with his idiosyncrasies."

"Blimey. So he doesn't use technology? At all?" I frowned.

"He uses his mobile for phone calls. And he uses his old-school laptop occasionally for a claim if he's got no other choice."

"That's...unusual."

"More like annoying." I kept my face neutral even though I wanted to laugh. She gave me a sly side-eye. "Very diplomatic. You'll do well."

With a snort, I said, "Well, I'll make sure I keep the app updated even if he doesn't."

Caroline swept into a bow. "The entire team at MagicAssess thanks you."

CHAPTER TWENTY

Monday morning started with a lot of tears. Mostly from me, of course.

Before Nic took her to the bus stop, Millie snuggled into me on the couch. She was all gangly limbs these days but no matter how big she got, she would always be my little girl.

"Mum?"

"What's up, little dove?" I asked as I stroked her hair.

She hesitated before saying, "Are you sure this is what you want? What if you kept working for Fiona and I picked up some after-school shifts at the pizza shop or something? Would that help with the bills? Insurance assessing sounds dangerous. What if you get hurt?" Her voice trembled a little on her last sentence.

"Oh, sweetheart," I squeezed her even tighter, resting my head against hers. The wayward strands of her fringe tickled my cheek. "My darling girl. Thank you for worrying about me. But you don't need to." With a soft chuckle, I said, "You've got your whole life to worry about bills. I don't want you to be stressing about that right before your senior years at high school. What I want is for you to be able to focus on your education. I do not want you worrying about whether to choose to work another shift to get extra cash, or to stay home and finish an assignment."

My heart squeezed as I said the words, remembering a similar time in my own teenage years. But *my* mother hadn't had this talk with me. I had chosen to work after school so we had enough money to keep the lights on in our rental, but as a result, I had barely passed three of my classes. Millie didn't need to know all those details though. I was determined not to force her to make the same choices I'd had to make at her age.

"I'll admit, the pay rise is one of the reasons I decided to take the job. But it's more than that." I pulled back to look her in the eyes. "You remember the griffin attack last month?"

She nodded silently, studying me.

"When its wing sent me crashing into the ground, I looked over and saw you. You were facing up to that creature, all alone. I thought you were going to die. And I couldn't do anything to save you. I never ever want to feel that way again. Yes, assessing has risks, but we nearly died just going to your netball game. We can't live our life in fear; so I decided to make a change. To take back control of my life. I want to learn how to fight so I can keep us safe. And if I get paid handsomely to be trained on the job, that's okay with me." I stroked her back. "Does that make sense?"

"Yeah, I think I get it. Just...be careful, okay? I need you to come back in one piece." Her voice broke on the last word and she enveloped me in another hug.

"I promise. I'll check in every day. Call me anytime, okay? Altan knows you're my priority. If you need me, I will drop everything and come back to you, I swear."

With one last round of hugs, and an oath from Nicole that she'd take care of Millie as if she were her own, they drove away, headed to the bus stop. It felt like my heart was being ripped out of my chest as Nic took her away. I'd already given my best friend three pages of instructions for looking after Millie but worried I'd forgotten something.

Having no real idea of what I needed for the trip, I threw together a bag of assorted outfits that should last me a few days and a variety of different scenarios. I was wearing my MagicAssess office uniform when Altan picked me up from the front of my house. As he drove us to Brisbane Airport, he spent most of the trip explaining the claim we were assessing. The Big Mango in Bowen had been stolen. While I'd heard about it on the news, I'd never expected to be involved. Our job was to interview the owner and the local police to confirm that it wasn't insurance fraud and that there was no chance of recovering the stolen item. I noticed the grimace of disgust cross Altan's face when he mentioned the Big Mango.

We had a lot of "Big" sculptures in Australia. So what? I thought the Big Pineapple, the Big Banana, and the Big Prawn were a lot of fun. But I wasn't about to give him a lecture. I was preoccupied with the bubble of anticipation sitting in my chest. Don't get me wrong, the self-doubt was still hanging around, as well as the guilt about leaving Millie. However, I was looking forward to travelling again. It had been years since I'd been on a plane. And Bowen was supposed to be a really pretty part of the Whitsundays. I'd researched it last night and the beaches looked stunning.

Leaving Altan's car in the long-term carpark, we headed straight to the domestic departures terminal. He checked us in, lifting my bag onto the conveyor before I could grab it.

Is he being gentlemanly? Or am I just too slow and making him impatient? I shook my head. I could not figure him out.

Finally, we boarded, and the plane taxied along the runway. A thrill raced up my spine. Even though I hadn't taken a flight in forever, I still looked forward to the sensation of the world dropping away and seeing the carpets of greens and blues laid out below me. Though I will say, as much as I loved flying, I wasn't sure about the sanity of the humans who voluntarily rode dragons. I mean, more power to them, but I liked the security of having a giant metal box to protect me from plummeting to my death.

The cabin rattled as the plane picked up speed, and a hiss to my right had me whipping my head around, cricking my neck in the process. My mouth dropped open when I realised the sound had come from between Altan's teeth. His canines had elongated, extra fur had sprouted along his jawline and on his arms, and his eyes were tightly closed. As he gripped his tail in his lap, the tip flicked incessantly.

I worried my lip, torn on what to do. My knee-jerk reaction was to offer comfort, but this sphinx hadn't exactly welcomed my friendship. Throwing caution to the wind, I asked softly, "Hey. Hey, Altan. Are you okay?"

"No," he snarled as quietly as he could, his eyes still squeezed shut.

I reached over and placed my hand on his forearm. "I'm here," I murmured. "Everything will be fine." I had no idea if what I was about to do was inappropriate, seeing as he was a magica and my boss to boot, but I gave him the same comfort I would give my daughter in this situation. I began rubbing soothing circles on the back of his hand. I glanced up at his face, afraid of what I would see. Instead of fury, a curious expression of wonder spread across his features. "Breathe with me," I whispered.

He began by sucking in short gulps of air, but as I kept my inhales deep, and exhales measured, he slowly began to mimic me. I continued with my circles. I watched, entranced, as the colour of his fur changed when the light fell over it in various angles with my movement. I noted how it went from a midnight black to a chocolate brown, with a hint of a blue sheen when the artificial light hit it just right. Out of the corner of my eye, I noticed his shoulders relax, and he leaned back in his seat.

"Keep doing that, please," he said and closed his eyes again. His hands were no longer gripping his tail, which in turn had ceased its twitching.

I gladly continued my circling, enjoying the sensation of his coat under my fingertips. A wayward thought entered my brain as I wondered how much of his body was covered in fur, and what it would feel like to run my hands over it without clothes interrupting me. I blushed and pushed the inappropriate thoughts out of my mind. Or at least, pushed them down into a box and then found a wardrobe buried in the back of my mind and threw the box inside, hoping it would get lost in Narnia.

Ten minutes later, he sighed and shifted, effectively removing my hand. I pulled back and laced my fingers in my lap.

"Thank you," he murmured, his eyes still closed, but his posture had relaxed. The fur had receded back beneath his jacket. "I don't like take-off, and that helped."

"You're welcome," I squeaked out in a small voice. Had Altan just shared something personal with me? And said something kind in the same breath? Heavens, I should have recorded it so I had proof. No one would believe me.

We passed the remainder of the two-hour-long flight in silence before disembarking at Whitsunday Coast Airport near the small town of Proserpine. The airport was tiny compared to Brisbane. While Altan busied himself at the hire car company's counter, I headed outside into the hot afternoon sun and surveyed the open-air carpark. Turning my airplane mode off, I texted Millie to let her know we'd arrived safely. She wouldn't see the message until she finished school and picked her phone up from the office, but it made the tightness in my chest about leaving her ease a little.

The thunderous expression on Altan's face when he eventually steered me towards the hire car scared me.

I chose to be brave. "What's wrong?"

He snarled. Like, literally snarled, baring his elongated fangs.

"The reason I took so long," he seethed, placing emphasis on every word, "is because those assholes wouldn't accept my driver's license. They claimed it was an error on their system not recognising my 'animalistic' features." His tail was whipping from side to side as he spoke. "But they made me call HO to confirm my identity."

My heart squeezed with pity. "I'm sorry."

"This isn't your fault. But I need you to leave me alone for a little while so I can calm down."

I nodded and kept my mouth shut as we drove out of the tiny Proserpine airport in a glaringly bright yellow sedan. The vehicle's interior wasn't quite as intimidating as Altan's personal vehicle, but it was still way nicer than mine. Best to avoid touching anything. I'd hate for MagicAssess to have to pay an excess because I'd broken the bloody thing.

In an effort to avoid Altan's black mood, I stared out at the flat paddocks filled with either grass or sugar cane. The grass looked almost grey, it was so dry.

"I thought this was the tropics?" I said automatically before biting my tongue, afraid to bring Altan's anger down on me.

He gave a cursory glance out the window before returning his attention to the road. "The sun is shining, there are palm trees every kilometre, and I'm already sweating. Why do you not think this is the tropics?"

"I just thought it rained a lot in the tropics. Isn't it usually a bit more...green?"

"They're coming out of their dry season." he replied curtly, effectively halting any further conversation. I closed my mouth and vowed not to make any more observations.

Altan navigated his way north to Bowen, a sleepy looking place, but the sight of the ocean glistening like a jewel ahead of us removed any doubts I might have harboured about the beauty of the town.

"It's so beautiful," I breathed, immediately forgetting my internal promise to shut my gob.

The sphinx glanced at me and quirked an eyebrow. "It's just the water. You see it every time you head to the beach at Maroochydore. I don't understand the draw. If you've seen one ocean, you've seen them all."

"I disagree. I've never seen this ocean. Or this beach. Or these trees. This water is new and wild and different. I know we're here for work, but can we visit the beach while we're in Bowen? Please?" I tacked it on at the end, unsure of whether manners would help my case or not.

A small smile flashed across his lips, and it was like the sun coming out after a storm. I unconsciously breathed out and relaxed at his change in demeanour.

"I'm sure we can make time for that," he replied.

I really shouldn't let his mood affect me like this. Focussing on my surroundings and not on the confusing sphinx seated beside me, I admired the town. Winding our way through the quiet streets of Bowen, I noted many of the homes were classic Queenslanders with gable roofs, weatherboard exteriors, and vibrant, if somewhat chaotic, gardens. There were a few modern properties mixed in with them, and I couldn't help but feel that they didn't hold the same charm and heart as the older homes.

As we weaved through Bowen, Altan said, "We'll check in to our accommodation first, then interview the insured at the site, and, if we have time" —he glanced at his watch— "we'll visit the cops to review their report with them."

"Sounds like a plan." I paused before asking, "Did you want to talk about the hire company's behaviour?"

He levelled me with a piercing stare, then sighed heavily, letting all the tension seep out of him. "All the humans that were in the line in front of me had no problem getting their vehicles. It's because I'm a magica. There are a thousand different ways we're treated like lesser beings. That's just the latest in a long line of prejudices."

"I'm sorry that happened to you." Reaching out, I gently squeezed his forearm.

He stiffened for a second, then pulled his arm away and steered the car into a carpark beside a caravan park. Jerking the hand brake on, Altan exited the car.

I stared after him as he went into reception. I had a basic understanding of the stigma associated with magical beings but hadn't been close enough with someone before to hear how it affected them on a daily basis. It was incredibly sad. We were all a part of this world. We all just wanted to find happiness. Was it really so hard to treat each other with some respect, regardless of whether we were human or magica?

Heaving a sigh, I unbuckled my seat belt and hopped out of the car, leaning against the hood as I took in the ocean to our left. The tide was in, and the waves rolled gently onto the white sand that separated the caravan park from the ocean. It was so peaceful. I sighed and rolled my shoulders, trying to relax them.

Seagulls hovered on the breeze above the units at the front of the park, squawking as they waited to spot a hapless victim trying to eat chips in peace. I jumped at the sound of a sliding door slamming shut and turned around.

The sphinx stalked towards me, his tail twitching. The poor guy had been pissed off for half the day already. Kind of seemed like he needed to see a psychologist to manage his anger issues even more than I did.

"I'm sorry, Trix. Head Office has stuffed up. I asked them to get two one-bedroom units for us. They booked us in for one two-bedroom unit." He massaged his temples.

"What's the problem? There are still two beds, right?"

"Yes."

"So, there is no problem then? It's all good. It's not like we need to share an actual bed."

I chuckled at the familiar trope. I loved reading romance novels where, gasp, there was only one bed. Whatever would the two main characters do in such an impossible scenario? Man, I was glad no one could hear my thoughts. Even I found myself corny sometimes.

His brows pinched. "Are you sure you don't mind? We'll have to share a bathroom. If it's a problem, I can try to find different accommodation. These guys are booked out aside from that one unit."

"Honestly, I don't mind at all. Fair warning though, I think I sleep talk."

"You think you do?"

"Well, it's been a few years since I shared a bed with someone, but I know I used to." I suddenly felt awkward, sharing something so personal with my boss, and looked at the ground.

"Hey." The sphinx moved closer and tipped my chin up. "I see what you're doing. You don't need to apologise for being yourself. You sleep talk. So what? It's not something you can help."

He was very close. My brain stopped working for a moment. The sunlight lit up the yellow in his eyes. They were captivating. Who even had eyes like that? It should be illegal. They weren't just yellow. I studied the flecks of gold swirling in the deeper amber. Oh no, I was leaning closer to him. There were only a few inches between our faces.

Did I brush my teeth this morning? Can he smell my breath?

Altan broke the spell first. He stepped back and gave himself a shake. Maybe my breath *was* terrible.

Tossing me the car keys over his shoulder, he said gruffly, "See you at unit thirteen," and strode away abruptly.

Why he thought tossing me car keys was a good idea based on my training days, I don't know. They fell to the ground before my hand was even moving. Darting forward, I scooped them up and took some deep breaths to calm my raging lady parts. I'd have to give them a stern talking to. I was here to work. Now was not the time to imagine doing the horizontal tango, especially not with my superior.

Come on, girl. Get your act together.

It took me four tries to get the key into the ignition.

Chapter Twenty-One

I MADE SURE I kept my speed below the five kilometres per hour limit as I drove through the caravan park to our unit. Obviously that was because I was being careful to avoid any small children that might be racing around the cabins on their bikes and had nothing to do with the need to calm down the fire raging below my belt. My libido (and my heart) had taken a vacation after Chris and I had split. The last month had seen all of my carefully constructed walls come crashing down. All of a sudden, my lady parts felt the need to inform me that they were still very much alive, thank you very much. Why now? I was supposed to ogle guys like Perry; not guys like my boss.

I pulled the sedan into the dedicated parking space beside our accommodation, grabbed both of our suitcases out of the boot, and walked up to the sliding front door. The exterior was covered in cream weatherboards with a few tropical plants screening the entry from prying eyes. Altan had his head in the fridge when I walked in. I probably needed to do that too to cool down the flames in my cheeks.

He straightened and looked at me, showing no sign of the earlier tenderness. He frowned and raced over, grabbing both of our bags as I heaved them over the threshold. "You should have called me. You didn't need to carry mine in."

Our fingers brushed as I let go of his bag's handle, and I jerked my hand back. Oh no, I was projecting my romance novel fantasies onto him, making something out of nothing. Ignoring the attempts by my body to insist that every moment was filled with sexual tension, I said breezily, "It's no problem. If I want equal rights, I need equal rights in all things, right? That includes carrying the bags."

He smirked at my comment and stepped back, keeping a careful three feet between our bodies. Thank goodness he wasn't the kind to lodge a sexual harassment claim. Poor guy must be feeling so uncomfortable.

He said, "I just did a quick recon. The main bedroom has a queen bed, and the other has two single beds. You can take the queen."

I frowned. "No way! You've got an extra appendage so you'd need more space, right?"

Altan choked out some sort of strangled cross between a laugh and a cough.

My brain finally caught up with my mouth when I realised that the extra appendage comment could be taken in a couple of different ways. My eyes grew wide in horror, and my mouth dropped open.

Maybe sharing a cabin wasn't such a good idea.

"Your tail!" I blurted out, dropping my bag and clasping my cheeks. Seemed like the beetroot blush was here to stay. "I meant your tail! I'm sorry! Sometimes I say things without thinking about how they sound. I'm not great with words. I don't mean to be rude or disrespectful or flirty or..." I threw my hands in the air. "I don't know how to do this. To speak to men, to be friendly without accidentally sounding flirty. I'm just... I'm sorry, okay?"

"Are you trying to flirt?" His voice held no censure, only a tone of curiosity. He cocked his head as he studied me, and his tail grew still.

"I mean, I do li... I don't know." I shrugged, my logic warring with my emotions. Clearing my throat, I straightened and lifted my chin. I had to keep my cool. Stay professional. And not hit on the boss. "No. Obviously not. That would be inappropriate. What do I want? I want to be a good worker. I want to help our clients. I don't want you to regret employing me. And I want to learn how to be a competent fighter so I can protect myself and my family."

Altan's tail suddenly drooped to the floor, and one of his ears gave a brief flick. He held my gaze and said, "I don't regret employing you. You're very...different to the people I usually work with. But I find myself enjoying your charm." He smiled and placed a hand briefly on my arm. "We're good. Please allow me to be chivalrous for once. Take the main bed. Me and my tail are fine."

"If you're sure," I said dubiously, chewing my lip.

Altan didn't respond; he simply walked away into the smaller bedroom with his bag and started unpacking.

I mimicked his actions, and it didn't take long to hang my clothes and set up my toiletries in the bedside drawer. The sound of the waves lapping against the shore out the front of our unit lured me away from the task soon enough, and I revelled in the fact that we were staying so close to the ocean. The salty breeze teased my hair, and I closed my eyes, enjoying the sun on my face.

A tingling raced over my skin, and I instinctively ducked, feeling an abnormal wind flurry against my head.

"Cheese and crackers!" I shrieked and threw myself onto the ground and away from the black and white demon that appeared in my peripheral.

Altan raced out of the unit. "What's wrong? Why are you screaming like a banshee?"

"Maggie!" I screeched and pointed.

He stared at me incredulously. "It's a bird."

"It's not just any bird," I spat at him as I sought refuge, scrambling along the ground as the bird swooped again. Maybe Altan would scare it away for me. Fat chance. But I'd been scratched by one of those black and white devils in the past and wasn't keen for another round. "It's a maggie." He returned my gaze blankly. "You know, a magpie? You think dragons are bad? You don't need a magical creature's help to die in Australia. Our native animals can do the job just fine. Woe is him who doesn't heed the magpie's song. You'll find your head split open before you can say, 'Boil a billabong.'"

The sphinx simply gawked at me, his brows pulled up in bewilderment. I didn't know if that was because my simplified David Attenborough impression of Australian birds was lacking or if he just didn't understand any of my colloquialisms. Either way, the poor guy needed an education.

"That's an unfair stereotype. We're not that lethal." The animated voice in my head stopped me in my tracks.

I groaned and dropped my head into my hands.

"Stone the crows," I muttered. "Or magpies, in this case." Dragging my head up reluctantly, I found the maggie, who was now perched on a nearby rock.

"We only attack if we think our young are in danger." He cocked his head. *"Although, I will admit we make a point of remembering the faces of all who dare to disrespect us. Also, just a side note, I don't think the crows like that saying very much."*

Staring at the bird, I moaned, "Not you too."

Altan looked between me and the magpie. "What are you talking about? I'm just standing here. What did I do?"

"No, I'm not talking to you!" I stood up and brushed the loose grass off my pants. "It's that bloody bird."

"Didn't I hear you say you swore off swear words?" He raised an elegant brow and crossed his arms. "And what in heaven's name do you mean you're talking to the bird?"

"Bloody isn't a swear word; it's a colourful adjective," I affirmed — as much for my sake as for his. "And I don't know what I mean!" I threw my hands in the air. "One morning a few weeks ago, I was heading out to my car and a tawny frogmouth communicated telepathically with me." When I saw his look of confusion, I added, "That's another Australian bird. And now this guy" —I gestured at the magpie— "is here for a chin-wag! Any thoughts you have on the matter would be extremely helpful as I've got no bloody idea what's going on! Except for the fact that I can hear voices in my head. And that's never a good thing!" I was almost shouting by the end of it, the frustration of not knowing getting the better of me.

I staggered to the shade of the unit's patio and sat down on the outdoor setting in a huff. Altan paused for a moment, then ducked inside to the fridge and returned with a water bottle.

Offering it to me, he murmured, "I can't say I've heard of humans speaking with animals before." He rubbed a hand over his chin as he considered the puzzle I'd presented him with.

The magpie hopped closer to the unit. *"Why don't you ask one of us?"*

"Ask you what?"

"What your new ability means for you."

"Great idea," I said sarcastically. "I already asked the tawny frog-mouth, and she just left me with more questions." I leaned forward, eyeing him. "So tell me, Master Magpie, if you're so smart, why can we communicate?"

He glared at me with his beady black eyes and ruffled his feathers. *"I didn't mean me. It's not like I know the answer. I'm just a 'bloody bird', remember? Talk to someone with more magical knowledge."* With a disgruntled shake of his wings, he flew away.

Who knew magpies had so much sass? Actually, scratch that. Of course they did. I shouldn't be surprised.

I groaned again and sunk deeper into my chair. "This is so frustrating."

Altan sat beside me and asked, "What exactly do you mean when you say you can speak to them?"

I waved a hand between us. "Turns out I can chat to them as easily as you and I are talking right now. Not that any of them are answering my questions." I gave a disgruntled sniff.

"Them? How many are we talking?"

"So far it's just been that magpie and Froggy." At his questioning look, I explained, "According to Froggy, I knew her when I was younger and gave her that name. It's a terrible name, I know. But I don't remember doing that. She indicated that some of my memories were blocked but couldn't say why or who'd done it."

He ran his fingers through his hair and stared out at the ocean for a long moment. "Curious. And how does the communication start? Do you initiate, or do they?"

"I haven't really thought about it." Frowning, I picked through my memories. "That magpie initiated the conversation after he swooped me. I think Froggy and I have both taken turns at starting our chats. Froggy told me she can't read my thoughts, only what I'm telling her. She said she couldn't tell me anything about my ability. She mentioned she made some sort of promise?" I kneaded my temples with my fists. "An Everlasting Oath was what she called it." I shot a nervous look at Altan. What if he decided I was a liability and needed to be sent away to a psych ward? Or worse, what if Millie was taken from me since I was mentally unstable?

Oh no, what had I done? I shouldn't have told him anything.

"That must have been a huge shock to you," he said.

"Yeah, it was… Hey, you're not… I don't know, going to send me away to a mental institution, are you?"

His brows pulled together, and genuine confusion crossed his face. "Why would I do that?"

I shrugged and looked at my hands in my lap. "It's not exactly normal when someone says they hear voices in their head."

If I was expecting any reaction from him, it wasn't this. He burst out laughing.

I straightened up in my chair, indignation colouring my voice. "Don't laugh! This is my future we're talking about here!"

If I wasn't feeling so worried, I would be enjoying the husky sound of his chuckle a lot more. I'm sure my overactive imagination would allow me to dwell on it later. When I was all alone and locked up in a padded cell. My heart rate spiked at the thought.

Altan held up his hands and quietened his laughter but couldn't stop the crinkle around his eyes. "You're not going anywhere. I think you're forgetting how much magic I've seen in my life. Hearing voices in your head isn't that weird. Don't worry." He squeezed my shoulder. "We'll figure this out. Just…keep an open mind and pay attention to whether it's only birds that you can talk to or all animals. Or even magicas." He shifted in his seat. "Let's experiment. I'm going to think of a question in my mind and try to project it to you. You tell me if you hear anything, okay?"

I nodded mutely and waited.

He stared into my eyes, and my lady parts started doing their internal salsa again. No man or magica had any right to be this good looking. Attempting to rein in my hormones, I forced myself to focus on opening up my mind to him.

"Anything?" he asked.

"Nada."

He stood abruptly and turned away, and I thought I saw a look of disappointment flash across his face. Very quickly, his mask of indifference was back in place. "That's good to know. I'll talk to some friends of mine." At my look of panic, he added, "I won't say anything about you. I'll just make some general enquiries about animal communication and see what they say. But before I do that, we have a claim to assess. Let's go."

Chapter Twenty-Two

On the drive to the client, I asked Altan for advice. "What are we looking for exactly?"

"Once we've interviewed the owner of the Big Mango, Gary Wells, we need to look at the police report. Depending on what we find there, we will also conduct our own interviews. We eventually need to provide a report to MagicAssess of the details of the stolen item and the reasonable cost to replace it. Based on the information we've received from the insurer, I'd also suggest we need to look into the possibility of insurance fraud. It could be Mr Wells himself or a close contact or family member." He paused as he considered the claim. "We also need to consider any enemies, personal or professional, that are trying to frame him. They could be human or magica, so keep an open mind."

I frowned. "I thought the police would handle all that?"

"It used to be that way before the Spark. But since magicas arrived on Earth, the majority of the world's police force haven't caught up with the times and simply don't know how to handle crimes involving magic. That's where we come in."

Bowen's Big Mango was located a few kilometres south of the town, just off the highway. I hadn't realised it, but we'd gone right past it when we'd driven from the airport to our accommodation. One small building behind an empty carpark was all you could see from the road. Hopping out of the car and into the humidity again made me wish to be back in

Maroochydore. It rarely got this humid on the Sunny Coast at this time of the year.

Altan pulled open the glass door to the shop and ushered me through first, the bell above the door tinkling as we stepped through. Cold air immediately caressed my face, and I bit back a moan. I wished I could just stand there and enjoy the air conditioning running over my body. Instead, I kept walking forward, through the shelves filled with souvenirs and beach toys. A large freezer display sat beside the front counter. I made a beeline for it to admire the colourful ice-cream within.

An older elven gentleman with a sweet smile stood up from where he'd been sitting behind the counter. He had salt and pepper hair and a solid frame. He could have been a rugby player in his youth, but time had caught up with him, turning his muscles soft. Greying whiskers covered his jaw, but he couldn't be above sixty.

"Hello, my dear. What flavour can I get you today?" His voice was mellow and kind, his brown eyes twinkling at my obvious enthusiasm for the sweet treat. Before I could answer him, Altan interrupted.

"Good afternoon, Mr Wells. We're not here for ice-cream. I'm Altan from MagicAssess. This is Beatrix, my assistant. We're here for our interview."

"You can call me Trix," I said and held out my hand with a grin.

The man reached over the counter and shook my hand firmly. One thing my mother had taught me was to always trust a person with a firm handshake. His was firmer than an unripe mango. Fitting, I suppose, considering what we were here for.

"And you can call me Gary. One thing I'd like to be noted before we begin," he announced, his expression turning solemn. "There is always time for ice-cream. Especially if it's in the form of mango sorbet." He winked at me and chuckled at his own joke. "You sure I can't get you a scoop?"

"We're fine, thank you," Altan replied.

Cupping my hand, I hid my mouth from Altan beside me and mouthed to Gary, "I'll be back for some later."

He winked and locked his mouth shut with an imaginary key. Shuffling out from behind the counter, Gary took a seat at one of the tables in the corner of the shop and gestured for us to join him. "Can I get you two anything else before we chat about the theft? Water? Tea? Biscuits?"

We both shook our heads.

He glanced outside at the carpark. "Sorry, we'll have to talk out here where I can keep an eye out for any customers that need assistance. My neighbour, Sylvia, sometimes helps me out with the café. She said she'd pop by today, but I'm not sure what time she's coming."

I studied the elf. He was wearing a white polo with the blue and yellow logo for Bowen's Big Mango above his shirt pocket. Navy shorts complemented the outfit, but my eyes snagged on his shoes. They were fish thongs.

When I say fish thongs, I mean that literally.

The flip flops were in the shape of bright green fish that appeared to be swallowing his feet.

Gary caught me staring and burst out laughing. He pointed at a display near us and said, "We sell these. And what better way to make a sale than to model them myself?" Sure enough, there were a dozen different sizes from child to adult out on display.

Altan shifted in my peripheral. I glanced at him, curious to see if he was amused or frustrated by the exchange. His face didn't give much away, but I thought I could see a glimmer of a smile being tamped down. Returning my focus to my leather handbag, I pulled out the tablet from Head Office. Pulling up the claim app Caroline had shown me, I prepared to take notes as Altan led the interview. Leaning forward, he asked Gary to repeat the details of what had happened.

"I've *already* told the police and MoonCorp all of this. Three weeks ago, I showed up to work as usual, and it was just gone. I didn't notice anything or anyone strange the day before or on that morning. The mango was there when I left Tuesday night and was gone on Wednesday morning. I only live just up the hill. I don't understand how I wouldn't have heard it being moved. It's ten metres tall and weighs around ten tonnes! It's not exactly easy to transport. And before you ask, yes, we have CCTV footage, and at one o'clock Wednesday morning, it just vanishes. It's there and then it's not. There are no cars around at that time, and none of our other cameras picked up anything. I've already passed the CCTV footage onto the police."

"Thank you for going back over the particulars," Altan said smoothly. "We just need to make sure the information we've been given is accurate and to ensure you haven't remembered any other details in the interim."

The doorbell jingled, and Gary excused himself to help the customers. I watched him smile and nod enthusiastically as he suggested some different local restaurants and cruises to the Great Barrier Reef. After a few minutes of chatting to the holiday makers, he served them mango sorbet with a flourish.

"He seems to really love his job," I murmured to Altan.

He pursed his lips and muttered, "It could all be an act. Don't let his friendliness cloud your judgement."

I snorted. "So what you're telling me is that I can trust you because of your prickliness and mood swings?"

Altan's ears flattened, and he turned to me with a wounded expression.

Gary sat back down between us. "Where were we?"

My boss had an amazing ability to shut down his emotions. *I must remember not to play poker with him.* Clearing his throat, Altan asked, "I wanted to ask how business has been lately?"

Gary raised an eyebrow at the two of us. "Are you asking that to figure out whether I got rid of the mango myself in order to commit insurance fraud?"

I started stammering, but Altan simply gave a curt nod.

Gary patted my arm. "Don't fret, my dear. You're just doing your job. My brother used to be a cop. I know what they look for in these kinds of cases. Business had been as good as usual up until the mango disappeared. Now there seems to be no pattern. I've had a few days where there were barely any customers because there's no reason to stop, and a few days where I was overrun with people coming to see where the Big Mango was stolen from. But I suppose if I looked at averages compared to last year, the business' income would be similar."

I made some notes on the app and, after the form prompted me, asked, "Do you remember the name of the officer who took your statement?"

"Um, Briggs, I think. Harry Briggs. I tried to make a joke with him about Dirty Harry, but I don't think he thought I was very amusing."

"Thank you," Altan said. "Do you mind if we have a look at the site of the mango now?"

"Of course! Come with me." Gary stood and pointed his hand at the door. "Ladies first."

I pulled the door and glanced around, confused as to why it wouldn't open for me. Altan silently pointed at the sign in front of my hand, which clearly said, "Push." I gave him a sheepish smile and leaned my body forward.

We left the air-conditioned room behind and stepped back into the heat. I smacked my arm when a mosquito landed on me. Thirsty little bloodsuckers. Oops. I couldn't say that word anymore. The Master Vampire had advised the Inter-Magical Community Council that the term was offensive to their kind. Seeing as they only drank animal blood or blood that was willingly donated from humans, I was happy to do whatever I needed to do to stay on their good side.

Gary limped ahead to the giant concrete plinth in the centre of the grassy area beside the shop. The metal legs were still bolted into the stand but no mango.

"No tyre tracks, no other damages, nothing else stolen." He shrugged and his eyes welled with tears when he said, "I just don't understand it." He cleared his throat. "I know you are here to place a monetary value on it so my claim can be paid. But that mango is priceless to me."

"Oh, Gary. I'm so sorry." I patted his arm, already feeling attached to the sweet elf.

"Thank you for the information, Mr Wells. We'll be in touch again tomorrow to discuss further and begin our formal investigation. If you think of anything, please give us a call." He handed over his business card and strode away.

I bade a hasty farewell to Gary and scurried after my boss.

Once we were safely in the car and out of earshot, Altan said, "Careful, Trix. He seems charming. But that could all be a ploy to get you onside so we don't suspect it's him."

"If that's the case, then why would he ask us outright if we suspected him of fraud?"

"A double bluff."

I sighed. "Look, Altan, I get what you're saying. I do. But my gut is telling me he's innocent." I held up my hands in surrender when he opened his mouth to argue more. "But I promise I'll keep an open mind."

"That's all I ask."

142   A. L. TIPPETT

"That's all I ask."

Chapter Twenty-Three

At my request, Altan dropped me off at the front of the supermarket while he made some phone calls. Maybe it was the mother in me or maybe I was too used to saving money wherever I could, but there was no way we were eating out for every meal while we were here, even if we were using the company credit card.

As I filled my trolley with essentials, I began worrying when I realised I had no idea what Altan ate. Milk, cereal, bread, jam, cans of spaghetti, and creaming soda. The yellow kind obviously; that pink stuff was fake news. Some bacon and eggs. I hesitated but grabbed Vegemite as well. I loved the brown spread but knew it was an acquired taste. I had no idea if Altan had ever tried it. I decided it was my job to give him the education.

When I made my way to the checkout twenty minutes later, a group of four magicas wandered past me, laughing loudly. A centaur, a witch, a spider weaver, and a satyr. They looked to be in their late teens or early twenties, but it was hard to tell with some of the species. The centaur wasn't wearing any pants so I politely averted my eyes. It was mandatory for all of the magicas that worked at Millie's school to wear clothing but, as far as I knew, there was no law in place for magicas in public spaces. To cover himself, the half-man, half-horse would need to wear pants on the horse section of his body, and it just wasn't practical.

The witch had embraced her stereotype and was wearing a floor-length black dress. She skipped in front of the group, teasing the spider weaver about her inability to cast a simple illusion spell. It sounded like the witch was goading the weaver into turning the satyr's hair pink.

The weaver looked like a human except for the additional two pairs of arms and the extra eyes in the middle of her face. She screwed her face up, all eight eyes focussed on the satyr, but all that happened was that the hair turned frizzy, as if it had been electrocuted. The satyr waggled his now-fuzzy tail in surprise.

Giggling, the witch wound her hands in a complex pattern before pointing at the satyr. His coat immediately turned fluorescent pink. The spider weaver laughed good-naturedly, and they disappeared into the aisles. It was nice to see the young magicas out and about all together. In Maroochydore, it was more common to see human-dominated groups with only one or two magicas.

Scanning my items through the self-serve counter, I paid with the company card, grabbed the receipt, picked up my two green reusable bags, and met Altan out the front.

He flipped his phone shut and tucked it into his shirt pocket. "The police station asked us to meet their officer tomorrow morning. So we'll head back to the caravan park now. Also, I've reserved us a table at a local restaurant for six o'clock." He grabbed the bags off me, ignoring my protests, and returned to the car.

The shop was only a few minutes' drive from our accommodation, so it didn't take long to get the groceries into the fridge. Altan helped unpack the bags.

Holding up the container of Vegemite, the sphinx asked, "What on earth is this?"

"An Australian staple. I figured you might not have tried it. Me and my kid like it, but it's a bit different. I believe the experts call the flavour umami."

Altan twisted the lid off and delicately sniffed it. His tail curled into a question mark shape. Pressing his finger into the black paste, he scooped up a teaspoon's worth and popped it onto his tongue before I could tell him to stop.

I winced. "Most people eat it with butter on toast. Not many like the taste by itself."

His mouth puckered, and his nose scrunched up. "That is very different, isn't it?" he choked out.

I chuckled. "How about I make you Vegemite on toast and show you the better version?"

He nodded silently. His tongue darted out repeatedly as if trying to forcibly remove the spread from his tastebuds.

My phone rang then, and I grabbed it off the bench. Glancing at the caller ID, I answered, "Hey, Nic, how's things?"

Millie's voice answered, "Ha! I won! I told Nicole you would say that." A disgruntled mutter in the background had Millie giggling. Once she'd settled her chuckles, she said, "Sorry, Mum, let me explain. I was going to call you on Nic's phone to check in, but she thought you'd know it was me calling on her phone. I said you wouldn't and that you'd say her name when you answered. So Nic promised she'd buy me ice-cream before dinner if I won the bet." As an aside, she said, "Nicole, you'd better turn right here if we're going to Baskins."

I grinned at the excitement in her voice. "Well done, sounds like you two are having fun. How was school? What did you get up to?"

"Yeah, it was fine. Not much." I could almost see her shrug.

"Did anything interesting happen?"

"I don't remember."

"You say that every day."

I could hear the smile in her voice when she answered, "Yeah, 'cause I don't remember what I did every day." She paused, then said, "We were trying to find Y in Maths. Corey made a joke about *why* we were trying to find Y. But Mr Lawson wasn't impressed and ended up sending him outside. Which I think is what Corey secretly wanted anyway. And I had choir practise at second lunch." Nicole said something in the background. "And Nic wants me to tell you that she was definitely right on time for pick-up from the bus stop. She absolutely wasn't three minutes late making the bus stay with me until she got there."

I sniggered at the obvious lie. "Well, you enjoy that ice-cream, and text me anytime, okay? Just because I'm not home doesn't mean I'm not there for you."

"It's all good, Mum, I know. Oh, I should have asked earlier, how was your first official day on the job? You keeping safe?"

"I sure am. The most dangerous part of my day was being swooped by a magpie! Try not to worry too much, little dove. I'm fine."

"Good," she replied firmly. "Did you enjoy your first day?"

"I did, actually. It's a steep learning curve, but at the end of the day, it's still about helping clients."

"What did you do?"

"Um, went on a plane, drove in the hire car, talked to people...I don't know. Work stuff."

"Haha, see, it's not that easy to remember specifics, is it?"

"Yeah, yeah, right-oh, Miss."

Before I could say anything else, Millie squealed in excitement. "We're here!"

"Have fun! But before you hang up, can I please talk to Nic quickly?"

"Sure, love you, Mum, bye!"

"Bye, little dove, I miss you!"

"Miss you too, Mum!" There was a scuffle as she handed the phone over.

"Hey, Trix!" Nicole's cheery voice always made me smile. "Hope you don't mind the ice-cream plan?"

"No, that's fine. Don't spend all your money on treats for Millie, okay?"

"Nah, don't worry about it. She's a good kid, and I'm enjoying spoiling her." The affection in her voice was obvious.

"All good with you two? Any questions or issues?"

"Nope, we're fine. But more to the point, how're you? What's happening in Bowen?"

I made sure I was out of earshot of the cabin and lowered my voice to be safe. I didn't really know how good the sphinx's hearing was. "I'm going out to dinner with my boss. What the heckin' heck do I wear?"

"Oooohhhh," Nic crowed in a sing-song voice. "Don't tell me the old maid is getting hot and bothered about her superior?"

"Nicole, shut your mouth. Millie doesn't need to hear you talk like that."

"Pffft, do you think I'm dumb? She's already in the shop. No one can hear us," she whispered conspiratorially. "Do you *like* him?"

I blushed for what felt like the hundredth time today. "No," I answered defensively. "And what is this, 'like'? Are we back in high school? I just want some help with my wardrobe. I never go out to dinner anymore. And I don't usually go to any after-work functions; that's your scene. Hence, my request for assistance." I finished with a prim note in my voice to make sure I got my point across that it was a serious matter and definitely nothing to do with trying to impress the handsome sphinx.

"Fine, tell yourself whatever lie you need to in order to function. I'll wait for you to realise on your own," she muttered darkly.

I chose to ignore her comment.

Nicole sighed melodramatically. "Tell me where you're going for dinner and what you've got packed."

"We're going to the restaurant overlooking Horseshoe Bay. I looked it up on my phone, and there's supposed to be a local band playing tonight."

"Sounds romantic," she purred.

"It's definitely not," I said firmly and began pacing. "Focus, Nic. I've got my office work uniform, which is a grey blouse and navy pants. I've got my work armour, which kind of looks like a leotard, but I won't be wearing that; that's in the unlikely case of a battle. I blooming hope there's no battles happening over dinner. I brought some denim jeans, tan shorts, a long-sleeved purple shirt, and a green polo. And a black dress."

My friend let out a long-suffering groan. "Trix. Trix, Trix, Trix. You're a smart girl. You know what I'm going to choose."

"But it's technically a work dinner! Maybe I should wear my office uniform?"

"Honey, no."

"It's pretty warm here, and it seems laidback. Maybe I should stick with my trusty shorts and shirt." My voice was growing higher as I grew more desperate. "Actually, how about I tell Altan to just order takeaway, and I'll eat in my room."

"Trix!" Her voice was exasperated. "Stop. Okay. Take a breath. Why don't you want to wear the dress?"

I stopped my frantic pacing and thought about her question. "What if I look silly? Or like I'm trying too hard? You know I have a Mum-bod now; it's not exactly perfect."

"Don't be daft. You're a total MILF. Speaking objectively, of course. Stop putting yourself down. Now, hear me out. How about you put on that pretty little number and look at yourself in the mirror and think how fucking gorgeous you are, okay?"

Unexpected tears pricked at my eyes. "I don't know if I can do that," I whispered.

"Honey, you deserve this. You've been a wonderful solo mother to Millie for all these years. It's well past time for you to put yourself first. Stop worrying about what anyone thinks about a woman wearing a black dress to dinner. Your fear is all in your head, Trix. Here's your mission. Wear your dress, tell yourself you look beautiful, ignore everyone else, and have some fun, girl!"

What would I do without Nicole? She was the best friend I could ever hope for. I sniffed and wiped my eyes one-handed. "All right, Nic. Mission accepted."

"Good. Please tell me you have heels?"

"Sandals look nice with dresses too, you know," I said defensively.

"What's wrong with you?" She made sure her horror was heard through the phone. "You are not allowed to wear sandals. Do you have heels?" she repeated the question.

"Ugh, yes," I finally conceded. "I brought a strappy pair with a very small heel."

"Thank God. Hey, make sure you text me if you get in your boss's pants." I could hear the wicked grin in her voice.

"Nicole!" I practically shouted. "I'm not having sex with my boss!" She hung up, laughing.

Locking my phone, I growled in the back of my throat. I loved that woman, but sometimes she was beyond cheeky. I turned back towards the cabin. Altan was standing on the patio watching me with a quirked eyebrow. Clapping my hands over my mouth, I stared at him, mortified, and heat swept over my entire body. Tears pricked my eyes as the humiliation consumed me. I hated that I cried when I felt embarrassed. "I'm so sorry," I stammered out. "That was inappropriate. My friend, Nicole, she's...full-on."

"I figured that out after having only met her for two minutes," he said drily.

"I really am sorry you heard that."

His ears flicked, and he cocked his head. "You can't control other people's actions. Your friend made a tasteless comment; you tried to correct her. It doesn't bother me."

"Are you sure?"

"It's fine, Trix. Don't dwell on it. By the way, I forgot to mention, we will be getting up at six tomorrow morning and going for a run. Just because we're on a job doesn't mean we stop training. Depending on how the day goes, we might try to sneak in a hand-to-hand combat session as well. I have your crossbow with me too, and I'd suggest we practise using that at some point, but we need to make sure we find a safe space."

"How did you get that through airport security?" I asked.

"I have a special permit that allows me to travel with weapons. You'll get one too once your paperwork is finalised." He checked his phone. "I called the local gun range to request a special session but had to leave a message. They haven't returned my call yet." He hesitated, and doubt crept into his eyes. He rushed to add, "I hope those arrangements work for you? Sorry, I'm used to organising my own calendar and have just lumped you in with my plans. I should have checked with you."

"You're my boss. You have every right to organise my work day."

He ran a hand over his head, flattening his hair. "I just don't want to overstep and become overbearing. Truly, I do want us to have a positive working relationship."

A peculiar feeling crept over me at his declaration. For the first time in years, someone was taking care of me. For a long time, I'd been the one organising everything about my life, and it was strange to have someone else take that mental load away from me. And the fact that he was being careful not to disregard my feelings meant a lot.

"Thanks, Altan. I really appreciate that."

The sphinx cleared his throat and shifted his weight awkwardly. "Good. Fine. Now that's sorted, it's five o'clock already. Why don't you get ready for dinner?"

"Yes, sir," I said and saluted. Walking past him into our cabin, I caught a glimmer of a softening around his eyes as he watched me.

Now what in the wolf's moon could that mean?

Chapter Twenty-Four

I STARED AT MYSELF in the sliding mirror door in my bedroom.

Parroting Nicole, I told my reflection, "I am beautiful. No one cares what I look like. They're all probably filled with self-doubt too. I'm going to have fun tonight." I scanned the image in front of me and admired the way the sleek black dress accentuated my natural curves. My dark hair hung loose, curling sweetly under my chin, framing my face. My brown eyes looked dark and alluring after applying some basic eye liner and mascara. I had never bothered to learn about make-up and didn't know how to create smoky eyes without looking like I'd been punched in the face. Maybe I wasn't too bad looking after all. At the end of the day, it didn't matter what anyone else thought. I felt beautiful. And that was all that mattered.

Now I just had to remember how to walk in heels.

I joined Altan on the patio and sucked in a breath at the sight of his crisp lilac-coloured long-sleeved shirt tucked into navy trousers. His eyes roved over my body, melting my previous sense of fierce feminism. I couldn't help the fear that coiled around my heart telling me he'd find me wanting.

A smile curled over his lips, lighting up his face. "You look lovely."

I bobbed into an awkward half-curtsy. "Why, thank you, sir."

He snorted and didn't say anything more, swinging himself easily into the driver's seat. The restaurant overlooking Horseshoe Bay was only a few minutes away by car. When we arrived, the band was already in full swing, and there were only a couple of empty tables left.

Springing out of the car, Altan opened my door before I had a chance to reach for the handle. He swept into a bow and said, "At your service, my lady."

I paused for a second, surprised at his ability to be playful.

Once I exited the vehicle and he grabbed his man bag, Altan offered his arm. Surprised for the second time in as many minutes, I slipped my arm through his. I was immediately thankful for his stoic presence beside me as my ankles wobbled in the unfamiliar heels. We turned away from the golden sands of the beach. The warm glow of garden lights hung over our heads as we walked up the concrete path. The smiling waitress took us to our reserved table in the centre of the room. Secretly, I was thankful that we weren't tucked away in a secluded corner with dim lighting. That was a recipe for disaster destined to confuse my feelings even more than they already were.

Both of us were given menus and a glass bottle of water before the waitress bustled off at the sound of the bell dinging from the kitchen. Opening the menu, I scanned the drinks page. They served mojitos! My favourite.

I glanced up at Altan, who was still studying the list. After I gave him another minute of perusal, I asked, "What are you having?"

"I don't drink much," he admitted. "I might just have a cranberry juice. But don't let my choice dictate yours; you have whatever you want. Alcoholic or otherwise. All I'll say is remember we have more interviews tomorrow, but you're a big girl. You can decide whether you want to work hungover or not." He smirked, the tip of his longer-than-usual canine showing.

At the mention of work, I drummed my fingers on the tabletop as an idea popped into my head. "Altan..." I hesitated. "I just had an idea." He cocked his head, waiting for me to explain. "I look fine, right?" I swept a hand over my body self-consciously.

His brows pulled together, obviously confused about where I was going with this line of questioning but answered anyway. "More than fine."

Tamping down the thrill that kickstarted my heart into overdrive, I glanced up at the bar where some men were sitting, nursing their respective drinks. I leaned closer to Altan and lowered my voice. "Some of these patrons are probably locals, right? Instead of waiting for the waitress to take our order, should I go up to the bar and" —I grimaced— "flirt? Then I can see if any of them have any insider knowledge about what happened to the mango. Maybe everyone knows that it was Gary, but no one is telling the cops. They won't expect someone like me to be digging for intel."

He leaned back in his chair and linked his hands behind his head. I tried not to notice the way his biceps filled out his shirt sleeves. "A creative idea." He nodded. "It has merit. You need a backstory though. What if they've seen you sit down with me? Who am I to you?" He ran a fingertip along his feline ears. "We're obviously not related. If you want to flirt, we can't be a couple."

I shrugged. "I'll just tell the truth with some adjustments. You're my boss."

"Why am I taking you to dinner?"

"Because I landed you a big client?"

"If they're local, they might know you're not one of them. Where will you say that you work?"

"If they ask, which I doubt they will, how about we say I'm an insurance broker from Mackay. I know the job, so I won't get caught out in a lie. You're the kind of boss who is out of touch with the reality of appropriate gifts. You thought a night away in Bowen would be a good reward."

He contemplated my words for a moment before agreeing with a grin. "Go get 'em, Trix. Give a whistle if you need a secret signal for help."

Channelling my inner Nicole, I summoned every ounce of confidence I could find and strode up to the bar, sidling between the two guys. Catching the eye of the young woman serving behind the bar, I gave a genuine smile. Her smoky eyeliner, dyed-black cropped hair, and choker gave me a flashback to my high school days when some of the girls had gone full goth. "Can I grab a mojito, please?"

Without being too obvious, I did my best to check out the men's ring fingers. The bloke on my right had a gold band, so I switched my focus to the more likely candidate on my left. Flicking my hair over my shoulder in what I hoped was a flirtatious manner, I leaned against the polished timber serving top. I glanced at the man beside me, and he looked up from his phone screen, meeting my gaze. I swallowed down my panic and focused on my job. This wasn't the real me. All I needed to do was play a part.

"Oh, hey!" I said brightly.

The young guy flashed a self-assured smile and put his phone down in what I hoped was a good sign. "G'day. How're you going tonight?"

"Oh, I'm fantastic. I'll be even better once I get some alcohol in me." I winked, wondering if that was too much. But the twenty-something year old seemed to be lapping the attention up.

"I'm Ben." He held out his hand. I shook it, making sure not to squeeze too hard lest he felt threatened.

"Nice to meet you, Ben. I'm Trix."

"Trix is a cool name. Can't say I've seen you around here before. And I feel like I would have remembered meeting someone like you."

Someone like me? What in the unicorn's mane did that mean? "Thanks! Nah, we've just come up for a visit."

"We?"

Shoot.

I saw his open expression shut down as I stupidly used the group term. *Stupid, Trix, why did you bring attention to your travelling companion?*

Ben looked over his shoulder, and I followed his gaze, my eyes landing on Altan, who was watching us. The sphinx was a lot smoother than me and allowed his eyes to flick over us as if he were looking at the TV behind the bar, acting like he didn't have a care in the world.

"Yeah, me and my boss." Ben turned back to me with a raised eyebrow. I rolled my eyes dramatically. "I landed a big client for him, and instead of giving me a voucher or a fancy pen like a normal person, he decided to bring me up to Bowen for an overnight holiday. Of course, *I* get to stay in a caravan park unit while he stays in some swanky hotel room." I pulled a face and then giggled, being careful to make it clear that the idea of a relationship between me and my boss was ridiculous.

Which it was.

Obviously.

Ben's shoulders dropped as he relaxed, the threat of another man removed. "Sphinxes, huh? They don't really seem to be in touch with reality, do they?"

I automatically bristled at that but bit my tongue. I couldn't afford to get him offside even though his rude comment made me want to shake some sense into him. Thankfully, the barmaid chose that moment to place my drink in front of me.

"Let me get that for you," Ben said, pulling his card out.

"That is so kind, thank you, Ben!" I squeezed his arm. Unfamiliar with touching a male as I was, I was screeching with panic on the inside, but I somehow managed to keep a winning smile plastered on my face.

"So where are you from then?"

"Mackay."

"Oh nice, only a couple hours away then. I have a sister who lives in Mackay."

Why was he telling me that? Why would I care? Far out, I did not know how to talk to men. "That's nice. Do you visit her often?" I batted my eyelashes.

Cheese and crackers, but I felt ridiculous.

He looked me up and down, smiled, and moved his chair closer to hook his arm around my waist. "I might have to visit her sooner than I expected. Guess we'll see what happens tonight? You wanna ditch your boss?"

Frick-a-frack. My attempts at flirting might have worked a little too well. I took a deep pull on the straw of my mojito, the minty drink doing nothing to quell my panic. "Maybe." I giggled again and tucked a strand of hair behind my ear. "I need another drink before I decide." I couldn't waste any extra time on baiting my prey; I needed to focus instead on what I came here for. "Your town is really beautiful. I've not been to Bowen before."

"It's all right, I guess." He lifted a shoulder non-committedly.

"Have you lived here for long?"

"All my life."

"Oh, wow! That's so cool. I've moved so much in my life. It would be nice to have lived in one place and know everyone." I took another sip of my drink.

"I guess. To be honest, I wish I had travelled more. Where have you liv—"

I cut him off. "Hey, I heard a guy today say that someone stole some giant mango..."

"Oh, yeah, it's been all over the news. That mango has been a tourist attraction since before I was born. The owner Gary is my dad's mate. He's a good bloke. Poor bugger is pretty cut up about it. He puts on a brave face, but that place is his life." Ben glanced at me apologetically. "Sorry, that's probably a bit boring. You don't want to hear about the local gossip."

"No, no!" Jeepers, that was exactly what I wanted him to talk about. Now I just had to convince him to keep talking without sounding like a cop. "I love visiting new places and learning about the people who make those places tick." He still didn't look convinced, so I tried a different tactic. "Plus..." I lowered my gaze, blinked a few times, then looked up at him through my lashes. "I love watching the way your mouth moves when you talk." Giving him one of those lazy winks I'd seen on old TV shows, hoping it looked as seductive as they did onscreen. I moved in close to his ear and whispered, "It's giving me all sorts of ideas for what those lips might get up to later tonight."

Fire truck, but I felt stupid. Although Ben seemed to be lapping it up. Those romance books were really coming in handy.

Who said reading was a waste of time?

Chapter Twenty-Five

BEN SEEMED A LITTLE dazed by my heavy-handed flirting. Poor guy mustn't get much action if he was this hooked by my feeble attempts. He shook his head and cleared his throat before paying for another round. The barmaid caught my eye and gave a knowing smirk. I winked back. This was the biggest winking workout I'd had in years. At this rate, my eye was going to be twitching by the end of the night.

Somehow or other, my attempt at seduction worked. Ben opened up and chatted about growing up in Bowen. His father and Gary caught up for beers at the pub every other weekend and Ben used to play with Gary's son, Michael. Mike had moved away after finishing high school, and Ben hadn't spoken to him since. Gary was the salt of the earth, and everyone loved him. His Big Mango had helped put Bowen on the map and catapulted their tourism industry to the next level. As he spoke about the landmark, I jumped in.

"Do you think Gary could be trying to commit insurance fraud? It sounds a bit weird that someone would bother stealing something so big. It's not like you can sell it on the black market. Its only real value is as a tourist destination." I tried to sound nonchalant about it, like I was gossiping, not fishing for information.

My new friend cocked his head as he considered the idea. "Honestly, I don't think so. I know they say it's the person you least expect when it comes to committing crimes, but Gary is one of best guys I've ever met... He's just chill, you know?"

No, I didn't know. That's why I was asking.

Instead of letting my frustration show through, I pasted on a big smile and gushed, "He sounds so nice! Maybe I should go visit him while I'm here...show some support even though the mango is gone."

"He'd love that. That mango means the world to him. I don't think he plans on ever retiring. He's so passionate about educating visitors about the region and talking about mangoes. It's the perfect job for him. Hey, maybe I could take you there?" He looked at me with those big brown puppy dog eyes.

Oh, God, what had I done? I'd laid the charm on too thick, that's what. And now I had to get out of it. To stall for time, I made a non-committal noise in my throat before gulping some more mojito. "Need to go to the ladies! Back in a mo'!" I squeaked out and leapt off my stool, stumbling slightly as my heels took my weight. Oops. I'd forgotten how quickly mojitos hit me.

I faltered and looked around before throwing the goth barmaid a desperate look. She noticed and pointed out the door, explaining they were at the back of the garden. I quickly made my escape. But it didn't last long.

This was why I didn't wear heels. They sank immediately into the grass until my toes felt like they were pointing to the sky. I sighed. They must irrigate this area because it was ridiculously soft and spongey compared to the dry surrounds. When I'd told Ben I'd needed to pee, it had been a lie to avoid giving him a proper answer. But now I really did need to go.

Pulling my leg up with a grunt, I trudged my way slowly through the picturesque garden. I didn't have the energy to admire the red and pink hibiscus flowers as each step was a sucking effort. Finally, I made it to the relative safety of the brick toilet block with its solid concrete floor. Stomping my feet to rid the heels of the dirt clumps, I headed inside. After finishing my business, I unlocked the toilet door and heard whispers. So many whispers. I hesitated and cleared my throat in case they wanted some privacy and didn't know someone was already here. If anything, that caused the whispers to grow louder.

I caught snatches of the conversations. *"New lady."*

"Another visitor."

"Walks funny."

"Who's there?" I demanded.

It all went quiet for a moment before the sound burst forward again, clearer this time. *"She heard us!"*

"How? Humans don't understand us."

"She's different."

"Special."

"Yes. Special. Special. Special." The susurration of that word repeating over and over had me shaking my head to dislodge the intense buzzing sound. Raking my gaze over the walls of the bathroom, I saw nothing except brown bricks and a dozen daddy longlegs. They were a staple of most public bathrooms. No matter where you went, you always seemed to find the tiny spiders hiding in one corner or another. One scuttled towards me.

I know a lot of people are afraid of spiders. Don't get me wrong, I don't love them. But so long as they're minding their own business high up on a wall somewhere, I can tolerate them.

But seeing the long-legged arachnid skittering towards me had me scrambling backwards.

"Frick-a-frack-frogs-legs!"

The spider stopped its attack, but the whispering started again. *"Why is she talking about frog's legs?"*

I stared at the daddy longlegs. "No way. This ability extends to freaking spiders?"

"You can hear us?"

I had no idea which of the dozen spiders were talking and couldn't discern any facial features on the closest spider to be able to read emotions.

"Exciting!" Once again, the word was repeated by the many spiders in their soft whispers, resulting in that buzzing again.

"I'm glad you're excited we can chat." After a beat of blessed silence, I held my hands up and, feeling like a fool, said, "I come in peace."

There was a tittering amongst them. One of the larger ones came forward then and said, *"You might come in peace, but there is danger coming here. A rumbling in the earth. We suggest you make haste and abandon this place."*

Thrown by their change of subject, I stuck with it just in case there was any truth to their warning. "What? Like an earthquake? We don't usually get earthquakes up here."

"*No. An unnatural disturbance approaches. It will arrive tonight. Good luck in the coming battle.*" With that ominous warning, the lot of them retreated towards a dark corner.

"Battle? What battle?" But no answer came.

Grumbling, I headed back to the bar, cursing my shoes as I trudged through the grass again.

In the surprise of speaking to the spiders, I'd forgotten to think of an excuse to give Ben so I wouldn't need to go home with him. Plus, their warning of an unnatural disturbance was playing on my mind. My new friend wasn't at the bar when I arrived, and I let out a premature sigh of relief.

The barmaid caught my attention and said, "Your friend wanted me to tell you that he's just stepped away to take a phone call." She pointed out the main entrance.

Ben waved and held up five fingers. So much for getting away scot-free.

The barmaid put down the cloth she was using to wipe the counter and leaned over the bar. Her eyes flicked around before she murmured, "I heard your conversation with old mate, and yeah, Gary is a good guy. I kind of get the feeling that your story might be different to what you're telling your friend." She looked at me expectantly, but when I said nothing, she continued. "If you *are* undercover looking for the thief, I'd be looking into Gary's son. Mike has come back to town recently. Not a lot of people know that yet. Rumour is, he's made some enemies in the big city and has come home to lay low. If anyone needed money, it would be him. Whether he'd go so far as to steal from his own father, I don't know."

Jeepers. I did not have enough training to know how to play this. I tried for cool indifference. "Hypothetically, if I were undercover, where might I find Mike?"

She snorted. There was no fooling her with my act. "Not sure, exactly. But I'd guess he'd be hiding out somewhere at his dad's house. A bold move if he did steal anything, but when you're desperate, you make stupid decisions."

"True. And your name?"

"Taylah Beckett."

I nodded my thanks and stood up, ready to report to Altan when I felt a hand on the small of my back. I yelped loudly.

"Woah, chill, it's just me!" Ben said with a chuckle.

Holding my hand over my racing heart, I went to apologise while frantically trying to think of an excuse to get out of any potential horizontal tangoes. Before I managed to squeak out two words, the building shook. Not a huge amount, just a little tremble, but enough for everyone to pause. The sudden lull in conversation made the following gabble of excited conversation that much more noticeable.

"Earthquake?" Ben asked, glancing around. "Crazy, we haven't felt one here for years."

The spider's warning blared in my mind. My eyes automatically sought out Altan, who was watching me. I muttered through gritted teeth, "I don't know if that was an earthquake." I was unsure if the sphinx heard me, was really good at reading lips, or could simply see the concern written on my face, but either way, Altan immediately stood. The ground shook again, stronger this time.

Both Ben and I grabbed hold of the nearest thing for balance. Each other. As the second tremor ended, Ben looked down at me, his hands wrapped around my waist.

His voice husky, he said, "That was a bit scary. Are you okay?"

"Nope," I replied in a forcibly cheerful voice and removed his hands from my body. Abandoning the poor sod, I made a beeline for my sphinx.

Not my sphinx. I didn't mean that. My boss. I made a beeline for my boss. No time to unpack my first sentence.

We met in the centre of the restaurant. He grabbed my hands. I spoke quickly, doing my best not to run my words together in my panic, "Altan, the spiders told me danger was coming here and to be prepared for the coming battle."

"Spiders?" He shook his head and held up a hand to halt my explanation. "We'll discuss later." He unzipped his man bag with a purposeful look in his eye.

I grabbed his shirt, halting him. "Shouldn't we call the police? I'm sure they can handle it."

"Police aren't really trained properly in the art of managing magica threats. Half the time they're of the mindset that they shoot first, ask questions later, but they usually just piss the magica off enough to wind up dead before they make it to the interrogation. It's up to us. Get ready."

"How the heck do you get ready for something when you don't know what's coming?"

"Lesson two. Be prepared. Armour, weapons, vials."

"But we're off-duty, and I'm wearing a dress." I gestured at my body.

He shot me a scathing look. "Have you already forgotten lesson one? Seriously, Trix. I thought you were more conscientious than that?" His lecture was interrupted by another rumble, larger this time. Someone screamed. "Shit. Here, take this." He handed me a dagger he pulled from his ankle and a small green bead. "Use that as a last resort. Try not to die."

Together, we jogged out the front doors, me tripping over the threshold while Altan looked like a vengeful god. He pressed a button on his sleeve, and his suit immediately switched to armour, looking like a second skin.

"Stupid, flipping shoes," I snarled and tugged them off, throwing them into the nearby garden. Better to be barefoot and mobile than dealing with those monstrosities for a minute longer. They made a satisfying thud, and I gave a grim smile. Adrenaline was already racing through my body, and it felt good to have control over one tiny thing.

Altan and I stood a couple metres apart in the carpark, and for a moment it was just us and the sound of the ocean waves. For a brief second, I felt completely badass. I just needed a leather jacket and leather pants like all those women wore on the movie posters.

My feeling of competency didn't last long.

Another tremor caused me to almost lose my footing. I flung my arms out wide for balance. The light from the restaurant didn't spread onto the shore, so I was relying on the moon to illuminate whatever it was that was causing the vibrations.

I didn't have to wait long. The beach in front of us erupted, sand flying everywhere as something massive appeared from a hole in the ground.

"Well, fuck," Altan cursed beside me. "It's a komada dragon."

Our prey had finally revealed itself to us.

Or were we its prey?

I guess we were about to find out.

Chapter Twenty-Six

Moonlight dappled the grey scales as the reptilian magica rose out of the ground. It hadn't even made it all of the way out of the earth, and it was already as tall as a two-storey house. The draconian snout scented the air, giving us a few precious seconds to stare in horror. At least, that's what I did.

I'm sure Altan was making a plan. But my brain was too busy imagining all the ways I was about to be disembowelled.

Hard ridges ran the length of its spine, but even though it was a species of dragon, this guy had no wings. Since the komada usually lived underground, its scales were dull and gave the appearance that each segment was made of rocks. A random fact popped into my brain, telling me it was considered an endangered species. For a change, it wasn't because of the humans. Komadas had done a good job of killing themselves off during battles over territory, and now there had been less than a hundred recorded sightings in the wild in the past two years.

Massive fangs jutted from its jaws as it weaved its serpentine body to and fro. Its red eyes seemed to glow in the dark as it regarded us. It hissed, the sound sending shivers up my spine.

Altan didn't wait for it to attack. He threw a bead at its face, causing the magica to scream and rear back. The sphinx blurred into action, leaping towards its exposed underbelly, his short sword raised.

Well. Maybe this would be over sooner than I'd expected.

When would I learn not to count my chickens before they hatched?

The komada's tail came out of nowhere. It slapped Altan out of the air mid-leap and slammed him into the sand. As he hit the ground, his head whipped and hit a piece of driftwood.

A strange ringing filled my ears, and my heart raced. His name ripped from my lips, and I took an involuntary step towards his body.

He didn't move.

But the komada did. Its gaze snapped to me. Then it was rolling, traveling along the beach in a weird spiralling movement. Unfortunately, its odd way of slithering didn't hinder it at all, flinging sand everywhere as it headed straight for me at breakneck speed.

So I ran.

If that thing had knocked Altan out of play within a minute of the battle, what chance did I have? Time to put those running lessons to good use. I sprinted up the beach, cutting through the carpark, ignoring the screams of the civilians still in the restaurant. At least I could draw the creature to me and save some people. Go out a hero and all that. But going out a hero meant saying goodbye to Millie. And I wasn't ready to do that. I pumped my legs harder, determined not to give up yet.

Bushland dominated the landscape on the southern side of the restaurant. I followed the wide hiking trail easily in the moonlight. That was good for me, less chance of tripping over a vine or tree root. Conversely, it also meant there were no easily accessible hiding places. Pushing my body to its limit, I grimaced when I heard trees crashing beside the path as the komada followed me.

It roared again. It was getting closer. But I didn't dare look behind me.

Instead, I gripped the green bead and dagger that Altan had given me even tighter, preparing myself for a last stand. My breathing was growing harsh. I wouldn't be able to keep up this pace for much longer. I should've listened to Altan and jogged every day. And added sprinting to my exercise regime.

And maybe just, you know, not left my nice safe job as an insurance broker. As they say, everyone has twenty-twenty vision in hindsight.

Was it my imagination or could I feel the hot breath of the komada against my shoulders?

I winced as my bare foot landed on a sharp rock, and I stumbled on the next step.

This was it.

My final stand.

I flung myself to the side of the path in the hopes my abrupt change of direction would confuse the komada dragon enough to avoid a direct hit. Narrowly avoiding taking myself out on a sapling, I managed to turn as I landed. I prepared to launch the green bead Altan had given me.

I wished I'd asked him what it actually did. Oh God, I really hoped he was still alive.

As I drew my arm back, ready to throw, the tail of the komada swung towards me, hitting my hand and pinning my arm against the small tree. The bark scraped the back of my hand. Combined with the unrelenting pressure of the boulder-like scales on the other side, it gave new meaning to being stuck between a rock and a hard place. But that was the least of my worries right now.

The komada hissed low in its throat and drew closer to me. As it brought its face down to my level, I stared death in the face, waiting for the inevitable crunch of breaking bones.

My heavy panting sounded so loud as I watched the red eyes inch closer. Nothing else existed in that moment. Just me and the komada, both of us watching the other, but only one of us expecting to die.

The beast opened its maw wide, and a foul smell immediately permeated the air. I gagged.

Why was it taking so long to eat me? *Just get it over with already.* I didn't want to hang around smelling this stench for any longer than I had to. Altan had been right. I hadn't had enough training to fight a magica, especially one this big. I had no idea what to do. I just wish I had my phone so I could let Millie know I loved her.

My poor girl. This would devastate her.

The komada whined, its mouth still hanging open. I tore my eyes away from its frightening gaze and looked inside the jaws that could easily fit around my torso. There was an abnormally shaped shadow in the furthest recess of its bottom line of teeth.

I sucked in a breath, doing my best to ignore the smell. "Are you...are you hurt?" I whispered.

The magica moaned and sank its head to the ground and finally released my pinned hand. It opened its mouth wider, distending its jaw, and tilted its head so the moonlight shone inside its mouth.

"Is there something stuck inside your mouth?" I asked, using the same soothing tone I used when Millie was in pain.

A soft huff answered me.

"Do you want me to try to remove it?"

It huffed again.

"This isn't some trick, is it? I walk inside your mouth, and you bite me in half or something?"

The red eyes rolled, and it made a peculiar sound as if to say it could have eaten me at any time in the past five minutes without the need for trickery. Was this giant rock dragon giving me attitude?

"Fair enough," I muttered and placed the green bead and the dagger carefully on the ground. Stupid, stupid, stupid. But I couldn't stop myself. The komada's head was almost as high as my shoulder. I took a steadying breath before leaning inside its mouth.

This was the dumbest thing I'd ever done.

But I could see it. Something long and dark was wedged in between two of its back teeth.

Gritting my own, I reached into the komada's mouth.

Seriously, if I was in a horror movie, I would be the first to die.

The fetid smell made me gag, but I held it together as I pushed my arm in further. My fingertips brushed the object. With a grunt, I leaned further, noting with some worry that my entire head and torso were inside the predator's mouth. The wet tongue was unmoving beneath me, but it didn't stop me from getting saliva on the front of my dress. Wrinkling my nose, I ignored the damp and managed to grasp the end of the stuck thing. The feel of bark told me it was a stick of some sort. With a few complicated wiggles, I dislodged it from between the komada's teeth. As I pulled it out, I noticed an angry looking wound on the inside of the magica's cheek.

"Oh," I breathed. No wonder the poor thing was so cranky. It was in pain. And that explained the smell. I withdrew from its mouth. "That looks infected, buddy. Do you have some way to get that healed?"

With a staccato rumbling, the creature closed its mouth and reared up. It bowed to me before plunging back into the earth, using its peculiar spiralling motion to tunnel a new hole. The komada disappeared as quickly as it had arrived.

Standing in front of the hole, I stared at the ground. My heartbeat was still pounding in my ears.

What the bloody heck had just happened?

"Trix!" Altan sprinted up the trail towards me. "Are you hurt? Where's the komada?"

Relief washed over me at the sight of him.

He's alive!

"I'm okay," I replied slowly, still not quite able to believe what had transpired. "And it's gone."

"Gone? What do you mean? Dead? Where's the body?" He peered inside the hole in front of us.

"Not dead. It left."

He whipped his head around to stare at me. "What did you do to scare it off?"

"I didn't scare it off."

"If you didn't kill it, and it wasn't scared off, why would it abandon the hunt?"

I hesitated. Pretty sure I was about to get my ear chewed off.

"Trix...what aren't you telling me?" There was an edge in his voice that I didn't like the sound of.

"Well...it appears the komada was just looking for help."

Altan pinched the bridge of his nose and squeezed his eyes shut. "What. Does. That. Mean?"

I scuffed my bare foot against the loose earth beside the hole while I avoided looking at him. "The komada followed me up here and when it was almost on top of me, I ducked to the side and tried to throw the bead. It squashed my hand against the tree before I could. It opened its mouth and I thought it was going to eat me, but it kind of...groaned, and then just waited." I winced as I prepared to own up to the stupidest thing

I'd ever done. I spoke in a rush, hoping that it would be like a plaster...if I ripped it off quickly, there would be less pain. Or in this case, I wouldn't get as much of a tongue lashing. "Then I had a look inside its mouth and found a stick stuck in its back teeth. It looked and smelt like it was causing an infection. So I wiggled the stick out and then the komada left." I spread my hands wide and attempted a smile. "All's well that ends well, right?"

Altan continued to stare at me. This silence was worse than a lecture. His eyes traced down my body, and not in a sexy way. The komada's saliva on my dress was obvious. When he spoke, it was halting. "You mean to say...you stuck your entire body...inside of that dragon's mouth?"

"Yes." Even to my own ears, my voice was shrill.

"Fuck me. Are you fucking kidding me?" He threw his hands in the air. "Why do I even bother. You could have died, Trix!"

I was wrong. His silence was better after all.

"The komada was in pain," I said softly. "I had to help."

He glared at me before slamming the flat of his palm against the closest tree. With bared teeth, he snipped, "You were fucking lucky. If that magica had been chasing a meal and not assistance, we would have been fucked. When we're on a job, always bring your armour and weapons. Even if you can't wear it out to dinner, it needs to be in the car. You were useless tonight, and worse, you put others in danger because you weren't prepared. This is why we train. This is why we bring our weapons, even when we're not on the clock. This kind of shit can happen anytime. It's not common, but you need to be ready." He turned on me, his fury palpable. "What's lesson one?"

I started, having been frozen during his tirade. "It's. Uh..."

"Lesson one," he roared.

Dropping my head, I muttered, "Expect the unexpected."

"Precisely." He stood there, panting heavily while he glared at me. I felt like sinking into the earth.

There was no point in arguing that no one got hurt this time. Or about the fact that the komada hadn't been here to hunt. Altan was right. It was only luck that both of us, as well as all the civilians, were okay. I made a promise to myself then that I'd train every day.

Next time, the magica might not be so friendly.

It wasn't until after we'd trekked in silence back to the hire car that I realised I was still holding the stick.

Chapter Twenty-Seven

AFTER A FROSTY EVENING of not much talking, coupled with jam sandwiches since we'd missed out on dinner, I didn't feel particularly excited about our Tuesday morning together. Altan kept his features neutral as we ate our cereal at the table.

Well, he ate. I mostly pushed the food around my bowl.

Finally, I'd had enough. "Altan, I'm sorry. I know I screwed up last night. I know it was pure luck that no one got hurt. I understand why you drill the lessons into me and want me fit." I glanced at the clock above the doorway. "I'm going for a jog. I'll be back before we need to leave for the police station."

A ghost of a smile flashed over his lips, but he didn't say anything. He simply nodded and kept eating.

Pushing my bowl away, I hurried to my room to change into my active wear. Altan had disappeared by the time I passed back through the dining room. After a quick stretch, I exited the caravan park grounds and found a concrete path that followed the shoreline. Forgoing music, I started my jog, limping a little from the small cuts on my feet from my barefoot dash last night. The scrapes on the back of my hand also clamoured for attention, but I shoved the pain away.

I was soft. I knew that. All my life, I'd only ever been a mum and an office worker. I needed to grow my resilience and increase my pain tolerance if I was ever going to make it as a competent insurance assessor.

And you know, not die.

Listening to the sounds of nature around me, I was careful not to open my mind too much in case I invited some more creatures to communicate with me. I didn't understand my powers but figured I should try to learn how to shut them out so random magpies or spiders didn't start chatting with me willy-nilly.

Seagulls squawked nearby, keeping their eyes peeled for suckers who'd give in and share their hot chips with them. Meanwhile, the caerulean ocean glimmered on my left as the waves murmured against the white sand. Palm trees lined the footpath, their fronds rustling in the gentle breeze. There were a few cars driving past, the occupants probably on their way to work, but Bowen's atmosphere remained relaxed. There was no sign of the 'rat race' here.

The sun was already well and truly on the rise, warming the air quickly. It didn't take long until I was gasping for air, sweat beading on my temples and dripping down my spine. I finished the five kilometres I'd promised myself, my limp even more pronounced by the end of it, before hurrying into the cabin to shower and change.

As I dressed in my armour, I stared at the stick I'd pulled out of the komada's mouth. I'd brought it back with me last night. For some reason, my gut had told me it was important. It was nothing special to look at: greyish-brown, about twenty centimetres long, and with a couple little knots in the otherwise straight stick. Following my instincts, I grabbed it and tucked it into my leather handbag. Redoing my hair, I pulled the dark locks up into a high ponytail and attached my spatha in its sheath to my belt.

I was ready.

Almost. I flicked a quick text to Millie to let her know I was thinking about her. I didn't bother telling her about the komada situation. No need to worry the girl when she was supposed to be focussing on school. I rubbed my chest. A dull ache had taken up permanent residence in my heart since yesterday morning. It was strange waking up without my girl. I took a few deep breaths to refocus myself.

When I exited my room, Altan was back. Dressed all in black once more, he looked intimidating even to me. God help the police officer dealing with us.

Looking me up and down, he nodded in approval. "Actions speak louder than words, Trix. I didn't mean to sound like an asshole when I blew up at you, but I'm just trying to keep you alive. If you'd only apologised for last night and done nothing else, I'd still be pissed with you. But you're trying to do better by following my advice. Thank you. Let's move on, be thankful that no one got hurt, and chalk it up to a learning experience. You don't need the spatha on you in the police station but keep it in the boot of the car just in case." He did a double-take and asked, "What's with the stick? I wondered last night, but I was too angry to ask."

I held it up. "This is the stick I pulled out of the komada's mouth. I know it sounds a bit mad, but it feels like I'm supposed to have it. I'm bringing it with me today," I added firmly, bridging no argument.

He quirked an eyebrow but didn't comment on my choice of accessories any further. With a clap of his hands, he said, "Let's get the day started!" Without waiting for me to answer, he headed out to the car.

We pulled into a carpark beside the lone cop car sitting outside a small brick building proclaiming to be the Bowen police station. I knew this was a small city, but it was a proper sleepy town. Tropical trees followed the sidewalk and a few dead palm fronds had fallen over the pavement. I glanced down and did an awkward leap over the fronds when I noticed the green ants' nest accompanying them. I didn't feel like getting bit by one of them today. As a child, I had taken a dare and knocked a nest out of a tree.

Never again. They bloody hurt.

Together, Altan and I walked through the glass doors. A tired looking woman manned the front desk. I let Altan take the lead while I watched and learned. He handed over his ID and announced our intention to speak with the investigating officer of the missing mango.

With a sigh, the woman nodded and said, "I'll get you and your partner to meet Detective Harry Briggs in the conference room. I'll let him know you're here." She shambled over to a door on our right, keyed in a code on the pad, and placed her palm over the crystal to release the ward on the door. Opening it, she waved us through. "He'll be in shortly."

We stepped into a room, and I thought a filter had been placed over my eyes. It was just cream on cream. Cream walls, cream vinyl flooring, cream chairs. The only splash of colour, if you could call it that, was a small brown desk in the middle of the room. A tiny red light flashing in the corner caught my eye and alerted me to the presence of a security camera. We'd just sat down when the door opened behind us.

I immediately jumped up and gave a smile. Briggs strode in and greeted us formally. He was on the older end of middle-aged, with a receding hairline and a beer gut that strained against his shirt buttons. Altan reintroduced us and explained we were here to review the police report for the theft of the Big Mango.

The detective crossed his arms. "Our office has already provided your company with a copy of the necessary information."

Altan cocked an eyebrow but didn't react to the man's somewhat disrespectful tone. "Yes, we received that, thank you. However, I understand that you haven't found the culprit as yet?"

"Correct. But really, it was most likely some opportunistic dick who managed to steal it in the middle of the night and sneak away. It was probably a dare." His eyes squinted, his voice accusatory. "This isn't the big city. It's not like our job is easy. We can't just sit in an office, watch a couple hours of CCTV to track their vehicle's movements, and catch them in five minutes. We do real police work here."

Holding up his hands in surrender, Altan adopted a placating tone. Only I noticed the tic pulsing in his jaw. "No disrespect meant, sir. I'm sure you do excellent police work. Our employer, MagicAssess, has been assigned by MoonCorp, Gary Wells' insurer, to assess his claim. Part of that job is assisting the local police in their investigation to ensure there is no chance of insurance fraud. It's your job to find the bad guy. It's our job to look after Mr Wells' claim. Based on the friends I have in the service, I'm sure you haven't been given enough resources to do your job to the best of your ability. We are here to help you with the magica aspect. If there is a chance that the Big Mango was stolen by a magica, we can help you figure that out. If it turns out Mr Wells has committed fraud, we can advise the insurance company while you arrange charges. We're not here to step on toes. We simply want to help."

Detective Briggs glared at both of us for a long while before finally releasing his breath in a long sigh. He lowered his large frame into one of the cream chairs and scrubbed a hand over his face. "You got one thing right. We don't have the manpower or the tech to do our jobs properly.

It's bullshit. When Gary called us, we investigated the scene. There was the usual mishmash of partial prints from employees, locals, and tourists visiting the shop. But absolutely no DNA could be found within a metre radius of the Mango's pedestal. It's as if the culprit wiped every blade of grass down."

"That's weird, isn't it?" I asked, casting a querying look to Altan. He rubbed his chin in thought but didn't respond.

The detective nodded. "The CCTV was no help either. The mango is there one moment and gone the next. Our tech department has confirmed the video hasn't been tampered with. We've interviewed everyone who works there and asked locals for any dashcam footage from that night, and nothing sticks out as unusual. So we're stuck." Briggs shrugged. "To be honest, we aren't throwing a lot of manpower at this one anymore."

My eyes narrowed. "Why's that?"

"What else can we do? There are no leads. Just have MoonCorp pay out his claim. Besides, Gary's a nice guy, but he's an elf. In my personal opinion, magica crimes should be handled by magicas. They shouldn't take up my time and resources when I'm already limited on both." He leaned back in his chair.

"But you swore to serve and protect. That doesn't just mean humans," I said, struggling to keep the accusation out of my voice.

"A common misconception. To protect and serve is actually a phrase adopted by American Police Departments. The Australian version is worded differently."

"Well, the intention of the oath is the same."

Briggs gave a curt nod but added, "Regardless of that fact, when the oath was written, there were no magicas in the world." He folded his arms.

I mimicked his posture, glaring all the while. "Well, I think that's—"

"Trix." Altan reached out and squeezed my arm.

Good thing he'd interrupted me when he did. I wasn't entirely sure if I'd been about to break my promise to never use an actual swear word.

I opened my mouth to argue, but Altan shook his head. The sphinx stood, an imposing figure in the small conference room, cutting off anything either of us might have said. "That's enough. This is not the time or place to get into an argument regarding personal opinions. Respectfully, sir, at this time, magicas aren't accepted into the police service, so for the time being, it remains your job to handle magica cases. We are here to assist you to do your job. If you would please just give us the evidence you have acquired in the course of your investigation, we'd appreciate it. We'll handle it from here and be in touch if we require you to make an arrest."

Detective Briggs stared at us for a long time before hauling himself out of the chair with a grunt. "I'll have Officer Mellor give you a USB with the CCTV footage along with a copy of the report. But I'm warning you now, there's not much to go on." He flashed a sardonic smile. "Good luck."

Together we watched the CCTV footage on Altan's laptop after we returned to the hire car. Unfortunately, the detective was right. One minute the Big Mango was sitting on its plinth; the next, it had vanished.

Altan drummed his fingers against the steering wheel. "Could be a transportation spell," he muttered, almost to himself. "You'd need a damn strong witch or wizard to perform it on something that size though. Or maybe a magica tampered with the footage and found a workaround so the police couldn't tell they'd hacked their system." He glanced at me. "Could a human hacker do that too?"

I shrugged. "I guess so, but I'm not super tech savvy. Admittedly, I'm better than you," I teased.

With a roll of his eyes, he rewound the video and watched it again, rubbing his chin.

I flopped back in the passenger seat with an explosive sigh. Squeezing the bridge of my nose, I muttered, "That chat with Briggs was...frustrating."

"I know what you mean but try to understand. The police are still playing catch up since the Spark. How many decades did it take the Force to allow women to be police officers? And then the world as people knew it exploded into a new age that included magical creatures. It was a huge shift for society, and humans don't tend to like change at the best of times. I'm sure the police will get there eventually, but they need more time to assimilate. It's our job to educate, not debate. On past jobs, I've found if I can assist them and show my value to their investigation, that does more to change their opinions than if I argue."

Blinking slowly, I stared at Altan. "That sounds very sensible." I hesitated over my next question but ploughed on regardless. "If that's how you feel about educating the police officers who openly admitted to not trying that hard on this case since the victim was an elf, why did you get your knickers in a knot about the hire car company?"

His jaw clenched, but he answered anyway, "With my dealings with officers in the past, most of them are willing to attempt to learn new ways when they see the value of a magica's help. The police put their lives at risk every day for the common good. They need to make split second decisions to minimise risk to the public. So while I don't condone it, I can understand their reluctance to change a system that used to work. But people like that woman behind the desk yesterday..." He squeezed his eyes closed and hissed air out from behind his teeth. "They are so damn narrow-minded that they simply view us as if we're no better than animals. I could see it in her face. She didn't *want* to hire the car to a creature like me. To people like her, we are lesser beings who don't deserve any respect. That's why I was so angry."

I winced. I really felt for Altan — and all the magicas that dealt with that on a daily basis. I had no idea what that was like.

I spoke in a small voice, "I'm sorry you have to deal with that."

He shrugged and put the car into gear. "That's life. Let's go chat with Gary again."

CHAPTER TWENTY-EIGHT

AFTER ANOTHER OFFER OF mango-flavoured goodies, Gary introduced Sylvia, his neighbour, to us. The woman looked to be in her sixties. Her hair had a beautiful silver sheen, and her clothing was immaculate. A fitted floral dress showed off her trim figure, and her easy smile found Gary quickly. She fingered the string of pearls around her neck as she greeted us.

"Welcome to Bowen! Are you here on holiday?"

Gary shook his head. "These are the insurance assessors who have travelled up from Brisbane to assess the claim for my mango."

"The Sunshine Coast is our base, actually," Altan corrected.

Gary made a shooing motion with his hand. "Close enough. What is it, an hour's drive to Brisbane?"

I nodded in agreement, but before I could say anything, Altan leaned forward and stared Sylvia down. "We are here to investigate the missing mango. We will need to interview you, Ms Silverwood."

Sylvia shifted uncomfortably under his intense scrutiny. "But why? I thought the police were handling that?"

I cut in, trying to deflect Altan's unblinking stare. "We are assisting the police with their investigations."

Sylvia cocked her head as she considered me. "I've already been interviewed by the police. If you're working with them, surely they would have given you a copy of the interview transcripts?"

Altan nodded, drawing her attention back to him. "Yes, they have. However, as a sphinx and an assessor, I am a little more attuned to the intricacies of claims where magicas have been involved."

"Oh!" She glanced between us. "Does Detective Briggs finally have a lead? Does he suspect a magica?"

"No, nothing concrete. They only suspect a magica due to the nature of the disappearance. Giant mangoes don't just disappear by themselves."

"I thought they were looking into video tampering?"

"They did, but their tech team said it's clean." Altan narrowed his eyes at her. "For a neighbour, you seem to be particularly well-informed with the investigation."

She laughed sweetly. "Of course I am! Gary's been bringing me up to speed every time I come to the shop to give him a hand. Plus, I care deeply about what happens to that mango. It's Bowen's crowning jewel."

Gary interjected, "I don't know what I'd do without Sylvia. She's always been a great support to me."

The bell above the entrance tinkled then, and a young family walked in. With a squeeze of Sylvia's shoulder, Gary left our trio alone to help the customers.

I repeated Altan's earlier question to get us back on track, "Do you consent to us interviewing you, Ms Silverwood?"

"Certainly. Anything I can do to help Gary." She cast a glance towards the elf behind the counter.

Altan shifted so he was blocking Sylvia's view and said quietly, "Let's go outside where we can talk in private."

With Sylvia leading the way, we exited the air-conditioned shop and braved the morning heat. As I followed my boss through the door, my handbag's strap caught on the door handle, stopping me in my tracks. Wincing, I managed to untangle it quickly without anyone being any the wiser.

I swear, Clumsy must be my middle name. The amount of times I'd tripped, dropped what I was holding, or got caught on something, was ridiculous.

We sat at one of the secluded outside tables with Sylvia so she could speak freely without worrying about the customers or Gary overhearing our conversation. Altan allowed me to take the lead once again. I began by asking her to clarify her version of events.

Refusing to use the app from Head Office, Altan took notes with a pen and paper. I bit back a sigh. In my role as his assistant, I suspected I'd be typing those up later for him.

Once Sylvia had recounted the same timeline of events to us, I asked her, "Tell us, what was Gary's reaction like when he came into work the next day?"

She shifted in her seat and clasped her hands. "He was devastated," she said. "I've never seen him so upset." Concern marred her delicate features as she cast a glance towards the mango's empty plinth.

"How long have you been working for Gary?"

"A little over a year," she said. "I have a mango farm just up the road. I supply the mangoes for Gary's sorbet that he sells here."

"Oh, okay, so you have a business relationship outside of your employment?"

"I would have been happy to volunteer my time here for Gary, but he insisted on paying me a wage for the couple hours a day I do for him. It's just to help him out so he can take a break during the day."

"So your main income is from your farm?" I clarified. She nodded. "Are you there alone or with a partner? And do you have any employees?"

She gave a sad smile. "I live alone. I retired from my full-time corporate job a few years back. No children, no partner. I sometimes employ backpackers when it's fruit-picking season. But for the most part, it's just me."

"Is there anyone you can think of that has a grudge against Gary who might have stolen the mango?" Altan asked.

Sylvia shook her head vehemently. "Gary is well-liked by everyone, and the mango brings tourists to the town. I don't know of anyone who would steal it."

After clarifying a few other details, we sent Sylvia back inside.

Tapping his pen against his pad, Altan leaned back in his seat and asked, "What did you think of Sylvia?"

"I reckon she's sweet on Gary," I replied with a smirk.

Altan furrowed his brows. "Really?"

"For sure." I chuckled. "She kept watching him, and I think I saw a blush when he touched her shoulder."

"But she's his employee. They shouldn't be fraternising."

Heat swept up my own cheeks then, betraying me. He was right. Employees shouldn't fraternise with their boss. They shouldn't even daydream about it. No matter how alluring said boss might be.

I cleared my throat, trying to focus on the current conversation. "I have a feeling it's one-sided. I don't think there's anything going on. She dotes on him, but he treats her like a friend, I think. Up to you if you want to interview her again, but based on that interaction, I don't think she would do anything to hurt him."

Not noticing my internal embarrassment, Altan stood and beckoned for me to follow him. He picked up a small stone from the landscaped gardens and then walked to the plinth that stood in the middle of the lawn beside the shop. He tossed the rock straight into the empty space where the mango used to be. It sailed through the air, before landing on the grass with a dull thud.

"What on earth are you doing?" I asked.

"Making sure it's not just a simple illusion charm. I didn't think so since it would take an extremely talented magica to hold one for this long, but best to check these things." He proceeded to open his man bag and for the next ten minutes, showed me how to perform other tests.

He placed a blue bead with red stripes on the ground in front of the plinth and lit it on fire with a lighter. It burned bright yellow before crumbling into dust. "Hmmm, no witches or wizards involved then. That was a spell recognition bead. It would have burned purple if a spell was cast here within the last week." He rubbed a hand over his jaw before picking a small spotted yellow bead out of his bag. Dashing it against the earth, he waited as the yellow spots flared away from the bead, drawing lines across the ground. They spiralled out from the plinth, before flaring white and disappearing. "The police were right. If there had been any biological evidence to detect, such as skin flakes or fingerprints, that bead would have left a powdery residue. It's strange though..." He trailed off as he stared at the ground.

"This whole thing is strange, but what in particular has you puzzled?"

"It's been a couple weeks since the Big Mango disappeared. People would have walked through here. The police said it was like every blade of grass had been wiped clean. It's still like that now, even though there should be general organic matter." At my puzzled expression, he explained, "Animal excrement, human hair, that kind of thing." Altan gave a heavy sigh. "Come on, let's get out of the heat and I'll have a think on that one."

The bell chimed again as we re-entered the shop. Sylvia was busy chatting with the visiting family while Gary sat behind his computer at the counter.

"Back again so soon?" Gary asked with a smile, softening any hint of accusation. "Any news?"

"Not yet, Gary." I smiled apologetically. I opened my mouth to continue but Altan interrupted me.

"We've come back to have another chat with you actually, Gary." He put his hands on his hips. Whether or not he meant to, Altan looked extremely intimidating.

With genuine surprise colouring his tone, Gary asked "Oh? How can I help you today?"

"Well, a source advised us that your son is back in the region after a long time away." Altan watched Gary closely as he spoke.

Ducking his head, Gary suddenly became very interested in straightening the brochures in the stand beside him. "So what if my son has come to visit? Why do you care?"

Altan's tone was brusque as he said, "We want to know if he stole the mango for you so you could claim the insurance money."

Gary met Altan's gaze abruptly. "Blunt, aren't you? Then allow me to return the favour. I can tell you right now, my son is not a thief. And I would never commit insurance fraud. My wife and I painted that mango together. It means more to me than just a tourist attraction. Honestly, I don't want the claim settlement. I want my mango back. It's the only thing left of her that..." He broke then and turned away but not before I saw the tears.

I shot Altan a glare, warning him not to make matters worse. "Gary," I soothed, placing myself in front of him, forcing the elf to meet my gaze. "My partner doesn't mean to be insensitive. We're just trying to do our job to ensure that the claim is legit, your insurance company isn't being taken for a ride, and that you get a fair settlement. We don't mean to be rude."

Gary snorted.

I grinned. "Perhaps I should say, *I* don't mean to be rude. My partner is just trying to find the truth. We were told to look into your son. The police haven't mentioned him in their report. And if you don't want to highlight his existence to the authorities, I understand. We don't need to bring him up if he's not involved." Altan moved forward and opened his mouth as if it to interrupt, but I held up my hand to stop him without breaking eye contact with Gary. "But let us interview him. Please. He might not have been involved, but he might have noticed something that can help us."

Gary's green eyes held mine, studying me. Finally, he nodded. "My son, Michael, got involved with a bad crowd down in Melbourne and has come up here to get the heat off. He's a good boy, really. He just made some bad choices when it came to his friend circle. For now, we're not advertising the fact that he's returned. Please keep it that way if you can."

"I promise," I said and placed my hand over my heart.

"Him too." He jerked his head towards the sphinx.

Altan crossed his arms and scowled. "This is Trix's claim now, apparently. Not sure I get a say anymore." With a roll of his eyes and a dramatic sigh, he dropped his arms. "Fine, fine. If your son's information is not pertinent to the claim, I promise neither of us will reveal his location to anyone else and certainly not to the police."

Looking between us, Gary gave a soft sigh. "Guess that's all I can ask for. Come with me."

He let Sylvia know he was ducking out for half an hour, then led us out the front, past the metal stand of the missing mango, and up a dirt driveway. Considering it was still spring, it was another unseasonably hot day. Flies buzzed around my mouth, and cicadas sang in the trees, hurting my ears.

We walked for five minutes before we found a house. The old Queenslander was kept in neat order, all the paint fresh, the deck newly oiled, and the gardens laid out in symmetrical patterns. We walked past Gary's home to the large iron-clad machinery shed out the back.

"Stay there," he ordered before swinging up into the seat of an old tractor. Upon the turning of the key, it started up immediately. Gary drove it forward a few metres before pulling the handbrake on again and turning it off. Without saying a word, he strode back inside the shed. A wooden trap door had been revealed. Gary knelt down and knocked out a complicated pattern before sitting back on his heels and waiting. After only a minute, the door pushed open and a head popped out. My first impression was of dark hair, green eyes, and a handsome twenty-something-year-old face with pointed ears.

Upon seeing us, Michael reared back and looked at his dad with accusation in his eyes. Gary held up his hands in a placating gesture.

"They're friends, my boy. Not cops. They just have a few questions about the mango. How about you come out and answer them so they can be on their way?"

His son looked between the three of us before furtively scanning the surrounding area. "Fine," he eventually ground out. He lifted himself out of the hole in the ground and stood, brushing his hands against his shorts. "But can we make it quick?" Michael kept a keen eye on the sky while he spoke.

With a silent acceptance, Altan nodded for me to take the lead. "Hi, Michael, I'm Trix and this is Altan."

"Everyone calls me Mike," he interrupted.

"Okay then, Mike. We are insurance assessors from MagicAssess. We are here to assess your dad's claim for the missing mango. Do you know anything about that?"

Michael might have come across as arrogant and paranoid, but he had the decency to look aggrieved. "No, it's got nothing to do with me. I know how much that mango means to Dad."

"Did you see anything the night it went missing?"

He shook his head, a lock of hair falling into his eyes. He pushed it out of the way impatiently. "As you can see, I've been hiding away in here most of the time. I didn't see anything."

Altan stepped closer then. "You sure? That deck looks real nice, and I have a feeling that at Gary's age, he mightn't be up to oiling it all by himself. If you've been out at night doing jobs for your dad, you might have seen something without even realising its significance."

Mike ran his fingers through his hair. "Look, yeah, I've been out of the bunker a couple of times, but I swear, I didn't see anything weird that night."

"Is there anyone who can prove your whereabouts?" I asked.

"I'll vouch for him," Gary interjected.

Altan held up a hand. "You're too close to this. Mike, is there anyone else who saw you that could prove you weren't involved?"

With an edge of frustration in his voice, Gary said, "He hasn't seen anyone here since he got back."

Michael shifted uncomfortably.

"Mike?" I probed, staring the young elf down.

He scuffed his shoe against the ground. "I...well, I caught up with Taylah that night."

Chapter Twenty-Nine

"Mike! You told me you had to keep a low profile for your own safety! Running around with some girl from the restaurant who has a penchant for gossip doesn't sound like keeping a low profile." Gary's shock was genuine.

"Not Taylah Beckett?" I clarified.

Mike gave a nod before lashing out at his father. "It's not some girl, it's Taylah! She would never out me!"

I interjected before things heated up any further. "Well, I hate to tell you this Mike, but it was Taylah who told me you were back in town."

"What? No, she wouldn't." At my sympathetic look, the young elf crumpled in on himself. "Oh." Raising his head, he looked at me and asked, "Why?"

Shrugging, I said, "You'll have to ask her that yourself." Looking at Altan, I asked in a low voice, "She pointed the finger at Mike. Could she be a suspect?"

He raked his fingers through his hair. "Add it to our ever-expanding list of questions."

Turning back to Mike, I tried a different approach. "Is there anyone you can think of who could have stolen the Big Mango?"

His eyes darted briefly towards his father before he met my gaze and shrugged noncommittally. "Nah, can't think of anyone off the top of my head."

I scowled, staring him down.

Altan cleared his throat and said, "Gary, would you mind stepping over here with me' I'd like to ask you some questions privately." The two magicas stepped out of earshot.

"Mike," I said firmly. "You're not telling the truth, are you? There is someone you suspect. But you don't want your dad to know."

The elf dropped his eyes to the ground and folded his arms. "I'm no snitch," he muttered sullenly.

"Yes, but you're not technically snitching. This isn't anything to do with organised crime. I'm not a cop. I just want to know what happened to your dad's mango. This will help him. It looks like he's helping you. Don't you want to return the favour?"

He glowered at me. Eventually, he heaved a sigh, dropping his crossed arms. With a furtive glance towards Gary, he finally leaned in close to my ear and whispered, "If I were you I'd be checking out Dad's worker Sylvia." He swiftly removed himself from my personal space.

"Sylvia?" She didn't seem the type. But I had no real experience in this sort of work, so what did I know? "Why is that?" I asked.

He shrugged again. "I don't know. Gut feeling, I guess. She swoops in here while I'm gone, gets all cosy with Dad, and now the mango is missing."

"So no evidence?"

Mike shook his head.

I chewed my lip, debating whether to ask my next question. "I don't want to overstep here, but do you think your feeling isn't to do with her guilt, and is more about how you're feeling like Sylvia is trying to take your mum's place?"

The crossed arms were back along with a vicious glare. "No!" His tone was petulant making it hard for me to believe him.

I sighed and rocked back and forth on the balls of my feet as I contemplated his information. I'd have to chat with Altan about it, but I couldn't see a motive for Sylvia either. "Okay, okay. Thanks for the info. We'll investigate that avenue. We promised your dad, and I swear to you too, that we won't tell anyone about your safe house. But you might want to make sure Taylah knows that as well."

The elf nodded silently, his eyes planted on his shoes.

Handing a business card to Mike, I added, "If you think of anything else, please give us a call."

"Fine. I've got to go now." He snatched the business card and lowered himself back onto the ladder.

I returned to Altan and Gary.

"What did he have to say?" Gary asked. When I didn't answer immediately, he rolled his eyes. "I know your tricks. I know your friend here only pulled me away so you could have a private chat with my son."

I looked to Altan for direction, and he gave a slight nod. "Well, Gary, I asked your son again if there was someone he suspects."

"And?" Gary probed.

"He thinks something's not sitting right with your employee Sylvia."

"Sylvia!" Gary exclaimed. "No, no, no. He couldn't have that more wrong." He placed his hands on his hips. "Listen. Losing my wife, Carrie, was hard on both Mike and myself. Since she passed on, he's become overprotective of me. So naturally, he's wary of any woman that hangs around. But Sylvia is just an employee," he protested. "There's nothing between us. But Mike can't see that. He was already against me having female friends before he left town. After his experiences in Melbourne, he's come back excessively paranoid." He shook his head sadly. "It's going to be a long road for him. He wasn't always like this. I have faith that he'll find joy in life again, one day. He just needs time."

Altan was staring off into the trees, listening to Gary intently. Once the elf finished his explanation, the sphinx placed a hand on Gary's shoulder. I couldn't figure out if it was supposed to be comforting or if he was securing Gary so he couldn't avoid his next question. "Mr Wells, tell us, who inherits your estate should something happen to you?"

"Everything goes to Mike. Not sure that he wants the shop, but I don't have anyone else. I guess it would be up to him if he decided to sell. Obviously, I wouldn't want him to, but it's his life."

"And Sylvia isn't entitled to anything?"

Gary huffed angrily. "I don't know what else to tell you. She's a lovely lady and a wonderful help. But we're not in a relationship. She isn't noted in my will, she has no control over the business, and when she came in the morning after it disappeared, she was nothing but supportive."

Altan ceased that line of questioning. "All right then. Who do you think stole the Big Mango?" Gary blustered about a random burglar but Altan held up a hand to stop him. "I want the unadulterated truth. If it *was* someone who knew you, who pops into your mind?"

With a furtive glance around, he shuffled closer to us. "I don't know that he would actually break the law, but I will say the mayor has been acting shifty lately."

"The mayor?" Altan's eyebrows raised.

"Yes. Mayor Brett Goldwin. I can call his office and request a meeting if you like, but chances are you'll run into him. He's been hanging around the shop ever since the Big Mango went missing. But surely it wouldn't be him? He's the mayor!"

"It seems unlikely," I offered.

"But we can't rule out any possibility until we have hard evidence," Altan said firmly.

Gary rubbed the back of his neck before giving a heavy sigh. After returning the tractor to its original position, he walked us back down the hill, with only the cicadas breaking our silence.

Before we re-entered the shop, Gary stopped us. "I've been thinking about what you said about the girl. About Taylah Beckett," he clarified. "Her father and I had a business together many years ago, but it went bust. Our friendship never recovered. If Taylah and Mike are going steady, I suppose that could be a motive for him to lash out and steal my mango. I hope it's not him." Gary pursed his lips. "He was a good man, so I don't believe it's in his nature. But I just wanted you to have all the facts."

Altan pulled out his pen and pad and made a note. "Thank you, Mr Wells. We will look into it."

When we arrived back at inside the shop, Gary took over from Sylvia. She squeezed his arm, then bustled into the kitchen to make us all an instant coffee.

The bell rang as the front door opened. A man in a grey suit walked in, full of pomp and energy. How the heck he was wearing a suit in this heat, I had no idea. He was in his fifties and had obviously dyed his greying hair a harsh black. Rushing up to the counter, he gripped Gary's hand before pulling him into a hug. It was then that I noticed the sweat stains under his armpits.

"Gary! My boy! Have you had any updates on the mango?" the man gushed.

Gary shot us a weighted look before shaking his head. "Mr Mayor. How kind of you to check in. Again. No, as I said two days ago, I will be sure to give you a call as soon as I have any news. Here, allow me to introduce you to the insurance assessors handling my claim. Altan and Trix from MagicAssess. This is Mayor Brett Goldwin."

"Oh, claiming already!" Brett started but recovered quickly. "So it seems the mango is gone for good then?" The mayor adopted a hurt demeanour. "If you've got assessors here, I suppose you'll be getting paid out soon?"

A flicker of pain flashed across Gary's face. I assumed it was because of the cold way the mayor was talking about his beloved mango.

I stepped forward and shook the pompous man's hand to draw his attention. "Mayor Goldwin," I started, but he interrupted me while continuing to pump my hand vigorously.

"No need to stand on ceremony! Call me Brett." He winked and held my hand for far longer than I wanted.

I cleared my throat and amended, "Brett, we are working alongside the police to ensure all avenues are addressed. Mr Wells would prefer the return of the mango over the receipt of funds. We hope we can help facilitate that outcome for him."

"Excellent. Excellent. Well, it looks like you've got a crack team handling things. I do hope you find the blasted thing. I've heard of some complaints from tourists that they can't see the Big Mango on their trip. Let's catch these ne'er-do-wells and make 'em pay, eh? If there's anything I can do to help with the investigation, you let me know, you hear?" Somehow, he puffed himself up even further. "As mayor of this great region, I have access to power you couldn't imagine!"

Altan and I shared a perplexed glance, and as I met the sphinx's amber eyes, I struggled not to burst out laughing. The mayor was ridiculous. Turning away, I coughed into my elbow in an effort to hide my chuckles.

Somehow, my boss remained professional and smoothly soothed the man's ego. "Absolutely, sir. We're right in the middle of the initial interview process. However, if we get stuck, we'll be sure to call for your aid." Brett smiled cheerfully at that. "Speaking of, where were you on the night of the fifteenth?"

Brett's face turned red and he spluttered, "I hope you don't have me under investigation! What a ludicrous notion. The very idea!"

"Oh, it's nothing personal, sir," replied Altan with an easy smile. "We just need to ensure we cover all bases for the insurer's peace of mind." He tapped his notepad with his pen. "So, the fifteenth?"

Brett folded his arms across his chest. "I was home with my wife," he replied sullenly. "All night."

"And she can corroborate that?"

The mayor looked like he was about to explode. "Of course, she can!" he barked.

Altan made some notes. "Fantastic, thank you, sir." He glanced at me. "Right now, my associate and I need to review our case files." Turning to Gary, he said, "Please pass on our apologies to Sylvia for not staying for coffee. We'll be in touch soon."

It didn't escape my notice that Altan chose not to shake the mayor's hand. Hurrying out of the shop and into our car, I couldn't stop my giggles any longer.

"What a pretentious man!"

"You can say that again," Altan replied and caught my eye. A chuckle escaped his lips, and I forced myself not to pay it too much mind. Thankfully, he distracted me quickly with a question. "Okay, let's work through it. Who do you think is on the suspect list?"

"After that little display, maybe the mayor should be on the list," I joked.

Flicking an ear, Altan affirmed, "He's not *not* on the list. People in power sometimes do strange things to draw attention to themselves."

"Huh. Okay then. I know you have Michael high on your list, but honestly, I don't think he did it."

"Why?"

"Gary seems one hundred percent trustworthy, and I believe him when he says Mike wasn't involved."

"I'll admit that Gary does seem genuine. But you do know that people lie?"

"I know, but I believe him."

"You're too trusting."

"You're not the first person to say that," I muttered.

He gave a light chuckle but didn't push further. "Who else?"

"Well, Taylah is on the list now that we know about her pointing the finger at Mike when he was under the impression he could trust her not to tell anyone about his return. Add to that Gary's comments about his history with her father..."

Altan nodded and prompted, "Anyone else?"

I ran through the known suspects on my hand. "The mayor, Mike, Gary, Taylah, and... Sylvia, I guess." Holding up my five fingers, I rounded on Altan. "I don't really get a bad feeling off any of them. Could it just be a random opportunistic thief? Who do you think?"

"It's always possible, but the planning that went into the burglary seems too careful for it to be a passerby. My money is on Mike, and the fact he tried to push you towards Sylvia reaffirms my suspicions." He shifted in his seat. "Trix...at the end of the day, it's our job to find evidence to support the fact that Gary didn't commit insurance fraud. If we can't figure out the guilty party and the police close the case, there's not much more to be done. Once the evidence of Gary's innocence has been secured, we simply write up our report and provide MoonCorp with our settlement recommendation."

"But Gary doesn't want the settlement. He wants his mango back. As part of our enquiry, can't we help him find it?"

"It's technically not our job. If we prove that Gary isn't committing insurance fraud, MagicAssess will pull us off the investigation," Altan said firmly.

"If Gary was your Dad and was being ignored by the police, wouldn't you want the assessors to help him?"

Altan paused before looking at me. We looked into each other's eyes for a long moment, and I thought I saw a softening in his gaze. He sighed and broke eye contact. "Fine," he grumbled. Stressing the '*if*', he said, "*If* we happen to find a concrete lead that gives us a clue to the guilty party, we will follow it. But the first priority is to ensure that Gary and his son are not at fault. All right?"

I nodded eagerly, glad he'd conceded to me.

Now we just needed to catch the crook.

Chapter Thirty

It was an honest-to-goodness stakeout.

I couldn't decide if I was more nervous or excited. Stakeouts always looked so exciting in the movies with lots of snacking going on. And I did love snacks.

But we'd just eaten lunch at the restaurant at Horseshoe Bay, where Altan had used a myriad of his intimidation tactics to get Taylah to talk. Turned out, she'd heard rumours that Mike was seeing another girl, so in a fit of jealousy, had pointed me towards him in retaliation. There was a lot of crying and shaking from the young woman, so unless she was an amazing actress, I had a feeling she was telling the truth. What she had mentioned that had spiked our curiosity was the fact that Mayor Goldwin had been asking her questions too. After finishing our burgers overlooking the ocean, we'd got back in the car, and with no other concrete leads, had driven to the street of the mayor's home.

Since neither of us were feeling snack-ish after our lunch, we sat in silence and stared out the open windows, settling in for the stakeout. It became boring very quickly. They didn't show this part on TV. Grey clouds heavy with the threat of rain rolled in from the coast. Birds flitted around the car, where we were parked up in front of the botanic gardens, opposite Brett Goldwin's house. The earth on this side of the street was dry, and small flurries of wind and dust swept past us. I began drumming my fingers on the door's interior panel but quickly stopped when I felt Altan's eyes on me. Curbing my nervous fidgeting, I returned to scanning the drive across from us.

As the minutes dragged on, I grabbed the tablet out of my handbag and began typing notes into the app of who we'd spoken to during the day. I lifted the tablet and took a photo of the mayor's house to include in the report. My work phone pinged loudly in the silence with a report request from HO.

"Turn that damn thing off," Altan snarled.

"Sorry," I mumbled, quickly switching it to silent. I'd respond later. I tucked both the phone and the tablet back into my handbag.

He gave a heavy sigh and rubbed the bridge of his nose. "It's all right. That wasn't your fault." He hesitated. "I know how boring waiting is, especially when you're not used to it yet. Sphinxes are more used to sitting still for long periods of time than humans are."

"Really?" I asked, surprised. "Aside from the obvious physical differences between the two species, what else is there?"

"Quite a lot," he said matter-of-factly but didn't elaborate.

After a lengthy pause, I challenged him, "Why do you do that?"

He glanced over at me with a twist of his lips. "Do what?"

"You shut me down all the time. If we're going to work together, Altan, I'd like to know you better. I feel like all I do is chatter away and make a fool of myself. And you sit there, watching and judging me and offering nothing in return."

A peculiar expression flitted across his face, but it was gone again before I could determine what it was. The next pause stretched on for so long, I didn't think he was going to speak to me again for the rest of the afternoon. So I settled into my seat and turned my attention back to our surroundings.

Then Altan cleared his throat. "I've been hurt a lot." He said it so quietly, I wasn't sure if I was supposed to hear. "Mostly by humans." His hands were balled up into fists, fur sprouting on their backs. "My sister and I were orphaned when we were very young. Shortly after the Spark. Eventually, we were adopted by a Welsh couple. A human couple. They treated us like we were their human children. They did their best to love us in their own way. Since they couldn't have children of their own, they showered us in gifts. Looking back, I think they thought their money could buy our love. But it wasn't what two young sphinxes needed."

I listened with bated breath, hoping he would continue. I didn't have to wait too long.

"They sent us to a human boarding school in England. I've now realised that my adopted parents thought spending all that money on us to go to a prestigious school was an act of love, but at the time, my sister and I simply felt abandoned."

When Altan didn't continue, I said gently, "I'm sorry. That must have been a confusing time for you and your sister. What is her name?"

"Cora," he whispered, keeping his eyes fixed out the windshield.

"Where is Cora now?"

He didn't answer me, instead, giving himself a shake and clearing his throat loudly. "That's enough for today." He was still avoiding my gaze. "Let's work on your observation skills. Tell me, what do you see?"

The white picket fence housed a manicured lawn. Mayor Goldwin obviously irrigated it as it was such a bright green, it almost hurt my eyes when compared to the surrounding grass. There was even a peacock roaming the front yard. Who even owned peacocks? The guy had a screw loose.

"I know Bowen seems like a nice little town, but that seems like pretty basic security for the mayor," I observed.

Altan froze at my comment.

The sphinx leant forward and squinted at the fence. "Show me that photo you just took."

Puzzled, I dug the tablet out of my handbag again and brought up my half-completed report, clicking on the image to enlarge it.

Looking at the photo, Altan glanced between it and the mayor's fence before uttering a low hiss. "See that?" He pointed to the right side of the photo on my screen. "It's an illusion."

I cocked my head. "What? Where? How do you tell?" I demanded.

"That glimmer in the corner of the yard." He zoomed in on the image to give me a better view.

A translucent square shimmering in the air above the white picket fence was the only sign of anything out of the ordinary. "That thing?" I pointed.

"Yes." He slammed his fist against the dash and cursed. "I've been looking at this all wrong!"

"But you said you tested for an illusion spell and nothing showed up?"

"Yes, I tested for a *spell*, not —" The tinny ringing of his phone interrupted whatever else he was about to say. With a cursory glance at the screen, he flipped it open and snapped, "Detective Briggs?" He listened for a moment before his eyes narrowed, his ears flattened against his head, and fur sprouted along the backs of his hands. "Officer, I told you we'd handle it. You've arrested the wrong man." His voice was all hisses and snarls. There was a long pause as he listened while I bounced on the edge of my seat, wishing he'd put it on speaker. "That is blatant discrimination!" he roared, making me jump. "Just because he's an elf doesn't mean he's a thief. Why would he steal from his own father?"

What? Why were they arresting Mike?

"Yes, we knew about Michael living at his father's, but with no evidence linking him to the crime, we didn't feel it was necessary to advise you of his involvement at this time." He waited, and it sounded like there was shouting on the other end. "We interviewed the Taylah girl, and she deliberately misled us due to her jealousy. Her testimony is not valid. You can't arrest Mike based on her word alone." The tip of his tail was twitching in agitation, growing more frantic as the conversation continued. "I don't care if the mayor is pushing you to make an arrest. You can't just believe the word of one human who is known to have a vendetta against the accused." He growled low in his throat. "You. Are. Incompetent." He pressed the end call button and looked ready to throw his phone.

I was glad I wasn't the one bearing the brunt of his anger.

With his eyes blazing and his fangs bared, he hissed, "Idiots!" Turning the car on, Altan threw it into gear and tore off.

With a yelp, I gripped onto anything within reach at the sudden turbulence. Teeth gritted, I stared at my boss. As we broke the speed limit heading back towards the caravan park, I waited for him to explain where we were going. When he didn't and I didn't feel like I was going to be tossed out the window anymore, I mustered the courage to ask, "Come on, Altan. We've talked about this. Communication, mate."

His eyes flicked to me before refocusing on the road. "Sorry, not used to having a partner. The police are on their way to arrest Michael thanks to that stupid girl letting her emotions get the best of her. Apparently, she called the police after we left the restaurant." He hissed out a long breath from between his teeth. "So now, it's more important than ever that we find the one responsible so an innocent elf doesn't wind up in jail."

I nodded in agreement. "Would it help if we went down to the station and talked to Detective Briggs?" I asked.

"That buffoon is useless," Altan murmured grimly. "To answer your question, no it wouldn't. He needs to make an arrest. The mayor and media are pressing him for an answer. He won't listen to reason unless we give him an alternative answer. Preferably one that comes with a signed confession on a silver platter and tied up with a bow." He sped up on a straight stretch of road. "What I started to say before the dickhead called was since we had no leads on the location of the missing mango, we've been trying to find a motive for someone to steal it. But what if it was never stolen in the first place?"

I stared at him. "But it's gone. I don't understand what you're saying."

"Grab my laptop and look at the CCTV footage again. This time, we need to watch out for signs of an illusion. It's not an illusion charm created by a witch or wizard. It is an actual illusion crafted by an incredibly skilled magica. Certain magicas have the ability to warp reality and only let you see what they want you to see." He shook his head in admiration. "The fact that they removed the physical reaction of things passing through the space where the mango was...incredible!" He took a hand off the steering wheel and jerked a thumb behind us. "The mayor's house looks like it has no real security. But I bet my bottom dollar that illusion is hiding a serious fence. Possibly electrified. The peacock is probably actually a guard dog. It's a complex illusion, made by a magica. But which one?"

Thanking the wolf's moon for my seat belt, I managed to reach behind me and pull the laptop carefully into the front seat. As I opened it, I kept a tight grip on it lest Altan's driving sent it flying off my lap. Somehow, I managed to bring up the CCTV footage without dropping the computer, but what with all the flying around corners, I couldn't focus on the images.

Thankfully, we made it to our cabin at the caravan park in record time. Altan jerked the hand brake on and leaned towards me so we could both watch the screen. I pressed play, and we studied the now-familiar footage. Altan's ear flicked, and the tip of it brushed my cheek. I bit back a shiver; this was no time to look at how close his face was to mine and analyse what that was doing to my body. That was future-Trix's problem to deal with.

"Look!" he exclaimed and pointed at the left corner of the screen.

There it was. A faint glimmer on the concrete pedestal where the mango sat.

Altan released a long breath and looked at me. "The tell-tale of an illusion like this one only shows up on cameras. We can't see them with the naked eye. Even within the footage, it's been cleverly disguised on the base. I wasn't even looking for that." He swore. "This is a large illusion and hidden well. Assuming the Big Mango is still there, only an extremely gifted magica can hold it for so long." He rubbed a hand over his chin. "I don't want to go back to the mango yet and risk showing anyone we know their trick."

Abruptly, he got out of the car and headed to the cabin. I hurried to keep up. Once we were inside, Altan grabbed my shoulders and stared into my eyes. "Trix, I'm going to do something now. But it's a secret guarded fiercely by all sphinx-kind. To my knowledge, no human has been told of this aspect of our magic. Can you swear to me that you will never tell another soul, human, magica, or other?" His amber eyes drilled into me.

What else could I say? "Of course, Altan. I've got your back. I'll never tell anyone anything, I swear it on—" I paused before committing to my next words. "Millie's life."

The sphinx held me for a moment longer, and the weird electricity between us started ramping up again. Seeming satisfied with my answer, he released me. When I didn't think he was looking, I let out a shaky breath and clasped my trembling hands behind my back. That had been entirely too intense.

Swiftly entering his bedroom, I heard him unzip his suitcase. Curiosity getting the better of me, I followed him into the room. He was pulling out a glass bottle of sparkling purple liquid.

He gave it a gentle shake and threw a smile over his shoulder. "Not for human consumption." Carefully placing the bottle on the bedside table, he began speaking as he rummaged through his case. "So. My secret." He pulled out a short black candle and placed it beside the bottle. "Sphinxes have the ability to See past events."

The way he said the word 'See' made me think he wasn't talking about using his eyes.

"Some magicas have access to a third eye. I can perform a ritual that gives my third eye the ability to traverse time and space itself. It is a...challenging ritual, and I'll be wiped out for a few hours afterwards. The items I need to complete it are also difficult to find, so I tend to avoid it as much as I can. But I think you're right that Mike is not guilty. My body will stay here, but my mind will travel back in time and find the magica who performed the illusion. They will have had to attend the site to perform the charm. It could have been any number of species. We need to know what we're dealing with." He trailed off for a moment as he stared at the blank wall. With a shake of his head, he continued, "When I resurface, I should have enough energy to tell you what I saw, but I won't be able to walk for a little while, let alone act on the information." He pulled out a smooth round piece of jade from his suitcase and sat it next to the other items beside his bed. He sat down on the bed with a thump. "Trix..."

His amber eyes caught mine once again, trapping me in their warmth. Trapping me in a good way. In a very good way. In a way where, if an elf's future wasn't on the line, I'd be taking those few steps to the bed, pushing him down onto the mattress, and kissing him until the world dropped away, and all we could feel would be each other. Instead, I pressed my body against the cool wall, praying for some reprieve from the fire inside me.

"I need you to promise me something else. When I come back to myself, do not, I repeat, do not go after the one responsible. Not by yourself. Wait for me to recover. Please."

That last word broke me. A hint of something more than a boss's concern echoed around the edges of it, but I refused to entertain the idea that he thought of our relationship as anything other than platonic. Otherwise, I'd be lost.

"Understood, sir. What do you need from me now?"

"Just close the door and curtains, then pay attention to what I say when I come back."

I nodded in silent agreement, then closed the bedroom door and pulled the curtains across the window, plunging the room into darkness. Pulling out a lighter from his pocket, he lit the black candle. A blue flame sprung from the wick and burned brightly, casting dancing shadows on the bare walls of the bedroom. After taking a swig from the bottle of purple liquid, Altan shuddered. Lying down, he cradled the jade on his stomach and began breathing deeply, the green rock rising up and down slowly.

I moved forward cautiously, watching him. His eyes were closed. I couldn't help myself. My eyes traced over the strong line of his jaw and admired his thick hair. All I wanted was to run my hands through it. But that would be crossing a line. I folded my arms over my chest, determined to keep my hands to myself.

CHAPTER THIRTY-ONE

I STOOD THERE AND watched him breathe for twenty minutes. Every now and then his muscles would twitch. The only sound that broke the peace was our combined breaths and the rustle of my clothes as I shifted my weight in an attempt to stop my leg from going to sleep. Out of the blue, Altan sucked in a strangled breath and threw the jade away from his body where it hit the wall.

I jumped at the unexpected movement and gasped, choking on my own spit as it went down the wrong hole. He reached over and pinched the candle's wick, extinguishing the flame and throwing the room into darkness. Deep, racking coughs came from him, and I flicked on the light switch to see what was happening. Altan was sitting up and staring around wildly, seeming to not know where he was.

When his eyes found mine, his panicked expression subsided, and he lay back on the pillow. He was so pale. "Spider weaver did illusion. Mango not stolen. Still there," he rasped before covering his face with his arm and croaking, "Water."

I rushed to the kitchen to grab him a glass. Filling it up from the sink, I noticed a huntsman spider sitting in the corner of the lounge. I hesitated for a second but gritted my teeth and ignored the massive grey arachnid. I ran back to Altan with his water. As I re-entered the room, I heard his steady breathing once again. He was asleep.

I placed the cup of water beside the bed and touched his forehead. He was burning. I winced. Heading to the bathroom, I quickly located a fresh flannel and rinsed it in the basin. Once more, I returned to Altan's side and placed the wet cloth on his forehead. He stirred and reached out blindly with a hand until he located my arm.

Gripping me tightly, he murmured, "Stay."

Both my body and thoughts froze for a moment at the plea. Could he want me as more than an employee? To be his safe harbour? To care for him? To be someone special? I banished the idea of him wanting me and reminded my traitorous thoughts that he'd asked me to not investigate alone. That was all he meant by his request for me to stay. Hurt curled in my gut.

Of course that was all it was.

My imagination had been having way too much fun lately. Carefully, I removed his hand from my arm and left the room. Crossing my arms, I stood with my legs shoulder-width apart, giving my best impression of Fiona's power stance.

Glaring towards the corner I'd last seen him, I opened my mind and, with as much authority as I could muster, said, "Huntsman."

There was a beat of silence before an answer came. *"Human."* The spider scuttled out from behind the couch. He was as big as my hand spread out, large even by huntsman standards. *"You seek the weaver?"*

I cringed internally at his scurrying movement but refused to show any fear. "Yes. He a friend of yours?"

"We are...distant cousins."

"Do you know where I will find the spider weaver responsible for the illusion?"

"Why should I help you?"

That made me pause. "Because if I capture him and dispel the illusion, it will save a young elf's life."

The spider made a noise in my head that sounded an awful lot like a snort of derision.

Panic started clawing at my insides. Of course the spider didn't care about some random elf. What would a spider want? What could I offer him to make him give me the information I needed?

"If I help you, you will owe my kind a favour. If a spider ever asks for your assistance, you are bound to give it."

I hesitated. Unknown future favours were never a good idea in the movies. But he was a spider. What kind of favour could they ever need from me? "All right then. I swear it."

"Good. You will find the weaver in a secluded cabin at the back of the mango woman's property."

"The mango woman? You mean Sylvia? He's hiding out on her farm?"

"I believe that is what the fleshbags call her, yes." He sniffed disdainfully. *"Follow her driveway, turn north before the creek, then turn west beside the old gum tree and walk the trail."*

"Thank you. Your help will stop an innocent elf being left to rot in jail."

"I don't care about that. Just remember: the weaver may have done the deed. But ask yourself, is he really the one responsible?"

I considered his advice before casting one last look back at the closed door of Altan's bedroom. "I have to go now, don't I?"

"If you want to catch him before he disappears forever, yes."

Chewing my lip, I took a few steps towards the front door, halted, then returned to Altan's side. Shaking his shoulder, I whispered, "Altan. Altan, can you hear me?"

There was no response other than a soft snore. I rocked back on my heels and debated with myself. I felt so torn. I'd promised Altan I would stay here. But the huntsman said it was now or never.

Altan shared his secret power with me and now it's wiped him out. I can't let all of his efforts be for nothing. I can't let him down.

If I was going to have any chance of catching the spider weaver, I had to leave now. I nodded to myself. I would just go to the weaver's hideout and have a look around. I'd shadow the weaver if he left the property and call Altan in an hour and hope that he had recovered enough to come and help me. Guess it was lucky I still had my armour on.

Grabbing my weapons and my bead kit, I didn't hesitate to include my stick. For some reason, the unremarkable piece of wood felt like it wanted to come along. Don't ask me why I thought my stick had needs.

Not trusting him to check his phone, I scrawled a note for Altan and left it on the bench beside the front door. Grabbing the car keys, I drove as fast as I dared, hoping I could find the weaver in time and somehow figure out a way to convince him to tell me his employer's name.

As I tore out of Bowen and onto the highway, I tried to work out why the weaver would have done what he had.

Like the huntsman had said, the weaver had no motive that we knew of to steal the mango. I shook my head. Not steal. Hide. And in plain sight too. The audacity of it floored me.

So why had it been hidden in the first place? The only other illusion we'd seen was at the mayor's house. It had to be Brett Goldwin's doing. He had already used the weaver's skills for his own home.

I pondered on why the mayor might have done it. According to the movies, the usual motives for any sort of crime were money, greed, or love.

If the town's biggest tourist attraction disappeared, what would it achieve? Media attention for the town? More tourists coming to see the lonely plinth on which it once stood? Or was there something more sinister afoot?

My mind raced. Was there a reason Brett could want Mike out of the way? Maybe he'd set this up so that the evidence led back to Gary's son? But why? Was there a connection to Mike's dodgy past in Melbourne?

I needed to talk to the weaver to figure this out.

Turning off the highway, I drove down the dirt driveway past Sylvia's house. I decided against advising her first. This probably wasn't following protocol, but at this point, I didn't care. Better to ask forgiveness than permission, and all that.

I figured it would be safer to avoid talking to her in case she had any sort of loyalty to the weaver. He was staying on her land, after all. I didn't want to risk him running off before I got there because she'd called him to let him know I was on my way. I couldn't help but look at her empty front verandah as I zipped past. The house looked empty anyway.

Following the huntsman's instructions, I travelled west until I arrived at the creek. Turning right, I bumped along the northward road until I found a massive gum tree. It had to be the one he was talking about. Growing directly beside the track, its trunk was over a metre wide, and the boughs spread out, casting shade over the entire section of road. I pulled up outside of its shade, vaguely remembering a warning about how easily a gumtree would drop their branches.

Pulling the handbrake on, I tucked my phone into a pocket in my armour, and attached my sword to my belt, hoping like heck I didn't need to use it. I double checked the contents of my bead kit on the other side of my belt. I had a couple of healing beads, a shield ward, and a fire attack. I pulled out the shield bead so it would be ready to throw at a moment's notice in the hopes that, if the weaver came out all guns blazing, I'd have at least a little bit of protection. Without hesitation, I grabbed the komada's stick in my other hand.

Here was another reason why I'd be the first to die in a horror movie. Why was I choosing a stick over a sword as my preferred weapon?

Even that burst of logic wasn't enough to convince me to switch my stick for my spatha. I rubbed my thumb over the grey bark. A tingle crept into my fingertips, causing me to almost drop the stick. I stared at it.

What in the world was that all about?

I didn't have time to address my stick's weirdness right now. Taking a steadying breath, I raised my chin and pulled up my imaginary big-girl pants. Gripping the small bead in my fist and ignoring the stick's tingles, I took the trail past the massive gumtree and followed the simple dirt track. Sweat coated my skin and dripped down my back. Glancing up at the tree canopy, I suddenly realised how quiet it was. There was no birdsong, and not even the cicadas were singing today. A shiver crept down my spine.

This wasn't my smartest idea.

On any other day, I would consider this a charming hike. But not today. Not knowing what waited for me at the end of my trek was petrifying.

Would there be a battle? Maybe I should have messaged Millie one more time. Just in case.

A small wooden cabin appeared between the trees. I tread carefully, doing my best to avoid making any noise. Tucking myself behind the trunk of a large paperbark gum, I hoped the smell of its eucalyptus leaves would hide my scent. Peering through the underbrush, I debated how to confirm the weaver was inside the cabin without alerting him to my presence. As soon as I had confirmation that he was in there, I'd contact Altan.

I'd almost decided to try to sneak around the side and see if there was a window when the front door flew open. The weaver stepped out into the sunshine. I froze.

"Trix! I know you're there. My name is Darius. There is no need to hide. Please, join me." He stepped aside and gestured at his front door with two of his arms.

"Mother trucker," I hissed. I was this close to using a real swear word. Instead, I straightened and casually said, "Oh, hey, Darius." I wandered out of the tree line like this was my everyday walking track. "How's your day going?"

Crikey, could I sound any more blasé?

"Not going to lie, I've had better. I'd really like to talk to you if you're free?" He kept his posture relaxed and waited for me.

"Of course. I'd love to chat." Faking a confidence I didn't feel, I marched up to his home, keeping a death grip on my bead and stick in case he tried any funny business. He didn't. At least not yet. He simply held open the wooden door for me.

Once I was inside, it took my eyes a few seconds to adjust to the sudden shade. Looking around, I noted it was a simple house. There was only one room, with a concrete sink, a couple of broken cupboards, and an oven making up the basic kitchen on one side. A hammock was hung up on the opposite wall. There was no sign of a mattress, a bathroom, or any sort of dining or lounge room furniture. Even though there were no lightbulbs, I could see well enough to tell the floor was packed dirt.

Darius shut the front door and leaned against it nonchalantly.

My exit was cut off. I didn't like this at all.

With a charming smile, the weaver said, "Sorry, I'd offer you a seat, but I don't have one. I'm not used to entertaining guests. Can I get you a glass of water?"

"No, thanks, I'm fine." Even though I was thirsty, I figured it was better to stay on the safe side. What if he poisoned me?

"Suit yourself." He shrugged and left the door unguarded, grabbing a glass for himself and turning the sink tap on. I debated making a run for it, but the entire point of my trek was to interrogate and capture him, and I couldn't do that from outside. The water spurted a couple of times as the air bubbles worked themselves out before the stream of water steadied. After drinking for a few seconds, he pulled the kitchen window's curtain open, allowing a patch of sunlight to hit the dirt floor. Dust motes swirled in the beam as he moved to zip up a backpack sitting against the wall.

"Colour me curious, Darius. How do you know my name? And how did you figure out it was me in the trees?"

"I know a great many things." He gave a secretive smile.

"Cool, cool, cool. That sounds super mysterious and all. But it doesn't really answer my question, does it?"

"I said I wanted to speak to you. I didn't say I'd be answering any of your questions."

"Well, you're no fun," I replied, keeping my tone light and playful in the hopes it would delay the inevitable battle. Who knew. Maybe my distraction technique could work? "So, what did you want to talk about then?" I prompted him.

"We have so much to discuss. But first things first, how did you find me, Trix?"

I couldn't tell him about Altan's vision, but I could give him half the truth. "A huntsman spider told me where to find you."

He paused at that, his back to me. "Did he now? How very interesting. Do you talk to spiders often?"

"It's a recent habit," I answered drily.

"You are a curious human. It's a shame I have to kill you." Turning around, he began picking out some dirt from under his nails without meeting my gaze.

"I mean, you don't *have* to. You could just give me a stern warning and let me be on my way."

He snorted and looked at me then, his eyes completely black. "Like I said, it's a shame. My employer requested no loose ends. And you have become one, I'm afraid."

"Your employer?" Maybe if I could just keep the weaver talking, I could find a way to capture him like they did in the movies. You know the ones. The bad guy ends up monologuing for so long that the good guys have time to lay a trap.

The weaver cocked his head and studied me. "Since you won't be leaving this cabin alive, it might be nice to share all the sordid details with someone." He sighed. "You humans don't think about how isolating it is to be a magica sometimes." He paused as if considering where to begin his tale. "Years ago, a human killed my mate. I retaliated in kind. The law didn't appreciate that, so I've been on the run for a while. Last year, I found myself here, in Bowen. Sylvia was kind enough to take me in and offer me accommodation and a modest wage for helping her around the farm." Darius chuckled, but there was little humour in it. The sound made my skin crawl. "Little did I know, she knew all about my past. Now she controls my actions. She threatened to reveal my location to the police if I didn't obey her command to make the Big Mango vanish."

"Sylvia is the one behind all this?" My mouth dropped open.

"Yes, she plays the role of the sweet old dame very well."

My mind whirred as I tried to process his revelation. To keep him talking, I said, "It seems like killing is your go-to method of dealing with problems. Why didn't you just take her out and disappear again?"

All his hands fisted, and he straightened up with a predatory hiss. "I would have loved to do just that. But I can't. She stole my egg. The last thing left of my mate. And she took it from me." The weaver began pacing. "She swore to me she would give my child back after this job. But don't worry, if she goes back on her word, I'll take care of her too."

I shuddered at his words. Both at his threats, and the fact that Sylvia had threatened his unborn child. What kind of monster was she? "What I don't get though is why she asked you to hide the mango in the first place? She loves Gary. Why would she hurt him?"

Darius shot me a disparaging look. "That's just it. She loves him, and he doesn't reciprocate that love. So she figured by taking away the thing that reminds him of his dead wife and being there for him as an emotional support during the trauma of losing it, it might force him to reconsider her role in his life." The weaver rolled his eyes. "The things humans do to chase the idea of love. You are all ridiculous."

"That's insane."

"Yes. From my interactions with her, I fear she has one or two screws loose."

"So, wait. What did the mayor have to do with it?"

Darius's brows drew together. "The mayor? Nothing as far as I know. He paid me to do an illusion on his house, and he has his own secrets, but he had nothing to do with the mango's disappearance." He sighed. "And I'm afraid we've run out of time for any more questions." He took a measured step towards me and raised his hands. "It is time to die, Trix."

Well, fuck.

CHAPTER THIRTY-TWO

MY PHONE RANG, BREAKING the heavy silence laying between the weaver and me. Reluctant to break eye contact, I still chanced a glance at the screen. It was Altan.

I looked back at the weaver, who had relaxed and was now leaning casually against the wall. My spidey senses were screaming at me not to trust him. "It's my boss. He'll think it's weird if I don't answer."

The spider weaver gave a wide smile. Unnaturally wide. His lips stretched and split his face in two. When he next spoke, saliva dripped from his teeth. "Answer away. Tell him whatever you want. He won't make it here in time anyway. I'll be gone, and you'll be dead. Give him a chance to say his last goodbye." It was almost a purr, and he licked his teeth with his peculiarly long tongue.

I shivered at the threat of my imminent death but hit answer anyway. "Altan?"

"Where the fuck are you?"

"I'm with the weaver. But it's Sylvia you want. You were right, the mango isn't stolen. Sylvia has leverage over the weaver and had him create an illusion to make it disappear. I'll explain it all later but you need to move on her now. It didn't look like she was at her house."

"What about you? Are you safe? Is the weaver cooperating?"

"Erm, not exactly. But I'll handle this; you get Sylvia."

He cursed again, loudly, and hung up.

I stared at the silent phone in my hand. Guess he'd taken me at my word.

Well, I had said that I'd handle it; guess I better do just that.

Throwing my shield bead at the ground in front of me, I switched my stick to my left hand and unsheathed my sword with my right. A shimmering bubble of air appeared in front of my body, and the tingling in my stick grew stronger.

Darius had remained in his nonchalant position against the kitchen wall. With a smirk, he said, "You're new to this, aren't you?"

He had no idea how new, but I wasn't going to give him the satisfaction of admitting it.

"Fine. Don't talk. I'll share some advice with you, rookie. Ward beads only last for a few seconds and are most useful when deflecting an immediate attack. Not as a long-lasting shield." He gestured towards the bubble, which was already beginning to disintegrate. "Not that it matters since you'll be dead shortly anyway."

Cheese and crackers. I should have known that. Guess I'd have to go on the offensive. I raised my spatha and took a step towards the weaver.

"I don't think so." He raised one of his hands and flicked it casually towards me.

My vision went dark.

Panic immediately overwhelmed me. My heartbeat drummed loudly, and I began to hyperventilate.

"Trix! What're you doing? Come lie down with me."

I froze at the sound of Altan's voice. Confusion swept over me as I looked around at the beach scene that appeared before me. It was close to sunset, and waves rolled gently onto the shore while palm trees nodded their heads above me. Altan was lying on a navy-coloured beach towel, propped up on his elbows, shirtless.

Goodness gravy.

The guy was hot. I'd already thought so when he had his clothes on, but now that he only had itty-bitty trunks covering his junk, there was little left to the imagination. The sphinx looked up at me and smiled wide, the most relaxed I'd ever seen him. His tail beckoned and he nodded to the rainbow-coloured towel laid out on the sand beside him. He repeated himself, his voice a seductive purr, "Come on, don't make me beg. Let's enjoy the sunset together." One of his cat-like ears flicked, and it took everything I had to stop myself from dropping to my knees and stroking them.

As it was, my legs automatically carried me towards him, but I hesitated once I reached the towel. I wanted nothing more than to lie down beside him, but I had a feeling I was supposed to be somewhere else. I frowned as I tried to remember what I was doing before I came to the beach. Something tickled my palm. Looking down at my hand, I realised I was still holding my stick. The tingling turned into a stinging sensation, burning away the illusion.

Altan and the beach faded away, leaving a dull ache in my chest. Reality came rushing back. The weaver.

Firecrackers.

The A-hole had tried to mess with my head to stop me from attacking him. Fury filled me at his ability to find my secret daydream and use it against me.

No more Mrs Nice Guy. Lady. Whatever.

"You bastard," I seethed.

Darius blinked in surprise and lowered his hand. "You broke free of the illusion. Impressive. How?"

"No bloody idea. But you'll pay for that."

He chuckled. "Sure thing, rookie. Look, I am a little bit sorry about this. It's not personal. Sylvia wants things tidied up, and I want my egg to stay safe, so I do as she says. Personally, I find you amusing. You look like a kitten that's trying its best to fight off a wolf. It's impossible, but you try anyway. You're adorable. Tell me, what's your plan now?"

With pure instinct guiding me, I dropped my sword and held onto the stick with both hands. Warm pulses radiated through my body, down to my feet, and into the ground. In a peculiar way, I felt intensely connected to the earth. In my mind's eye, I couldn't detect any signs of animals nearby, but an alien awareness stirred as my consciousness brushed it. Ignoring the magic prickling through my body for the moment, I replied with gritted teeth, "I'm just a woman with a stick standing in front of a magica, asking him to surrender."

He laughed outright. "And if I don't?"

"Well, I guess I'm going to have to take you down." The being from underground pushed towards me, and somehow, I knew it was offering its help. As it moved closer, I finally realised what it was. The paperbark gum tree I'd hidden behind when I'd got here. Its roots ran deep beneath the cabin and, using my stick as a conduit for my power, I managed to coax them closer to the surface of the earth.

How on earth a stick that was stuck in a komada's mouth was the magical conduit I needed to channel my newfound power, was a question for another day. Preferably, a day when I wasn't about to get to get killed.

The weaver padded closer, each step measured, his confidence obvious. "And how exactly do you plan on doing that?"

"Like this," I said and threw all my energy into yanking the roots of the paperbark gum up and out of the dirt floor and sending them towards my would-be attacker. The thick tendrils wrapped around the weaver's neck. The look of astonishment in all eight of his eyes was priceless but didn't last for long as he began clawing at his throat. His cheeks began to change colour, making me feel ill. I didn't want to kill the magica. Just hold him until the police could get here. Mentally, I tried to force the roots to loosen the hold they had on Darius, but as I took a step towards him, a wave of dizziness rushed over me. Blinking furiously, I couldn't stop myself from keeling over. Darius fell at the same time and grew still, one thick root still around his neck.

This was not how I'd envisioned this day ending.

The last conscious thought in my mind was of my daughter. Then darkness claimed me.

"Fuck, fuck, fuck!"

Something was tugging at my body. Everything felt so heavy. My head lolled as I was rolled onto my side.

And why was that noisy something swearing like a sailor? How rude.

"Wake up, Trix! Fuck, don't leave me."

Leave? I wasn't going anywhere. The noisy, rude something smelt nice. Like...sandalwood. A frown flickered over my brows as I tried to remember why I was on the ground.

"Snap out of it. Come on!" Something thumped me.

"Stop itttt," I slurred, attempting to bat the noisy thing away but failing because my hands didn't want to cooperate.

"Thank God, you're alive."

Of course I was alive. Why would anyone think otherwise?

Squinting through my eyelashes, I couldn't stop a small gasp from escaping my lips. Altan's ear was a hairsbreadth away from my lips. The late afternoon sunlight coming through the windows highlighted the fur on the tips, and I just wanted to lean forward and rub my cheek against it.

Even my addled brain knew that would be a bad idea. Why was I addled anyway? That was a good question. I just needed to figure out how to make my body work again, then I was sure I could figure it all out.

Blinking, I looked past him and saw the timber walls of the spider weaver's cabin. It all came rushing back. The weaver, the attack, my sudden rush of power. The tree! I hoped it would be okay after I'd disturbed its roots so aggressively.

I sucked in a lungful of air. A bubble of hysterical laughter burst out.

Altan stared at me, concern marring his handsome face. "It's over now," he murmured, his tone soothing, his fingertips stroking my cheek.

Closing my eyes, I enjoyed his touch for a moment before jerking away. "What about Sylvia? Did you get her?" I rasped out.

"Yes, the police have picked her up. I left them while they were arresting her because I thought I was rushing in to save you." He chuckled softly. "Turns out, you'd already saved yourself and taken down the most powerful weaver I've ever come across."

"What about the egg? Did the police save it? The weaver told me that Sylvia was using the weaver's unborn child as leverage over him."

"Yes, they located a spider weaver egg inside her house. It was safe." He screwed up his nose at his next sentence. "The constable gave me a walkie-talkie when I left them and I heard them report it. But don't worry about the egg, let's focus on you for now."

He raised my hand to his mouth and kissed it gently.

As his lips connected with my skin, I forgot how to breathe. His eyes squeezed shut, and he muttered, "I feared the worst. When I saw you unconscious...I thought..." He opened his eyes and captured my gaze. "I'm so glad you're okay," he whispered hoarsely.

"Me too." I cleared my throat, trying to ignore the sudden heat sweeping over my cheeks.

Much to my disappointment, he released me. Dusting his trousers off as he stood, he came around behind me and helped me stand up. I was as wobbly as a baby taking its first steps.

"So...you should probably call your daughter," he said sheepishly as I finally managed to make my legs hold my weight.

"Why?" I put my hands on my hips. "Altan, what did you do?"

"When I thought you were in mortal danger, I called your emergency contact Nicole. But Millie overheard the conversation, so she might be...a little anxious to hear from you."

"Why would you do that?" I screeched.

"I'm sorry!" He had the decency to look ashamed. "I know how much you care about your family, and I figured you'd want them to be updated."

"No!" I yelled at him, all semblance of sexual tension forgotten. "That's not how it works!" I threw my hands in the air. "I never want to worry them when I have a problem, okay?"

Altan's face creased as he puzzled over my comment. "But you want them to come to you with *their* problems?"

"Obviously. They need to tell me every single detail if they're ever in trouble so I can try to fix it."

"That seems extremely imbalanced."

"Maybe so, but that's how mums work, okay? Do not tell them next time!"

After a few tearful minutes of consoling my hysterical daughter over the phone, I hung up with a promise to call back as soon as I had wrapped up the case. Altan and I greeted the police and paramedics when they arrived at the weaver's hut. Detective Briggs was frosty and distant while another officer helped a paramedic load the still unconscious weaver onto a stretcher. The other paramedic gave me a quick check over and told me to take some painkillers and rest up, but that otherwise, my vitals were fine. They assured me I'd only knocked Darius out, not killed him, so I was thankful for that.

Our procession of six slowly followed the trail back to the dirt road and loaded Darius into the waiting ambulance. Altan kept a tight grip around my waist the entire walk as I was still wobbly. I couldn't decide if I was thankful for his help or still pissed off about him scaring Millie.

The young officer who was taking my statement, Constable Casey, listened with wide eyes as I repeated the story the weaver had told me. Altan confirmed that, when the weaver had lost consciousness, the illusion had dispersed and the Big Mango had returned in all its orangey-yellow glory.

"One question remains though," I said. "Why was the mayor so weird about it all? According to the weaver, he wasn't involved."

Constable Casey glanced over her shoulder at Briggs before whispering, "To be honest, I've always found Mayor Goldwin to be a bit odd. He's over-friendly, loud, always needs to know what's going on, and is slightly paranoid. It wouldn't surprise me if he was on your suspect list simply because he acts suspiciously. But to my knowledge, he's essentially harmless."

Shrugging one shoulder, Altan said, "Some people in power become too big for their boots. He obviously felt public pressure to find the culprit, so forced Briggs to make an early arrest."

I shook my head. Small towns and their politics. I didn't think I'd ever understand.

While Briggs continued to ignore us as he climbed into the paddy wagon's driver seat, Casey thanked us for our service to their investigation. She shook our hands and assured Altan and I that both Darius and Sylvia would be sent before the Inter-Magical Community Council to stand trial. With a smile and a salute, Casey left us and joined her superior in the police car, where they drove away swiftly, bumping along the uneven road.

I jumped when Altan squeezed my shoulder. "Well, Trix. I need to say congratulations. You did it. You survived your first claim. And more than that, you stopped an innocent elf from being sent to prison by taking initiative. I will say though, I'm not a fan of you ignoring a direct order."

I sighed happily, the stress of the past few hours leeching out of my body as I processed that the ordeal was over. "It all worked out in the end though."

"This time," he muttered.

I opened my mouth to give a smart retort but my phone pinged loudly, interrupting me.

Frowning, I pulled my phone out of my pocket and skimmed over the text. My eyes widened.

"What's wrong?" Altan asked, going still.

I stared at him, horrified.

"My mother is coming to stay."

Links

If you enjoyed Mother Trucking Monsters, please leave a review:

https://altippett.com/rl/3566883

Dive into Trix's next adventure with Gosh Darn Griffins, Book Two of the Magic and Motherhood series:

https://altippett.com/rl/3938847

Want to read more books by A. L. Tippett?

Read A Dragon's Mind, Book One in The MINATH Chronicles:

https://altippett.com/rl/3937325

Claim your FREE short story when you subscribe to my monthly newsletter:

https://altippett.com/latest-updates/subscribe/

Get to know me by visiting:

https://altippett.com

Or by following my socials:

https://facebook.com/altippettauthor

https://instagram.com/a_l_tippett_author

https://tiktok.com/@altippettbooks

https://bookbub.com/profile/a-l-tippett

https://goodreads.com/altippett

Acknowledgement

Firstly, I want to thank you. Yes, you there, holding this book. Whether you are reading these pages on your Kindle, phone, tablet or if you've got your hands wrapped around the spine of a paperback. I want to say a heartfelt thank you for reading this story. I hope you loved reading it as much as I loved creating it.

If you enjoyed this book, please consider leaving a review on Amazon, Goodreads, or BookBub. But please remember to be kind. I poured a part of my soul into these pages and, while my brain knows that it won't be everyone's cup of tea (and that's okay), my heart craves acceptance. I'm always happy for readers to email me with constructive feedback.

And don't forget to preorder your copy of book two: *Gosh Darn Griffins*. Poor Trix was left with more questions than answers so make sure you join her as she uncovers secrets about her powers!

I want to sincerely thank the professionals who helped make *Mother Trucking Monsters* the best story that it could be. In particular, thanks to my editor, Miranda Grant, for her sound advice, kindness, and patience with me during a challenging year.

A HUGE thank you to my friend and mentor, Heather G Harris, for her invaluable suggestions and ongoing support. As a thank you, she is now immortalised forever as a succulent in this series!

A massive thank you to my cover designer, Chris from Taurus Colosseum, for the brilliant cover. His talented wife from Ravenborn Covers has assisted with the paperback and will continue the series.

Many thanks to my wonderful alpha and beta readers (and unofficial cheer squad), Claire, Zoe, and Kara. You three are truly wonderful!

A thousand thank yous to all the family members and friends who have continued to support me as I follow my dream.

Last, but not least, thank you to the most important people in my life.

Mum and Dad, you continue to inspire me. Your unwavering support and love means so much to me. Love you uttmasaba.

To my children, you bring me so much joy. Thank you for inspiring me to be a better person. I love you both beyond words and beyond worlds.

Fly fierce, strike strong.

April xo

About the Author

I was born in the South Island of New Zealand before my family and I moved to Australia when I was two years old. We lived on a yacht for a few years and travelled along the east coast of Aussie and across the Pacific Ocean to New Caledonia. My parents home-schooled us while we sailed the seas until we bought a house on the Sunshine Coast in Queensland. I finally got to go to "real-school" and loved it – I couldn't understand why we had weekends (because, apparently, I am, and always will be, a big nerd).

Shortly before beginning high school, we moved north to a rural property near Mackay. The big draw card was that I could finally buy my own horse, a dream I'd had since I was a little girl.

Then, I started writing. I began work on my first fantasy novel when I was twelve but abandoned it after deciding that being an author wasn't a "real" job and therefore not worth pursuing. After completing my secondary schooling, my parents encouraged me to experience the real world before committing to a university degree. So, I applied to be a rider in a travelling horse show! Unfortunately, I wasn't successful so instead I did the complete opposite and got a job as an insurance broker. I worked in insurance for seven years before leaving to start a family.

I am now the mother of two wonderful children. It's tricky finding the time to write with two young kids (whilst combatting sleep deprivation!) but, as they say, where there's a will, there's a way! I can't wait to get started on my next book and am looking forward to sharing many more stories with you!